# DRIVEN TO KILL
## CHRIS WARD

# DRIVEN TO KILL

## CHRIS WARD

©2015 Chris Ward
All rights reserved

The right of Chris Ward to be identified as the Author of the Work has been asserted by him in accordance with the Copyright, Designs and Patents Act 1988.

No part of this publication may be reproduced, stored in a retrieval system, or transmitted, in any form or by any means without the prior written permission of the publisher, nor be otherwise circulated in any form of binding or cover other than that in which it is published and without a similar condition being imposed on the subsequent purchaser.

ISBN – 10: 1515117871
ISBN – 13: 978-1515117872

This book is a work of fiction. Any similarity between the characters and situations within its pages and places or persons, living or dead, is unintentional and coincidental.

## Table of Contents

CHAPTER 1 .................................................................. 1
CHAPTER 2 ................................................................ 22
CHAPTER 3 ................................................................ 35
CHAPTER 4 ................................................................ 60
CHAPTER 5 ................................................................ 64
CHAPTER 6 ................................................................ 76
CHAPTER 7 ................................................................ 78
CHAPTER 8 ................................................................ 95
CHAPTER 9 ................................................................ 99
CHAPTER 10 ............................................................111
CHAPTER 11 ............................................................120
CHAPTER 12 ............................................................127
CHAPTER 13 ............................................................139
CHAPTER 14 ............................................................143
CHAPTER 15 ............................................................152
CHAPTER 16 ............................................................156
CHAPTER 17 ............................................................161
CHAPTER 18 ............................................................177
CHAPTER 19 ............................................................181
CHAPTER 20 ............................................................197

| | |
|---|---|
| CHAPTER 21 | 205 |
| CHAPTER 22 | 216 |
| CHAPTER 23 | 219 |
| CHAPTER 24 | 240 |
| CHAPTER 25 | 246 |
| CHAPTER 26 | 250 |
| CHAPTER 27 | 257 |
| CHAPTER 28 | 262 |
| CHAPTER 29 | 277 |
| CHAPTER 30 | 282 |
| CHAPTER 31 | 285 |
| CHAPTER 32 | 290 |
| CHAPTER 33 | 297 |

# CHAPTER 1

In the mid-July heat, fifty-one-year-old Michael Fletcher and his two boys, eighteen-year-old James, and seventeen-year-old Harry, splashed about in one of the outdoor heated pools at the five-star Real Marina Hotel and Spa on the Portuguese Algarve.

Francis Fletcher, forty-seven, lay on a thick multi-coloured towel on the ubiquitous white sunbed in her one piece, blue swim suit. A white table next to her had a red and white umbrella, which shaded her from the burning midday sun while she read one of her customary romance novels. She put the especially-bought-for-the-holiday book on the table and glanced over at her boys. This would be their last real family holiday, as James would go off to Plymouth University in September, and Harry planned to take a year off to backpack in Australia and New Zealand with a couple of pals.

Francis smiled. They were good, responsible, handsome young men full of character, and would go far. She congratulated herself on being partly responsible, along with Michael, for giving them such a good start in life.

Her seven hundred pounds rotary gold watch showed the time at two p.m.; half an hour before she was due at the hotel spa for some divine massage treatment. She leant back on the sunbed and picked her book up. Ten minutes more, and then she would head off to the spa.

This trip made the third visit to the Hotel for the Fletcher family, and they adored the five-star opulence.

This time, as it would be the last family holiday, they had booked fourteen nights instead of the traditional ten. As usual, Michael had stuck it on his gold credit card—one of the benefits of being a senior executive for the National Trust Bank. Cash bonuses may have gone down, but perks had improved tremendously as the Bank tried to get around the government's anti-bonus culture.

Ten minutes passed like a flash and Francis slipped her bright red varnished toenails into green flip-flops, and gathered her number fifty suntan lotion, expensive leather purse, romance book, and Hello magazines together and made off in the direction of the Spa for her massage. When she reached the hotel pool entrance, she turned back for a final look at her husband and the two boys. A smile lifted her lips when she saw the boys grappling with their father and trying to get his head under the water. Only two days to go before they had to leave. Francis felt in high spirits that they'd had the most amazing holiday, and her only concern was that next year it would be just her and Michael. Hopefully, they would find enough to talk about.

After she entered the hotel, Francis ambled to the bank of lifts and took the next available one to the first floor, where she sauntered along the thickly carpeted corridor. At room eighteen, she slipped the room card into the lock and opened the door. She tossed all her bits and pieces onto the double bed, stepped out of her swim suit, and strolled into the gleaming white bathroom. Next, she pulled the shower curtain across, turned the bath shower on, and stepped in.

For exactly two minutes, she soaped and washed herself, then jumped out feeling refreshed and clean. She took one of the huge, soft white towels and dried herself. While she rubbed, Francis hoped Michael would stick his big cock in her later that night. They hadn't done it that often while at the hotel, and following the massage, a delicious dinner, and a couple of glasses of chilled Rioja white wine, she would absolutely be in the mood.

After she'd pulled up a pair of tiny white panties, she threw on a long, thin, wavy green and blue dress, tied her long brown hair back, and left the room. Five minutes later, she lay on a towel-covered, long massage table in the spa. Tony, the masseuse, used his strong hands to massage her from head to toe. She loved it when he got close to her vagina and massaged her arse cheeks with warm oils. She had heard stories that he would fuck anybody on his table, but Francis easily resisted the temptation to see if it was true.

\*\*\*

Michael lifted his head out of the water again, gasping for air. The two boys were stronger individually than him, and together made a formidable team. They leapt on him again and dragged him under. After what seemed like an eternity, he once more shot to the surface and, this time, held his hands up and yelled, 'I surrender. You win.' After a short pause, he shouted, 'How about a cold beer?'

James and Harry didn't need any further persuasion. The three of them swam like hell to the bar situated on a small island in the middle of the pool, and Michael, of course, came in last, well behind the boys. A group of older teenage girls lounged in the bar, wearing skimpy bikinis. The outfits left their breasts hardly covered, and also their bottoms, and James and Harry couldn't take their eyes off them. Michael wished he was twenty again, and then quickly changed his mind—he'd had enough womanising in his time and had settled into a happy and contented middle-aged relationship with his still-desirable wife of twenty-seven years.

Michael stood at six feet, had a medium build, and still looked handsome in a rugged way, dressed in his usual conservative pair of grey trousers with a dark-blue Van Heusen designer shirt, and also a smart pair of open leather sandals that he would only ever wear while on holiday. The two boys had underdressed as usual in torn, scruffy denim jeans and plain white tee shirts. Michael had insisted that Harry remove his original white tee shirt with the words *FUCK THE WORLD* on it.

The undoubted star of the show, though, had to be Francis, who had dressed in a beautiful, white lacy summer dress that showed off her slight tan and figure to the full. She had paraded around their room naked, and her slim, sexy body still turned Michael on even after all the years they had been together.

Dinner was an immense buffet with a multitude of choices for starters, mains, and desserts. The boys ate gargantuan meals that never failed to amaze their parents. Michael also ate well, while Francis took a long time to decide what she wanted, and then ate sparingly to keep her trim figure in shape. The family reminisced about previous holidays, discussed the fortuitously rising

Euro exchange rate, and Michael gave the boys a short lecture on behaving themselves when they visited the hotel nightclub later that evening. What Michael and Francis didn't know was, that boys being boys, Harry and James had both taken French, Polish, and German girls up to their shared room on three nights of the holiday already, and as they were nearing the end of their stay, were determined to pull on their last couple of nights. In next to no time, dinner had finished, and the boys disappeared to the bar while Michael and Francis took a stroll in the beautiful hotel grounds.

'It's been a lovely holiday. One of our best.'

'I agree,' Michael said with a smile, as he had more on his mind than a little stroll. They held hands and had soon reached some distance from the hotel. The day had turned into another fabulous evening with a clear sky and a profusion of bright, shining stars. Michael saw what he was after: a small recess surrounded by hedges where nobody would be able to see them. He felt so horny that he almost dragged Francis into the grassy enclosure. Francis laughed.

'Michael, what are you doing?'

And then she found out.

He took her arms, wrapped them around his neck, and leant forward and kissed her passionately. She replied in kind. His hands grasped her bum cheeks and squeezed, then they transferred to her breasts.

He stopped for a moment.

'You're still a beautiful woman, and I love you so much.'

Francis looked around her, and Michael followed suit: outside and on the grass, just like when they'd been teenagers. She giggled like a schoolgirl while she pulled the straps down on her flimsy dress and let it sail to the ground. Her matching white knickers and bra entranced Michael. Next, she slipped the bra off to reveal full, pert breasts. She always liked Michael to pull off her knickers. He held her again and licked her nipples, and then she sank to the ground, using the dress as a makeshift blanket. As expected, he slipped her knickers off, and they made passionate love outdoors for the first time for over twenty years. The last time, she had commented that the grass got everywhere, and said it again now, and the wonderful memories flooded back of their youth and Michael taking her virginity.

The holiday over all too soon, the horrible time of packing had arrived, and it made for a sad moment for all, as holidays would never be the same again. The Fletchers boarded their plane, and after an uneventful flight, landed back at Heathrow in the early hours. A thirty-five-minute minicab ride to Kingswood in Surrey and they were opening the door to their beautiful five-bedroom detached house.

At seven-thirty in the morning, James and Harry hadn't had any sleep yet, so carried their luggage in and duly dumped it next to the washing machine and went to bed. Francis just shrugged and couldn't be bothered to comment.

'Cup of tea, Michael?'

'Love one, darling,' replied Michael as he scooped up handfuls of letters, Indian Restaurant and Pizza flyers, and the odd small packages. He carried them into the kitchen and dumped them all on the kitchen table.

Francis put the kettle on and turned toward Michael.

'Anything interesting?'

Michael sorted the pile into bills, personal, and rubbish.

'Haven't seen anything yet.'

He picked up a thick, expensive looking envelope addressed to him with the National Trust Bank stamp on it.

He hesitated, and Francis asked, 'What is it?'

Michael smiled. 'A letter from the bank. Just work. Nothing untoward.'

He placed the letter to one side with a few other items addressed to him.

Francis served him a piping-hot cup of Tetley, and Michael disappeared into his small cubbyhole office at the back of the house. He loved his little office where he worked from home as a regional manager for National Trust bank, and once he'd closed the door, he entered his wonderland of numbers. His life had been spent looking at numbers, and he had responsibility for four area managers, who each managed twenty bank branches. With a turnover in the hundreds of millions, he loved his job.

He had been with the bank for twenty-eight years and considered himself indispensable and part of the bank family. He swung round in his expensive, black swivel chair, grabbed the stack of letters from the edge of the desk, and looked for the one from the bank. He couldn't put his finger on why, but he felt anxious. With a certain amount of trepidation, he picked up the silver paper knife, sliced open the top of the envelope, took the letter out, and unfolded it.

He couldn't take it all in as he speed-read the first few lines.

*Report to head office Monday morning at eleven a.m.*

*Meeting with the Commercial Director Tony Morgan and Head of Human Resources Helen Montague-Smith.*

*Do not make any contact with your area manager team or other colleagues prior to the meeting.*

He couldn't move, and a shiver ran down his spine. With a shudder, he put the letter on the desk and just looked at it. How could he but think the worst? Instinctively, he knew it was all over. What to do? He pulled himself together, picked up his mobile, and pressed speed dial for Graham Hawkins, the regional manager for the East. Graham, his best friend, would know exactly what was going on. It rang and rang.

'Pick it up, pick it up.' And then a voice answered.

'This phone is no longer in use.' And the line went dead.

Michael didn't particularly like swearing but muttered to himself, 'What the fuck is going on?'

Panicky, he opened his bank-issued Dell laptop and pressed the start button. In half a second the machine hummed into life, and he keyed in his password. He went straight to the bank website and again typed the password, but nothing happened. Funny. He re-keyed in his password, and still nothing happened, and then something did happen: a message came up on the screen.

*You are no longer authorised to enter this Website.*

Just then his Blackberry rang, and he grabbed it, but looking at the number, he didn't recognise it. He pressed answer.

'Michael, is that you? Thank God, you're back. I didn't know what time you were landing.'

'Graham, I've just been trying to phone you. What the hell is going on? I've got to see Tony and that bitch Helen Montague on Monday morning.'

'I was called in yesterday. I no longer work for the bank.'

'What?' Michael said, stunned. He felt shocked to the core.

'Bastards. I was in the office, and someone actually went to my house and picked up files and removed my computer.'

'Jesus, that's unbelievable. Honestly, I don't know what to say.'

'Well, I don't want to alarm you but you may well get the same treatment on Monday.'

Michael fell speechless for a moment. 'I've given them twenty-eight years of my fucking life, for God's sake. I've just spent five grand on a bloody holiday. So, what did they give you?'

'Well, I'm not even meant to be speaking to you but wait 'til you hear this, they gave me the legal requirement—not a penny less or a penny more. It's a few thousand, but after fifteen years it's a real kick in the teeth.'

Michael seethed and had to force his jaw to unclench so he could speak. 'If I'd known this was going to happen I wouldn't have spent all that money on the holiday. Bastards.'

'You've done twenty-eight years, and you'll get a big payoff, don't worry.'

Michael still had difficulty taking it all in. 'I'm in shock, and I need to speak to Francis. Are you going anywhere today?'

'No, I'm starting the hunt for a new fucking job, but you know what the industry's like. It's a young man's game, and it'll be tough.'

'I'll call you later. I need to take stock and speak to my solicitor, so I'll call you later.'

'Sure, later then.'

Michael clicked his phone off and leaned back in his chair. They were going to fire him—well, make him redundant—which amounted to the same thing as far as he was concerned. The deep breath didn't stop his brain from thinking about how much mortgage remained on the house, and soon his brain worked overtime on what to do first, and then he knew. He got up and opened the door.

'Francis, can you give me a hand for a minute, please?'

He sat back down and heard Francis approaching from the kitchen.

'What is it, darling?'

She entered the office, and her face clouded at the tense atmosphere. Michael put his finger to his mouth to signify that she should speak quietly. She lowered her voice and said in a concerned tone, 'Michael, what's wrong?'

For answer, he held up the bank letter, and Francis took it and read it. She stopped after a minute and gave it back to him.

'What does it mean?'

'It means that on Monday morning at eleven a.m., I am going to lose my job.'

Francis was now the one in shock.

'Surely not. It could be a number of things. You've been there twenty-eight years, for God's sake. Call Graham. He'll know what's going on.'

Michael looked at her, and a momentary silence fell between them.

'I already have. They made him redundant yesterday. He no longer works for the bank.'

'What? Oh my God. What are we going to do?' She looked to be in total shock.

Then panic set in and Francis burst into tears.

Michael stood and took her in his arms.

'Don't worry, it's not the end of the world, come on, we're both tough cookies. Look, with my experience, I'll get another job easily. In fact, this could be a blessing in disguise.'

Francis didn't quite see it like that but cheered up a little with Michael's confidence rubbing off on her.

'Look, darling, let's not worry the boys with this; they're both going away shortly, okay?'

'Yes, of course, we must protect them as best we can.'

'Good.' Michael smiled. 'So, I want you to get some rest and then cook us a nice dinner for tonight, okay, darling. I've got some calls to make so that I get as much as possible from the bastards.'

Michael hadn't sworn like that for years, and the aggressive tone of his voice shocked his wife. She headed for her bedroom to relax. In his office, Michael spoke loud words, 'Twenty-eight years. Fucking bastards.' It was a good job the boys were dead to the world in bed.

Michael got no answer from his solicitor and golf playing partner's mobile, so phoned him at home. His wife, Audrey, answered and said that Steven had gone out. Michael left a message to say that Steven should call him the minute he came through the door.

'You sound terrible, Michael. What's wrong?'

'Just get him to call me, please.' Then he pressed the red button to disconnect.

He took a deep breath. He'd heard one or two rumours the bank wasn't doing as well as it should be. This could only be the fault of the bastards at head office; they'd been losing money hand over fist in the futures markets, and the profitable retail sector would pay for it.

At eight, Michael answered the phone. Steven Coker had returned his call.

'Hi, Michael. Audrey said you sounded awful. What's the problem?'

'Thanks for calling back. I'm almost certainly going to be made redundant on Monday morning, and I need to know my rights—what payments I should get. You know, all that stuff.'

'What the hell is going on at the bank, for Christ's sake?'

'Reorganising, restructuring—call it what you want, but it's a pile of shit.'

'How long have you been there?'

'Twenty-eight years.'

'Music to my ears: big final salary pension?'

'Yes.'

'Salary this year and bonus?'

'One hundred thousand, and a twenty percent bonus.'

'Yo, buddy, they're going to have to pay you off big time. Let me look at the numbers and I'll call you at lunchtime tomorrow.'

'Thanks, Steven, I really appreciate it.'

'No problem. Speak tomorrow. Keep your pecker up.'

'I will.' He laughed and clicked off. Michael felt better. By lunchtime tomorrow, he would know what he could expect the redundancy package to be. Whatever it was, they had credit card debts, Hire Purchase agreements, and bank loans amounting to over thirty thousand pounds, and that didn't include the mortgage left to pay—about two hundred thousand. It was all tied up with the bank, so it would be interesting to see how Tony Morgan played it.

Dinner proved somewhat difficult, even though the one hundred percent pork sausages and mash with onion gravy tasted delicious. Husband and wife tried to appear normal, but Francis found acting a part difficult and just sat brooding. When Harry asked what was wrong, she replied that it was because she'd enjoyed the holiday so much and was just missing the sun, swimming pool, and not cooking for two weeks.

Steven Coker called back at two p.m. on Sunday, just as the Fletchers finished their Roast Chicken lunch. Michael had been waiting desperately for the call and went straight to his office, sat in his chair, and started swivelling.

'So, Steven, give me the good news.'

'Okay, so first, I'm going to tell you the absolute minimum that the bank has to give you. Don't get annoyed or start shouting, because this isn't what they will give you, okay?'

'Sure, let's hear it.'

'Based on everything you told me, the absolute minimum they could give you would be eleven two fifty.'

'Sorry, did I hear that right—eleven thousand two hundred and fifty pounds?'

'Yes, but that's based on the absolute minimum legal requirement by law.'

Michael wanted to scream, but he kept cool.

'You better give me some good news, or I'll be bombing the bank.'

'Careful what you say. You never know who's listening.'

'What? Yeah, okay, please carry on.'

'Okay, so if the bank gave you two weeks for every year, then you're looking at just over one hundred and twenty-nine thousand; of course, then there's holiday pay and bits and pieces, not forgetting your pension pot, which they may like to top up if you push.'

'Now you're talking. What if they gave me three weeks per year?'

'Just under two hundred thousand. You won't be worrying about the shopping too much.'

'You say that but it goes quickly, we'll have to cut back considerably.'

'What are you going to do?'

'I only know banking. I'll look for a job. What else can I do?'

'I'm a friend, yeah. Look, there are thousands of banking redundancies all over the country. Listen carefully: have a backup plan or be prepared to take a job at a vastly reduced salary to what you're used to.'

'Thanks for that, but no, seriously, thanks for all your help. I'll let you know how I get on in the morning.'

Michael spent the evening making some notes—experience told him that it would be easy to forget things when under stress, and whatever the meeting was like, it would certainly be stressful.

Michael got up early on Monday morning. Francis cooked up some delicious scrambled eggs and bacon—one of Michael's favourites. A stickler for punctuality, he left a little early at nine-thirty. He walked to the tiny suburban Kingswood railway station, picked up a free Metro paper and waited for the train. He felt calm and almost looked forward to the dance, which was to take place at eleven a.m.

The train arrived on time and slid out of the station two minutes later. Thirty minutes later, the train pulled into London Bridge Station. Michael dumped his Metro on the seat with the hundreds of others left behind, then walked briskly to the tube entrance, and soon stood on the steel escalator descending into the bowels of the station. The tube train pulled in just as he reached the platform, and he squeezed on last, having to push slightly to make sure the door would close. Two stops on the northern line would take him to Moorgate, where the bank's head office was. The journey was over in a flash, and he walked down Moorgate towards Coleman Street. Four minutes later, he turned into Coleman Street and checked his watch: ten-thirty. Right on schedule.

Michael ducked into Luiges Italian coffee shop and ordered a small latte, then sat down at the back and mentally prepared himself for the battle to come. Nerves had him check his watch every minute. Finally, quarter to eleven came, and he got up and walked the hundred yards towards the bank. At exactly ten to eleven, he stood at the plush, marble-topped reception.

'Good Morning. Michael Fletcher to see Tony Morgan.'

'Good morning, Sir.' The receptionist checked a list on her computer.

'That's fine, Sir. Would you take a seat? Someone will take you up in a minute.'

People visiting the tenth floor were always escorted up, as it was the Directors' floor. Solemn, Michael looked around. Shortly, this would all be history. Twenty-eight mostly enjoyable years. He shook his head. A concierge approached.

'Good morning, Mr Fletcher. Do come this way, please, Sir.'

Michael felt like saying, *I know the fucking way. I've worked for this bank for twenty-eight fucking years.* But held his tongue. They stood in the lift, and he watched the floor buttons light up one by one, and then they were there: number ten. They got out and approached a rather intimidating reception with a battery of attractive women in smart uniforms, seated behind a huge wooden desk. The concierge announced him.

'Good Morning, Mr Fletcher. Emma will take you through,' the oldest-looking woman of the group said.

'Thank you,' Michael said, impressed as always by the slickness and professionalism of the staff. They knew, of course, why he was here. Another one bites the dust and all that. If they ever even gave it a thought.

The woman ushered Michael into a small, insignificant meeting room.

'Mr Morgan will be with you in a moment. Can I get you something to drink?'

'Yes, a bottle of still water, please.'

'Certainly, Sir. I won't be a moment.'

He stood up and looked out of the window and across the city. Still daydreaming, a loud voice interrupted him.

'Michael, how are you?' The ebullient Tony Morgan had arrived.

'Fine, thanks, Tony, and you?'

'I'm hanging on in there. Look, I want to have ten minutes with you before Helen Montague arrives. Let's sit down.'

The water arrived, and Michael took a sip, as his mouth had already gone dry.

'Michael, we've known each other a long time, so I'm not going to insult you by pretending you don't know what is going on. I'm sure you've been on the phone to Graham, so you know why we're having the meeting today.'

'Of course, twenty-eight years is a hell of a long time, so it's not easy for me, but I'll try to keep the emotions in check.'

'It's a bad time. We're losing thousands of good people and closing hundreds of branches. The most important thing is that the bank continues, and to do that prudently, we've had to take these desperate measures. So, look, we've put together a more than generous package. Helen will go through it with you, and I'm sure you'll be happy with it.'

As if on cue, the door opened, and Helen Montague-Smith breezed in. For a moment, Michael wondered if the room was being monitored.

'Michael, so good to see you again. It must have been at least a year.'

Michael's hackles rose immediately; he hated this woman with a passion.

'Hello, Helen. Yes, it's a pity it's not under more positive circumstances.'

Helen took the cheesy smile off her face. 'Yes, quite. I couldn't agree more. Well, shall we get down to it.' She opened the folder and picked up a single sheet of A4 paper. 'So, I'll run through the offer. If you have any questions, please do interrupt.' She glanced at him, and then resumed:

'Number one, a one-off redundancy payment of three hundred thousand pounds, which will be reduced by clearing your loan and credit cards and thus enabling you to be debt free to the bank. So, your net payment from that is two hundred and seventy-nine thousand and thirty-six pounds. Number two, there is a holiday payment due to you of four thousand six hundred and fifteen pounds. Number three, you are owed expenses up to the end of June of one thousand two hundred and eighty pounds, which will be included in the payment. Please submit your July expenses, which of course, will also be honoured in full. Number four, you may keep your company car, and this will be signed over to you. Number five, as regards your pension pot, the bank has decided to make a one-off three-year contribution, which in the circumstances, is generous. So, the total amount due is two hundred and eighty thousand and three hundred and sixteen pounds. We took the liberty of paying that exact amount into your savings account this morning. You are, of course, free to consult financial specialists and dispute the payments, but in truth it's a generous package, not forgetting that the car is worth twenty odd thousand.'

Silence fell. Michael had sat through it all without saying a word. The offer was indeed generous, and they had given him his lovely car.

'I accept the offer, thank you.'

'Good. There's just the small matter of your laptop and mobile phone.'

'All in here.' Michael passed over his computer bag, which had the laptop, mobile, Bank ID, and some files.

'Excellent. I'm glad you're taking it so well.'

Tony grimaced when Helen said it.

'Helen, I can assure you that I am *not* taking it well. I've given blood to this bank for twenty-eight years, making profits and contributing, and all you do is sit behind a desk and do fucking paperwork, so don't patronise me, please.'

'No need for bad language, Michael. It's not my fault you're being made redundant.'

'No, maybe it isn't.' He turned to Tony. 'The fault lies with the board, who have tried to join the big boys and make huge profits on the futures markets. Well, it hasn't worked out and the profitable retail division, as usual, is going to pay the price—true or not?'

'It doesn't matter does it? Thanks for coming in, Michael. This meeting is over.'

The door opened, and Emma appeared as if by magic.

'Please, follow me, Sir.'

Michael stood up, didn't bother saying goodbye, and followed Emma back to the reception. He couldn't take his eyes off her cute arse, which was a delight to scrutinize with every step. The concierge appeared, and a minute later, Michael stood outside the bank in a trance, not knowing what to do. A man entering the bank stopped and held his arm.

'Are you all right, old chap?'

That seemed to wake Michael up. 'Less of the "old", matey.' With that, he strode off back towards Moorgate tube. His mind ran riot. He could open a coffee bar or backpack around the world—the opportunities were endless. He smiled and felt a weight lift off his shoulders that he'd never experienced before. With his lovely family, a beautiful home, a fabulous car, and a substantial amount of money in the bank, it could be far worse. He went to his pocket for his mobile to call Francis, said loudly 'fuck', and strode on.

# CHAPTER 2

Detective Inspector Karen Foster stood at her office window and gazed out as cars whizzed up and down Ashley road, and a small number of elderly pedestrians sauntered along the pavements. Although already July twentieth, it certainly didn't feel much like summer. The weather had been awful, and this particular day proved no different, being cold and windy. Karen thought about Esme. She loved having her at home, as she was witty, sharp, warm, and above all, the sexiest woman she had ever met other than, perhaps, Chau, who she always remembered so fondly. Life seemed splendid. She had stopped seeing Friday and now had become a one-woman woman.

In fact, she felt like she was getting old. At forty-two, she felt that the years of stress in Bermondsey and even the serial killer case in Surrey had caught her up, and much of the thrill had gone. Karen turned away and sat back at her impressively large, solid wooden desk. The bane of her life was still there: a mammoth pile of paperwork, and she resorted to how she always dealt with paperwork—she got up and went for a stroll around the police station.

First, she went downstairs and said hello to the unsung heroes of police work, the admin team. The ladies were well and seemed happy with their lot. Next, she headed to the front desk to see if she could find any action there, but it was so quiet she could have heard a pin drop. She walked back to the CID office to see if Mick or Ted were about, as she could always have a coffee with them for ten minutes. When she pushed the door open, a death-like emptiness met her. Fuck. Her watch showed eleven-thirty a.m., and Karen did the only sensible thing possible, and that was to have an early lunch.

*** 

Meanwhile, Freddie and Anne Rogers stood at the cash point at HSBC in West Ewell high street. They had been married twenty-six years and were both challenged. Freddie stood at five feet seven, with an immense paunch through enjoying his food too much and doing no exercise. He had such bad eyesight that he couldn't see further than five yards and always relied on Anne to put out his clothes to wear every morning. His wife stood an inch taller than him and looked slim. She had trouble stringing sentences together, and even the simplest maths gave her difficulty. Both fifty, they had met at a council-run day centre in Leatherhead.

Anne managed to press the right buttons and snatched up the twenty-pound note that appeared as if by magic from the cashpoint machine. She tucked the note into her small, silver-coloured cloth purse, and the two of them went next door to the Co-op convenience store. This Monday lunchtime, as with every day, they kept to a rigid schedule of where they went and how much money they spent. Freddy grabbed a black basket and knew exactly where they were going. First, two litres of semi-skimmed milk, and then a Kingsmill thick-sliced loaf, which they loved to toast. The third and last item was their Monday treat: two packets of fruit pastilles.

Anne paid at the till, then they left the Co-op and made their way along the road a short distance to the bus stop.

Their shoes made a clatter on the pavement while they marched in unison hand in hand. Freddie heard the same matching noise not far behind but thought nothing of it. They got to the bus stop at exactly eleven forty-five; the bus would arrive at eleven-fifty. The red double-decker arrived, they showed their free bus passes, and soon sat comfortably on the downstairs of the bus, headed home. The bus ride took ten minutes, and as they approached their stop, Anne rang the bell, and they both stood up, making sure that they held tight onto the safety rail. They waited 'til the doors had opened fully. Freddie shouted a 'thank you' and they stepped out onto the pavement.

Freddie and Anne knew every single one of the bus drivers, café owners, shop assistants, and post office workers in Ewell and Epsom. After all, they had been going to the same places for twenty-odd years. They lived in Ewell Road near Nonsuch High School for Girls, in a small one-bedroom council bungalow.

Anne took the key out of her bag and inserted it in the lock, turned the key, and pushed—they were home. Once they'd taken their coats off, as always, Anne went straight to the kitchen to put the kettle on. Freddie went to the toilet. The doorbell rang. Anne felt startled, as they weren't expecting anyone. She looked for Freddie and remembered he was in the loo, so went to the door and opened it an inch. Two young, scruffy men stood there, and one of them spoke in broken English.

'Hello. Me and my brother are handyman looking for working, do you need any job doing?'

Immediately, Anne felt frightened and didn't like the look of them one bit. 'No, thank you.'

She went to close the door and pushed it, but it wouldn't shut. When she looked down, she saw that the man had put his foot in the way. She didn't know what to say or do so she continued pushing, and then she went flying backwards onto the floor when the man smashed the door open with both his hands and feet. Anne tried to scream, but one of the men pinned her and had his hands around her throat in seconds. She could hardly breathe.

The other man swept past her and checked the kitchen and bedroom. The man stopped when the toilet flushed. Freddie opened the bathroom door and took a step. The man battered his head savagely with a small hammer, and Freddie fell to the wooden floor, with blood seeping from the wound.

Stanislav and Cedomir Kasan, the two well-built Serbian brothers, had stayed in the United Kingdom after their student visas ran out and were now in the UK illegally. Always on the lookout for easy pickings, especially from vulnerable people such as the elderly or mentally handicapped, they had seen Freddie and Anne at the cash point and followed them home. Stanislav was the elder by a year and the leader. Cedomir, nineteen, did exactly what his brother told him.

Cedomir found some tape in the kitchen and used it on Anne and Freddie to keep them quiet. The two brothers dumped them on the long, brown three-seater sofa, and soon Freddie began to stir.

The two men had ransacked the flat from top to bottom, and had loaded two carrier bags with watches, mobile phones, jewellery, cash, credit cards, ID Documents, a laptop, a spare set of property keys, and even two cans of lager from the fridge.

Freddie awoke and looked at Anne. His eyes said everything: What's happened? Are you all right? Neither could speak, and both felt terrified beyond belief. The two thugs returned to the lounge and stood in front of Freddie and Anne.

Stanislav spoke while Cedomir glowered at them in a frightening manner. 'We want pin number for cash point. You give, then he collect money, and we go no problem.' He leant forward and ripped off both their tapes. Anne howled in pain, and Stanislav put his left hand around her throat again. Freddie made an attempt to intervene, and Stanislav hit him across the face with the back of his other hand. Freddie reeled back, and blood pooled at the corner of his mouth, and then Cedomir grabbed him by the throat as well.

'Listen, you make no noise, if you do ...' He shook his head. 'I will beat you to death. You understand death, yes?'

Freddie understood. A small amount of warm urine ran down his legs and stained his trousers. Anne saw and smelt the urine and felt for Freddie. The fact that he had any pee left, after having just been, surprised her. She felt so terrified that she was amazed that she hadn't peed herself as well. Also, the thought that they might rape her or torture Freddie petrified her.

'So give pin number, sooner get money sooner we go.'

Freddie spoke up quickly, as he didn't want to make the situation worse. 'Three, five, nine, one.'

'Good. Now, how much is in account?'

'N-nearly three hundred pounds.'

'How much can you draw in one time?'

'Two hundred and fifty.'

'Good. You see, cooperation is nice, eh.'

Stanislav spoke in their language and told Cedomir to go and get the money, and that if he encountered any issue he should phone from the cashpoint.

Stanislav stared at Anne. 'Go make coffee, strong, three sugar.'

Anne stood up. Her body shook in terror while she walked past Stanislav. He grabbed her shoulder, and she froze.

'Don't worry, you play ball, everything all right.'

He looked at her ample breasts and slim figure and undressed her with his eyes. She shook even more. He pushed her towards the kitchen.

'Be quick, stupid bitch.'

Anne scuttled into the kitchen, grabbed the kettle, and held it under the tap. Because she shook so much, the water ran everywhere. Eventually, she had the kettle half full, and she turned it on. While she took a mug from the cupboard, she prayed.

'What you saying, bitch?'

Anne nearly jumped out of her skin, and turned to see Stanislav enter and shut the door. He took a six-inch flick knife out of his pocket, and it flashed open. Anne whimpered in terror.

'No, please, no no.' She backed into the corner and sobbed uncontrollably. Stanislav took two steps and stood right in front of her face, so that she could almost touch his rotting, yellow teeth. When he leant in close, she smelt his bad breath.

'If you make noise, I will cut your throat, you understand?'

Anne took a deep breath—anything to stay alive, that's all she could think about, staying alive. She nodded. He lifted up the front of her flower covered dress, and then pulled her knickers down and fingered her. Anne went to another place. With her eyes closed, she heard singing and dreamed of harps playing, and fluffy white angels, and hardly felt him as he probed with his filthy, rough fingers.

Forcibly, he turned her around, pushed her against the marble-topped unit, and shoved her legs apart. Then he ripped her knickers off and undid his trousers. Far away with the fairies, she had no idea what was going on. When she felt the intrusion, it was like an out of body experience. Something was happening, but she wasn't sure what it was. Stanislav held her hair tight and pushed in and out until it was done. When he released her, she couldn't move, didn't even know where she was, and she had disappeared into a fantasyland of make believe. He pulled his dirty trousers up and looked at her, but still she didn't move.

He shouted in her ear, 'Now make the coffee, bitch.'

She heard him faintly as though he stood some distance away, but couldn't move. Her feet seemed stuck in cement, and she tried desperately to lift her right leg, but it refused to obey. Then she felt a sudden rush of movement when he dragged her by the hair back to the lounge and threw her onto the sofa next to Freddie.

*\*\**

Freddie cried that he'd done it to her, the bastard had raped her, and that he could tell. Stanislav went back to the kitchen and made coffee. While he was gone, Freddie held Anne's shoulders, looked into her eyes, and whispered, 'Anne, don't worry, they will be gone soon. I promise.'

He looked at her, but she gave no reaction at all. Where had she gone? Stanislav returned with his coffee and some biscuits he had found, and sat in the single chair opposite the sofa.

'You got nice place here, would suit me.'

Just then the door opened, and Cedomir walked in.

'Everything all right?'

He held up the big wedge of cash, which Stanislav took and shoved in his jacket pocket. Stanislav turned back to Freddie and Anne.

'We go. You tell anyone, we come back and kill you.' He waved his knife in front of Freddie's face. 'You understand not be nice if I cut your throat.' He made a cutting motion with the knife. Freddie shook and nodded furiously, and at the same time prayed for them to leave.

'Good, so remember, I'll be watching you.' And with that the two thugs walked to the front door and left.

Freddie held his face in his hands and sobbed again. Then he held Anne and told her, 'They've gone, Anne, they've gone. We're safe.'

Still, she made no response: she had withdrawn into herself and gone to a different world, and goodness knew when she would return. Freddie lifted her up from the sofa and helped her to the bedroom, where he laid her on the bed and covered her with a duvet, then brushed the hair back from her forehead with a tender hand and kissed her on the cheek.

'Sleep well, my darling.'

Freddie went to the kitchen, re-boiled the kettle, and made himself a strong cup of tea, then went back to the lounge and sat on the sofa. He sobbed some more.

What sort of pathetic man was he? Couldn't even defend his wife. He felt so ashamed of himself. He wasn't a real man, but just a useless cretin.

He continued to cry, and then he stopped. What were they to do? Call the police? The thug, he said they'd be watching. Freddie rushed to the side of the window and peeped out, but couldn't see anyone. He'd only said that to scare them—they couldn't be watching all the time. What if they came back? He couldn't cope with all the maybes, ifs, and buts: it was all too much for him; he sat back, closed his eyes, and prayed for sleep.

Freddie woke with a start and thought that someone was attacking him. To protect his face, he brought his hands up, then kicked his legs in the hope he could push the assailant away. The two thugs had returned already. Then he heard a voice.

Anne sobbed. 'Freddie, it's me, Anne, wake up, I need you, please, wake up.'

Thank God. Anne had come back. He opened his eyes, and she stood there right in front of him. They fell into each other's arms.

'I just needed to know you were all right. Are you okay?'

'I'm fine, but you, that man, I can guess what he did, I'm sorry I couldn't help you, so sorry.'

Anne moved her hands and held Freddie's cheeks. 'It's not your fault; they were animals. We are alive and have survived.' With a smile, she asked, 'Now, how about a nice cup of tea?' He nodded, and she went to the kitchen.

Freddie shook himself more awake and thought again about what they should do. Perhaps they ought to move. They could tell the council and, hopefully, get an exchange. Then he got angry. Why should they move? They hadn't done anything. Should they tell Anne's elderly parents? No, they couldn't help. Anne's two brothers would help, and that could be the answer. He would mention it over the tea. Anne reappeared with two steaming mugs.

'Freddie, I've been thinking about what we should do, and maybe the best thing to do is nothing.'

Freddie looked at her and shook his head. 'If we do nothing, and they come back, and I think they will, when they are desperate for money one night, they'll come, knowing we are an easy touch.'

'I'm scared. That man, he did things to me, and I don't want to go through that again.'

Freddie stood up and held her. 'In that case, we have to get help, but who we turn to is the question.'

'We have to tell the police. Dial 999,' Anne said in a shaky voice.

'Yes, I agree, and then we'll call your parents and brothers.'

Freddie looked for his mobile, then remembered they had taken the phones. He picked up the landline and called the police.

Everything happened quickly. Soon, the whole area swarmed with police. Sergeant Mick Hill asked for descriptions, and Freddie and Anne did as much as they could to help. Anne's parents arrived, followed closely by her brothers, Steven and Philip. Mick interviewed Anne and Freddie at length, and then Anne—accompanied by her parents—went to the Special Rape Suite at Guildford Police Station. Freddie still sat answering questions by the time the crime squad team arrived and sealed off the Bungalow, looking for forensic evidence. Last to arrive was Detective Inspector Karen Foster, who sought out Mick and found him quickly.

'I've heard some of it. Disgusting, no-good bastards, picking on two defenceless, vulnerable people. Make no mistake, we're going to catch these scumbags, and the sooner the better.'

'Couldn't agree more, Boss. The poor lady's been raped, and the man got a hammer blow on the head. They'll both be okay, but have had a terrifying ordeal.'

'Okay, let me have the works.'

'Freddie Rogers is sure they were followed home from the cashpoint in West Ewell. The two thugs must have seen them collect the money and thought they were an easy target—'

'Which, of course, they were,' Karen said. 'Get someone over to the cashpoint right now and seal it off. You never know, we could get lucky with fingerprints.'

'They forced their way in when Anne answered the front door.'

'Don't they have a chain or eyehole to look through?'

'Council told them to pay for it themselves. They were saving.'

'Jesus, it gets worse.'

Mick nodded. 'They took the debit card, and one of them took two hundred and fifty quid out of the account, then the other raped Anne. They warned them that if they told anyone they would come back and cut their throats.'

'Did they recognise the accents at all?'

'Not really, but Freddie thought they were East European and definitely not British. They're both terrified those bastards are going to come back for seconds.'

'I'm not surprised. I want an officer outside 'til further notice. We need to catch these animals before they do any more damage.'

Sadly, when the police caught them, they would get two years, serve a year, all at tax payer's expense, and when they came out they wouldn't be able to deport them because of their human rights—a right load of bollocks.

***

Stanislav and Cedomir Kasan got back on the bus and headed to Leatherhead. The squat they had been living in had been repossessed, and they had to move on. A friend had given them the name of a fellow Serbian who would give them a room in a flat for a small rent. Not ideal, as they wanted to get their own place, but that was out of the question at the moment. First of all, they had to get as much cash as possible for the phones and stuff from the Rogers' flat, and with the cash they had on them, that would tide them over for some time. The next day, one of them would watch the post office while the other stayed at the Barclays Bank cashpoint—both near the Epsom clock tower.

***

Good news for the police: the two Serbian thugs had left fingerprints all over the bungalow. They also had positive DNA for one of them from the coffee cup, and from Anne having being raped. The police checked the fingerprints and DNA on the national registers, but nothing matched. Although a shame, once the police caught them, the evidence would still implicate them in the crime. The two men's descriptions were poor, but the artist had done his best with the information provided, mostly by Anne. Mick and his team circulated the pictures to all officers in Surrey and also informed the Metropolitan Police at New Scotland Yard.

# CHAPTER 3

Michael got home absolutely shattered. The journey and the overall morning's stress had caught up with him, and he needed to lie down, but before he could do that he needed to tell Francis exactly what had happened and what the redundancy package was. The large sum of money and the fact the bank seemed to have just given them the car, worth a considerable amount of money whether they sold it or not, gave Francis a pleasant surprise. The fact that they had cleared the outstanding loan and paid off the credit cards also delighted her.

Francis told Michael to lie down for a couple of hours, and he did exactly as she told him and collapsed onto the bed. His wife would feel a little less guilty; she didn't work and sometimes felt she should be contributing. Michael had wanted her to be at home looking after the children from birth, and continually told her that this was her contribution and a brilliant one. Once a week, she had her hair and nails done, and shopped at Waitrose and Marks and Spencer without looking at the prices. Life had been good for her—for them both.

Michael woke at four o'clock, had a shower, went into his office, and started to take stock. Firstly, they had no immediate concerns about money in the bank. They had enough to last a few years if they stayed sensible. He would take a further week off and get used to being unemployed, and the following week he would start looking for another job. He felt confident of getting something, even if he had to take a cut in salary, as Steven his solicitor and friend had suggested. Later, he sat in the lounge and discussed everything with Francis.

'So you see, hun, it's not the end of the world.'

'As long as you can get a job. You're over fifty now. Banks want young tigers, not middle-aged pussy cats.'

Michael laughed. 'I'm no pussy cat, and I'll prove that later.'

'You better had now you've said that.' They both laughed. 'Just promise me one thing.'

'What's that?'

'Don't do anything stupid with the money without talking to me. You promise?'

'Francis, I'm a banker. When have I ever done something stupid with money?'

'Just promise.'

'I promise. Cross my heart and hope to die.' He laughed.

The week went by at speed while Michael rushed to start and finish numerous jobs Francis had been nagging at him to do for months. The entire garden got tidied up, trees and bushes cut back, flowerbeds weeded, and hanging plants purchased and hung at the front and back of the house. Then he painted the shed with the stuff that does what it says on the tin, washed and cleaned the greenhouse, and bought some new garden furniture for a (hopefully) very hot August. He didn't tell Francis, but one day when she'd gone out shopping, a van pulled up at the house and delivered several cases of good quality wine. He laid them out in the cellar and stood looking at them, then smiled and rubbed his hands together. Plenty of wine always made him cheerful. The bills kept arriving and got duly paid without a thought. Standing orders and direct debits, as usual, flew out of the account. The week finished, and Michael woke on Monday morning with determination to find a new position as soon as possible.

'If you hear anything, let me know, okay. Keep in touch.' He put the phone down for what seemed like the hundredth time.

Michael, seated in his office, had spent five hours calling contacts made over his twenty-eight years in the banking world. The first thing that shocked him was how many people no longer worked at the same place, be it a bank, Insurance company, stock brokers, wealth management company, or Financial advisors. It seemed that half the contacts he knew had left their jobs for one reason or another.

The morning proved fruitless, and by lunchtime, he knew that finding a new job would be difficult, if not impossible. Companies were laying people off by the hundreds and thousands across all financial markets. You had to be a leaner, more focussed business, and to be that, you had to have fewer people. One thing Michael was not was a quitter, and after a lunch break he got back on the phone. It was all, 'Thanks for letting us know. If we have anything, we'll be in touch.' They may as well have played a tape with the same words. He carried on all afternoon, and at five p.m., Francis opened the office door and gave Michael a big mug of tea.

'I think I need something stronger. What a day.'

'Don't worry, it's only day one.' But Francis looked worried. It would be tough. Anyone over fifty had problems getting a job in just about any industry.

Tuesday came and gave more of the same. Wednesday and Thursday proved just as bad, and on Friday morning a letter arrived in the post that gave Michael an issue. He took the letter to the kitchen and showed Francis. Club renewal, seven hundred pounds. Michael had been a member of the banker's club in Marylebone for twenty years and usually just sent them a cheque.

'What do you think?'

Francis said, 'It's up to you, but it's a lot of money to go somewhere for lunch and a drink occasionally.'

'I agree, but there could be some good contacts. Remember, it's all bankers and financial people.'

'True. Look, Michael, it's a decision only you can make, but it is a hell of a lot of money.'

Michael smiled. Francis always remained so damn sensible. 'I've just resigned from the banker's club,' he said and ripped the letter in half, then chucked it in the bin.

The rest of the day felt tough, and at three o'clock, he finished early. He opened a bottle of red wine and poured himself a large glass, then sat in the lounge and relaxed. Francis came in, having been upstairs, looked at him, and stopped dead in her tracks.

'And when did we start drinking at three o'clock in the afternoon?'

Francis's words shocked him. But she had it right: he had never stopped work at three in the afternoon and started drinking.

'Hell, what's happening to me? I need to relax. Sorry, Francis.'

'As long as it doesn't become a habit, no harm done. Where's mine?'

Michael's expression changed to a weak smile, and he jumped up. 'Coming right up, Mrs Fletcher.'

They sat together and chatted about the boys, and about anything other than jobs, banks, and bills. Francis had the one glass, and Michael had polished off the rest of the bottle by five.

'So, what's on the agenda for this weekend?' Michael asked rather loudly.

'Nothing planned.'

'We could do the theatre and a meal,' Michael said.

'And how much will that cost?'

'Couple of hundred, if we're a bit careful.'

'We can't afford it,' Francis said with a frown.

'Jesus, what a fucking life.' Michael stood up and went to the wine cellar, then returned with another bottle of red. Francis glared at him, daring him to open it.

'I hear Graham's got a job.'

It was such a shock that Michael couldn't speak. He looked at Francis and finally spluttered, 'Doing what, exactly?'

'He's working for the local Council in the finance department.'

'How do you know that?'

'Mary told me this morning. They're over the moon.'

'What's he earning?'

'Thirty thousand a year.'

'Thirty K a year? How can they live on that?'

'They used the redundancy to pay off their mortgage, and cut back on everything. They'll have to change their lifestyle, but they'll survive.'

'Thirty K a year, that's unbelievable.' Michael shook his head in disbelief.

Francis's next words shocked Michael even more, 'Why don't we sell the house and downsize? The boys will be gone soon, and it's only us. We don't need this big house.'

Michael couldn't believe what Francis had just said.

'I've worked my whole life to get this house, and now you think we should sell it?' he said, shaking his head. 'Sell it? I'd rather jump off a fucking cliff and kill myself.' He grabbed his glass and the bottle of red, stormed off to his office, and slammed the door.

\*\*\*

Francis understood that the house was his sign—the sign that he had achieved, that he was a somebody, and exactly what he had worked for during the last twenty-eight years. A tear rolled down her cheek, and she felt terrible. They had never been like this before. She sat and sobbed quietly for a minute before disappearing to her bedroom to lie down. Without telling Michael, Francis had already cut her hair and nail appointments to every other week—every little helped, and they both had to make sacrifices.

\*\*\*

Michael sat in his favourite chair in the house and poured himself a full glass of the French St Emilion—one of his favourites. At first, he sipped at the red, and then just knocked it back. After only a week, he felt completely pissed off. Jesus, some people were unemployed for months or even years. He refilled the glass. Perhaps he should consider Francis's idea to downsize, and maybe even buy a flat. They could then spend a lot of time travelling. But his house. His fucking house. No, he couldn't let it go.

Michael sipped at the red. Thirty K—fuck, Graham was insane—how could you live on that? Michael finished the bottle, made a pathetic attempt to look at online jobs, and went to the spare bedroom, where he lay on the bed and fell asleep.

\*\*\*

The two boys had noticed the changes taking place. Dad was always around, and neither he nor their mother had said why. They were out most of the time anyway, so it didn't really affect them, but they had also noticed some tension creeping in between their parents. Harry was the first to say it.

'Dad's lost his job.'

James concurred, and they decided to say something, so they made their way to the office, knocked, and went in. James said to leave it to him, and Harry nodded.

\*\*\*

'Dad, we know there's a problem. If we can help in any way, you just have to ask.'

Michael looked at them and smiled. The time had come to spill the beans. 'I should have told you earlier.

Sorry about that. I just didn't want any fuss. Look, I no longer work at the bank, I've been let go—I think that's the expression nowadays. There's no need to worry, we have money in the bank, they gave me the car, and hopefully I'll soon have another job.' He wasn't sure about the 'soon have a job', but he wanted to appear confident and relaxed.

Harry laughed. 'They gave you the car, and that's worth at least twenty K.'

Michael chuckled. 'So if things get really bad, your mother and I will live in the car.'

They all laughed. James spoke again when the boys turned to leave, 'Glad to see you're on top of things, but we're here if you need us.' Harry backed him up by nodding.

'Thanks, boys. I appreciate the thought. Now, disappear and let me get on trying to find a job.' He smiled at his two big lads.

They shut the door behind them, and Michael frowned as he leant back in his chair. Getting a half-decent job might not be as easy as he'd originally thought. That morning, he'd gotten up early, made some coffee, and gone straight into the office. Before he got going, though, he needed to find Francis so he could apologize and make up with her.

He shuffled into the kitchen. Francis turned around from where she stood doing the washing up.

'Oh, it's you then.'

'Darling, what can I say except I'm really sorry. I didn't mean to be such an obnoxious git. Really, it's the truth.'

Francis smiled. 'I know, it's a difficult time for us both. Apology accepted. Now, how about some nice bacon and eggs?'

Michael put on a serious face. 'Only if we can afford it.'

Francis grabbed a tea towel and chucked it at him, and Michael laughed and ran for the door. 'Two eggs for me, please.'

They had a family breakfast, and everybody enjoyed chomping down masses of eggs and bacon with strong coffee.

The boys finished first and rushed out to meet friends in the town centre. Michael went back to his office and called recruitment companies. He registered with several, who said they would get back to him should anything suitable come in. He rang the next, Bank Solo, specialist recruiters for the banking industry.

'Good morning. My name's Michael Fletcher, and I'd like to register, please.'

The receptionist passed him through to a recruiter named Fiona.

'Hello, Michael, how are you?'

Michael hesitated, nearly asked if she called all her clients by their first name when they hadn't even met, and then decided against it. 'I'm fine, thank you. And you?'

'Good, thanks. If you want to register, you have to come in so we can have a chat about what you've been doing, what you're looking for, and such—you know the drill. We have opportunities coming in all the time, so when's the soonest you can make it?'

'Tomorrow morning, or is that too soon?'

'Not at all. Shall we say ten? You have our address from the website?'

'Great, I'll see you at ten, then.'

'Yes. Ask for Fiona Mizzen. Bye.' The phone went dead.

Michael felt happy; he would have to put on a good show at the recruiters so when something came in they'd have him in their thoughts. He opened the office door and called, 'Darling, I'm going to see a banking recruiter tomorrow morning. Need my best white shirt ironed, please.'

'Okay, I'll get it done later.'

The rest of the day made for a long trudge through a long list of recruiters, who all seemed happy for him to register. It got to five o'clock and Michael felt exhausted. Not having a job was more stressful than managing a three hundred million pound budget at work. He spent the evening updating his CV and writing notes on key areas he wanted to highlight to Fiona, the recruiter.

The next morning, he woke early and jumped out of bed with a spring in his step, and prayed that the perfect job had arrived at the recruiters and that he would be offered an interview. He put on his superbly ironed white shirt and tied the diamond cufflinks. His best dark-blue suit followed, and he finished off with a matching tie and handkerchief set of blue with white spots. Beautifully polished, nearly new, shiny black brogues finished off the smart city look.

'Wow, you're looking good, Mr Fletcher. I'd give you a job any day.'

'Well, thank you, Mrs Fletcher, that's very kind of you to say so. Coffee and toast?'

'All ready for you, Sir, in the kitchen.'

'Good, I have a feeling today could be a good day indeed.'

'I hope so, Michael. Give me a call when you come out.'

'Sure.'

Michael finished his breakfast and made for Kingswood Station. The recruiters was in Victoria Street near Scotland Yard, and he arrived at nine-forty-five.

'I'm here to see Fiona Mizzen. My name is Michael Fletcher.'

The young receptionist asked him to take a seat while she informed Ms Mizzen he had arrived. Michael took a seat and flicked through the financial times, which had been on a table with a collection of daily papers and magazines. He glanced at his watch to confirm the time when he heard a clock strike ten. Time stood still, and every minute seemed like ten. Soon, ten-twenty came around.

The receptionist spoke to him, 'Sorry, Mr Fletcher. Fiona is running late and will be with you shortly.'

He nodded and smiled. Several recruiters came out into reception either to collect people or to say goodbye after meetings, and Michael couldn't help noticing that they all looked so young. It got to ten-forty, and Michael got peeved; ten minutes late was okay, but forty minutes? He looked at the receptionist and smiled. Two minutes later, a young girl who looked about sixteen came out into reception and spoke to the receptionist. She motioned towards Michael, and the young girl then approached him with a smile.

'Michael, good morning. Would you follow me, please?'

Michael assumed that this was an office junior come to take him to see Fiona Mizzen. He followed her until she stopped, opened a door, and entered a small meeting room. She stood to the side, let him in, and then shut the door.

'Please, have a seat, Michael.' And with that, she also sat down.

'My name is Joanna. I'm a trainee on the recruiter team. I'm sorry, but Fiona is tied up, so you got me instead. Now, let's get a few details down.' She took a piece of paper out of a file.

Michael felt shocked. A girl younger than his children was interviewing him; he felt uncomfortable but tried hard not to communicate that by his demeanour.

'I brought my CV, which has all the information you would require.' Michael handed it over.

'Thanks.' Joanna placed the CV into the file. 'So, how old are you, Michael?'

Michael thought that was an inappropriate first question. 'Fifty-one, going on twenty-one.'

Joanna looked at him and smiled. 'I haven't got long, so if we could just shoot through the questions. What have you been doing?'

'Regional Director for the National Trust Bank with four direct report area managers, eighty-three branches, and a budget of three hundred million.'

He thought she might comment on that, but nothing.

'And what are you looking for?'

'A senior management opportunity within the banking sector.'

'Salary?'

'Hopefully, a hundred K.'

Joanna looked up. 'Not many of those jobs come in nowadays. You may like to re-think that.'

'I'm flexible.'

'That's the name of the game. Now, Michael, be as flexible as you can.'

'So, do you have anything interesting at the moment?'

'No, but stuff comes in all the time. I'm sure we'll be in touch soon. Thank you so much for coming in.'

Michael wanted to say *thanks for wasting my fucking time,* but thought better of it.

'I'll walk you back to reception.' She led him out of the office. 'Thank you again for coming in.'

'A pleasure. I look forward to hearing from you.'

They shook hands and Michael made for the exit. When he got close to the door, he noticed three new fifty-somethings sitting in the waiting area. Good luck, chaps, you'll need it.

Michael shut the door and stood out on the street. He could have screamed—what a complete waste of fucking time. A slip of a girl, a crap five-minute interview, and it was all over. Furious, he swore he wouldn't make the same mistake again. Would he ever hear from them again?

At only eleven o'clock, Michael didn't want to go straight home. He walked down the road fifty yards and into the first pub he came to—The Grapes. He ordered a pint of Guinness and sat at a side table so he could see who came in. Michael fumed: fifty-one, looking after a three hundred million budget, hundreds of staff, a salary of £120 K, and interviewed by a fucking kid who probably didn't know her fucking times tables. He took a long drink of his Guinness—deliciously cold and smooth—then finished the pint in double-quick time, and ordered another. He thought he'd had a job for life. What a big fucking mistake. Should have put more away and not spent so much on holidays and all the rest. Oh well, no point regretting it now.

Before he realised it, the pint glass stood empty again, so he ordered another, with a whisky chaser. What a fucking life. Interviewed by a fucking scrawny trainee girl, and she didn't even have a nice pair of tits to look at. He would end up drunk and couldn't care less. If Francis didn't like it, tough shit. He'd drink what he liked, when he liked, and fuck everybody. With a morose look, he downed the whisky and held the empty glass up to the barmaid, who nodded, and a new whisky duly arrived. He had been the first person in the pub, and now it filled up slowly. He wanted some company. Not particularly a woman for sex, but just to talk to. Two women came in giggling like school kids, both attractive, about forty, and he detected American accents. They looked out of place, and he guessed they were in The Grapes to experience a real British pub. They got to the bar and discussed what to order. Michael sauntered up next to them and smiled at the one closest to him.

'You're from the States?'

The lady replied in a deep American drawl, 'How did you guess?' She laughed. 'What the hell should we be drinking? Can you advise us?' She fluttered her eyelashes at him in jest.

'Now there's a question. What do you usually drink at home?'

'White wine by the bucket, and vodka martinis.'

The other woman said, 'And we're kinda partial to a whisky nightcap.'

'I'm Michael.'

The brunette spoke first, 'Barbara.'

Followed by the blonde, 'Sally.'

'What I suggest you do is get a bottle of white and join me at my table. In fact, I'll get the wine. You just sit down and make yourselves comfortable.'

'What a nice gentleman, and you are so well dressed,' Barbara said.

Michael ordered a bottle of the house wine and two glasses, and then sat down with the two American women.

'So you're here on holiday then?'

'No, we're here on vacation.' They both thought that was hilarious and laughed uproariously. It could be a big mistake talking to these two. Michael tried to find the comment funny and gave a weak laugh.

'Where are you from?'

'The windy city, and we bet you don't know where that is?' Sally said.

Michael felt fed up. He had landed himself with two idiotic American women who believed that America was the only country in the world and that Americans knew everything, and everybody else knew nothing.

He rubbed his chin. 'I don't know, but I'll take a guess. There are so many big cities in the States.'

The two women looked at each other with a 'he hasn't got a chance' look.

Michael said, 'I need an incentive. You know, a prize if I get it right?'

Sally looked at Barbara. 'Now, that sounds interesting. What could the two of us possibly offer Michael as an incentive?'

Barbara replied with a glint in her eye, 'How about ...' She leant forward and whispered in Sally's ear.

Sally reeled back and laughed. 'I'm not sure if Michael would be up for that?' She turned to Michael. 'Would you?'

'Would I be up for what, exactly?'

'Well, if you were to get the city right, then Barbara says we could show you where we're staying—our hotel room.' She grinned.

Michael smiled the smile of a huge lottery winner and laughed.

'I accept the prize, and the city is Chicago,' he said with a theatrical flourish.

The two women stopped smiling and looked at each other.

Sally lifted her finger and wagged it at Michael.

'Naughty Michael's a cheat. He knew all along what the answer was.' And with that she stood up and motioned to Barbara. 'Let's go. I've gone cold on the idea.'

Barbara stood up, and they marched to the exit door, swinging their handbags.

Michael felt even more pissed off and grabbed the half-full wine bottle. Oh good, at least they hadn't finished it. He poured himself a glass and knocked it back. The wine finished, he had two more whiskies and another pint of Guinness. By two o'clock, Michael had gotten completely drunk and definitely didn't want to go home. He staggered to his feet, waved at the barmaid, and crashed out of the door and onto the pavement.

The fresh air hit him like a tornado, and he felt like throwing up. Leant against the building, he focussed on his shoes, and although he recovered quickly, he waited a minute before setting off down towards Victoria Station looking for some action. First of all, he needed to eat, and couldn't drink anymore on an empty stomach. After passing Costa Coffee, he saw a Burger King. Lovely. A big juicy burger and chips—just what the doctor ordered. Soon, he found himself seated at a window seat, chomping on a large quarter-pounder and chips. They'd asked him what drink he wanted, and he'd asked for a whisky! By the time he'd finished the food, tomato ketchup and bits of burger covered his white shirt and smart tie.

He sat and stared out of the window, and whenever a half-decent-looking woman went past, he waved and invited her in. Of course, he remained on his own for the duration of his stay. When he left the Burger bar, he continued towards the station. The big London stations always had something happening. He arrived and sped into the Iron Duke, which was part of the front of the station. He just made it to the bar and grabbed the rail before falling over.

'Pint of Guinness, please, Landlord.' He looked around for service. As if by magic, a young girl with huge breasts appeared, and he imagined fondling them. 'Eh, pint of Guinness, please,' he said without taking his eyes off the gargantuan mammary glands. While she poured the Guinness, he looked around the bar. Fuck all happening. He frowned.

'I'll have a straight whisky—no ice with that.' He lifted the pint to his lips. The food had settled, and he felt a bit better. Next, he grabbed a table with a good view of the entrance, as he didn't want to miss out on any gorgeous women coming in. He sat and he drank, and he sat and he drank. Three men had entered during the whole time he had been there. This must be the most boring pub he had ever been in, in his entire life. He glanced at his phone. Shit—five missed calls. Without checking, he knew it would be Francis. He put the phone back in his pocket, said 'bollocks' out loud, and drained the whisky glass.

A sudden commotion broke out at the door, and a group of women entered, laughing and joking around. Michael wondered why they had come in, and it dawned on him. He looked at his watch: quarter past five—they'd just finished work. Of course, everybody else had work to do, and he was the odd one out. He picked up his empty pint glass, and then staggered to his feet yet again, and went to the bar.

'Hello, my lovely ladies. Who wants a drink?'

A shout came from amongst the group, 'We only drink Champagne.'

Michael had gotten into a state where he couldn't care less about anything, and that included the cost of a couple of bottles of Champers.

'Two bottles of your finest Champagne,' he shouted out.

The seven women cheered as the barman opened the first bottle.

Michael stuck to whisky and Guinness, as Champagne would go straight to his head. He said hello to a couple of the ladies, but they seemed to disappear quickly, which wasn't altogether surprising considering how drunk he was. Michael had given the barman his credit card and some of the women were now putting drinks on his tab. It was a riot of booze and more booze, and then Michael hit a brick wall. He put the whisky to his lips but couldn't drink it. He knocked back the half-pint of Guinness, retrieved his credit card, and left the bar. Unsure where he was, he stumbled along until he got to the barrier, and then searched for his ticket. He couldn't find it and kept going through all his pockets to no avail.

'Are you all right, Sir?' a station attendant asked.

'I can't find my bloody ticket, it's a return to Kingswood.' He continued to rummage around, and then decided that it was lost. He took out his wallet and produced a receipt for the ticket bought that morning. When he addressed the station worker, his words slurred, 'I have the receipt.' He waved it in front of the statuesque railwayman. 'This proves that I bought the ticket, so can I get on the train?'

'I'm afraid you can't, Sir, because that is not a valid ticket.'

Michael stumbled as he spoke in a louder than normal voice, 'I just told you, I have the receipt for the ticket I bought this morning.'

'Somebody could have given you that receipt. I repeat, it is not a valid ticket.'

Michael became well pissed off with this jobsworth. 'So, what do you suggest I do now, then?'

'Go to the ticket office and purchase a new single ticket.'

Michael couldn't believe what he'd heard. 'Are you completely fucking insane? I bought a return ticket this morning, and I have the fucking receipt here in my hand to prove it.'

The railway worker looked tired of dealing with drunks—even well-dressed ones. 'Let me see the receipt?' He held out his hand.

'Now we're getting somewhere at last,' Michael said, as he handed over the receipt while nearly falling over.

The receipt was for a round of drinks at the Iron Duke pub.

'This receipt is invalid.' He handed it back and walked off.

Michael chased after him. 'You fucking jobsworth. I've a good mind to report you or even give you a slap, you fucking arsehole.'

The man had taken enough, and turned away from Michael and spoke into his radio. He walked away again, and Michael followed him, hurling a continuous stream of abuse in a loud voice. Then Michael went quiet. Two tall, heavily built armed police officers walked towards him.

Michael became incensed and trotted after the railwayman. 'You fucking wanker. Had to call for help, did you? Fucking tosser. What a fucking wanker.'

The two officers stood right in front of his face. 'Something troubling you, Sir?'

'Yes, that fucking jobsworth won't let me get on my train.'

'Do you have a ticket, Sir?'

'How many times do I have to say this? I have lost my fucking ticket.'

'No need to use bad language, Sir, or you could be spending the night with us.'

'I lost my ticket, and that dickhead told me to go and buy another one. I even have the receipt for the ticket.' Michael duly rummaged in his pocket, brought out the receipt, and shoved it under the officer's nose.

The officer moved his face back and smiled. 'Let's have a look at this, shall we, Sir. I see, well ...' The officer couldn't help but laugh a little. 'This is a receipt for drinks purchased at the Iron Duke this evening. Look, Sir, you want to go home. You can obviously afford it, so for all our sakes, go and buy another ticket.'

When Michael closed his eyes, he swayed on his feet.

'You know what, officer, that's a great idea.' He turned about and staggered off towards the ticket office.

Michael had absolutely no intention of buying a ticket. What he needed was a drink. The Iron Duke being the nearest pub, he staggered back in to be met with a loud cheer from the group of ladies at the bar. Soon, he propped up the bar and bought more rounds.

Michael had another couple of pints and felt decidedly ill. Yet again, he staggered to the door and made it outside. He turned into the station and looked at the timetable. It took him a minute or two to focus so he could actually read what trains were going where and at what time. Then he saw that his train would leave in seven minutes. He looked around and couldn't see any railway workers or police officers. When he tried to jog, he fell over. Quickly, he got up and dashed as best he could for the barriers, where he lunged at the plastic barriers and crashed over them. In a heap on the floor, he shook his head, looked up, and saw the blue of police uniforms. A minute later his arms were behind his back, handcuffed, and the police half-walked and half-carried him on each side. The presence of the police officers had a sobering effect, but Michael still made a nuisance of himself by shouting out loud.

'I have the right to phone my lawyer. Do you know who I am?' He giggled. 'Francis, where are you?' Shit. Never around when needed. He called out again, 'I demand to see my lawyer.'

Two minutes later, the officers bundled Michael into a small cage in a white police van and drove away from the station. Fifteen minutes later, they booked him in at Belgravia Police Station in Buckingham Palace Road. By ten past ten, Michael had been digitally fingerprinted, had a cotton bud wiped in his mouth to collect DNA for the national database, and had a mug shot taken. An officer then took him to a cell. He looked around the sparse space, lay on the bed, pulled the blanket up round his neck, and went straight to sleep.

\*\*\*

'I'm so worried. I didn't know what else to do.'

'Don't worry, Mrs Fletcher, you have done the right thing. Can I just confirm you have contacted his relations and friends?'

'I've phoned everybody. Nobody has heard from him or seen him. I'm worried sick.'

'You haven't had an argument or fallen out at all?'

'No, nothing like that, and it's completely out of character for him to just disappear.'

At eleven p.m., having thought about it for a long time, Francis had finally called the police. She had visions of Michael lying in some hospital, having been hit by a car or having had some sort of accident. Frantic with worry, she had been unable to go to bed.

'Don't worry, Mrs Fletcher, we will make some enquiries and I'll come back to you as soon as possible.'

'Thank you so much.' Francis put the phone down, went to the kitchen, and made her fifth coffee of that evening.

The phone rang at two a.m. Francis had been lying on her bed half asleep. She sat up and grabbed for the phone.

'Hello?'

'Is that Mrs Fletcher?'

'Yes, speaking.'

'It's PC Mary Travers here. I have some news for you.'

'Oh God, is he all right?'

'A Mr Michael Fletcher was arrested at Victoria Station for a breach of the peace. Basically, he was drunk and disorderly, and is now sleeping it off in a cell at Belgravia Police Station.'

'Arrested!' Francis screamed. 'Oh, thank God for that. He's all right.'

'Yes, he will be interviewed in the morning, and more than likely let free at about ten a.m.'

'Thank you so much for calling, I do appreciate it.'

'Good night, Mrs Fletcher.'

Francis breathed a sigh of relief. Drunk, arrested ... what the hell was going on with that idiot? Relief turned to anger. All the stress she had been through—he would need a good telling off after this, and she meant to give him one.

***

Michael pushed the door out into the reception area of Belgravia Police Station, and then looked up and headed for the main entrance—he couldn't get out of the place quickly enough. Then he stood stock still. Oh fuck. Francis came straight toward him. 'Hello, darling. So good of you to come. I'm not feeling very—'

'What have you done to your best suit?'

Michael looked down. One of the arms was missing. 'Hell. What happened? Police brutality, I'm sure. I feel like shit. Let's go, please.'

He got closer to Francis.

'My God Michael, you stink.' She turned away in horror. 'How did you get in such a state?'

'Well, the interview was a complete fucking waste of time, and I went for a quick drink. I'm sure someone spiked my Guinness.'

'Why on earth would someone do that? How much money have you spent?'

'Fifty quid. I know, it's a lot, but I had to stand my rounds.' When he woke up, he'd looked at the bits of crumpled up paper in his pockets—receipts for drinks that added up to nearly four hundred pounds. He had screwed them up and flushed them down the toilet. If Francis ever found out, she would go crazy.

Francis looked at him closely. 'You look terrible, and you've ruined your best suit, and I have absolutely no sympathy for you at all. You had better grow up, Michael, and quickly.'

As they trudged to the tube station, Michael tried to hold himself together. It didn't last, and he had to dash to some bushes at the side of the road to throw up. Francis just looked on in repulsion, and then stormed off up the road.

# CHAPTER 4

Karen Foster couldn't remember the last time she had been so excited. The drive through Bermondsey had brought back so many memories, good and bad. She had been invited back to Rotherhithe nick for a farewell party. Although she didn't know Jack Lemon, who was leaving after twenty-five years' service, it gave a great excuse for her and Jeff Swan to meet up again having not seen each other for a couple of years. Richard Philips, the notorious gangster, had shot Jeff in McDonalds down the Old Kent Road. He'd had six months off work in the end, before returning full time.

Karen smiled to herself when she remembered the cheering as Jeff got out of the Audi when he went back to Rotherhithe for the first time. Now, that had been a very very special moment. When she entered Lower Road, her heartbeat increased dramatically. The police station came into view, and Karen could have cried. *Pull yourself together, you stupid cow.*

Karen pulled into the car park and manoeuvred into what must have been the last space. She got out of the car, slammed the door, and pressed lock on the key fob. Then she turned around, and there he was—five yards away.

'Jeff, oh my God, I'm so pleased to see you.' She ran into his arms, and they gave each other a huge hug. They eventually let go of each other and looked one another up and down.

'Well, you haven't changed one bit.'

'Jeff, you look so well after that terrible ... anyway.' She grabbed his arm and whispered in his ear, 'Someone told me they serve the best latte's in the Met here.'

Jeff laughed out loud. 'Yes, it's true, so we better find one.' They headed towards the reception area. While they walked they talked, and talked, and talked a bit more. Karen told Jeff how she'd had a quiet introduction to Surrey Policing, and then a couple of lunatics had gone around cutting people up with Samurai Swords. Jeff told Karen that Bermondsey had quietened down since she'd left. They shared another laugh, and then Jeff added that it was also probably because Tony Bolton was still in Broadmoor high-security Psychiatric hospital and would most likely never get out.

'Oh, by the way, I have something for you.' Jeff handed Karen an envelope.

'What is it?'

'Open it and see.'

She did exactly that and took the single sheet of paper out and started reading.

*My dearest friend, Karen*

*I'm sorry we have not kept in touch. You saved Lexi's life, and for that I still owe you. The debt has not been paid. Remember what I told you: any time you need me, I will be there. I am now running a legit business; well, very nearly, anyway! Things are good. We are all well, and I hope you have found what you were looking for in Surrey. God bless you, with love XXX*

*Paul*

*078334101234*

'That's nice, it's from Paul Bolton.'

'Yes, I know. I bump into him now and then.'

'Has he really gone legit?'

'Yes, as best he can. He's got about twenty clubs now. It's a massive business.'

Karen became thoughtful. 'I shouldn't really say this, but I always liked Paul.' She frowned. 'But as for his lunatic brother Tony, let's pray no bunch of do-gooders ever get him let out of Broadmoor.'

'Amen to that.'

She smiled and squeezed Jeff's arm. 'So, what's been happening?'

'Honestly, not a lot. We've got a couple of kids who think they're the new Krays, but generally speaking, it's quiet.'

'You sound slightly disappointed?' Karen said, surprised.

'Since you left, it hasn't been the same. I'm not asking for a gang of ruthless killers to turn up but, you know, something challenging and a bit exciting would be welcome.'

'I know what you mean. When it's quiet in Epsom, IT IS QUIET. Perhaps we're a bit long in the tooth now?'

'Yeah, maybe a bit of that, but you can't beat a few years of good experience. So, what happened with Chau?'

Karen didn't want to talk about it but said, 'She wanted a more settled life. She was always terrified that when I left the flat I would be killed or maimed for life. You can't live like that. She's with a restaurant owner and, wait for this, I heard from a little dickey-bird that she's pregnant. I'm happy for her.'

'And you?'

'Oh God, it's a long story, but I'm living with a French ex-police officer—oh, a woman—my private life isn't perfect but it never has been.'

'As long as you're happy?'

'Yes, I am. Now, what about a refill?'

'Good idea, and let's grab some food before the greedy bastards eat it all.'

# CHAPTER 5

On the train, Francis ignored Michael and sat on her own. He stank of stale sweat, booze, and bad breath, and she felt so sorry for the people near him. Halfway through the journey, she had noticed him fall asleep, and then something awful happened—he broke wind, loudly. Two of the commuters sitting opposite and next to him got up and walked off, holding their noses and frowning. She had a good mind to leave him on the train—he would miss the stop and wake up in Tattenham Corner, the last station on the route. Most of the other passengers had left the train, so just before they pulled into Kingswood, she shook him awake. He just managed to get to his feet and stumbled to the exit. The door opened, and he fell forwards onto the platform.

Francis had never been so embarrassed in her entire life. He managed to get up and then threw up all over the platform. Francis was beside herself and, once again, felt like leaving him, but she couldn't do it and helped him up and half-carried him towards their car. She opened the passenger door and pushed him onto the seat. Then she slammed the door and cursed him loudly. She opened the driver's door only to hear him puking onto the floor in front of the passenger seat. Annoyed and repulsed, she swore he would clean it up when he sobered enough. Francis drove home with all the windows open while Michael slept or had gone into a coma. Francis pulled into the driveway, scattering stones in every direction, and parked right in front of the house door, where she got out, slammed the door, and left Michael snoring exactly where he was.

***

He opened his eyes not knowing where he was, what day it was, and whether it was morning, afternoon, or nighttime. The smell hit him first, stale vomit, and then he looked to see where he was and felt better when he saw his green front door. He'd obviously been asleep in the car, and then it came back to him: Francis had been at the police station. As to how he got home, he had no idea.

He pulled the door handle and pushed at the door at the same time. A breath of fresh air rushed at him, and he took a deep breath. He went to move and felt pain all over his body, so he lifted his arm and grabbed the stabiliser loop and pulled, then stumbled out onto the drive. After he'd rubbed his eyes, he looked around again. Although he was home, that feeling of not knowing what he had done or said enveloped him from head to toe—a ghastly, horrible feeling. He felt in his pockets for his bunch of keys but couldn't find them. Francis must be inside. Thank goodness for that. Hold on … why the hell did she leave him in the car? He must be in serious trouble if she had actually left him to sleep in the car. God, he must have been bad for her to do that.

He dreaded the reckoning that would come soon enough, but his immediate problem was how to get in the house—he couldn't possibly ring the doorbell. More grumpy by the second, he searched for his new mobile. Shit, the battery had gone flat. He could try throwing stones at the boy's windows, but had little to no chance of waking them up. Decision made, he opened the rear door of the car and crashed onto the seat, and then promptly fell back asleep.

\*\*\*

At nine-thirty-six a.m., Francis was up and in the kitchen making coffee. The doorbell rang, and she assumed it must be Michael. She opened the door with a scowl on her face to be met by the smiling postman.

'Good Morning, Mrs Fletcher.' He handed over a pile of letters.

'Yes, good morning.'

'Not that it's any of my business, but is your husband all right?'

Francis took a step out of the front door and saw Michael asleep in the back of the car. She knew he was all right because she could hear him snoring.

'Thank you for your concern, but he looks very well to me.' She went back in the front door and shut it. The postman took one last look at Michael and strode off.

\*\*\*

Michael didn't open his eyes again until eleven-thirty. He could hardly open his mouth, it was so dry and sticky, and he felt disorientated again, and then he heard her voice.

'I suggest you get out of the car, go and have a shower, and use lots of soap. Brush your teeth properly for ten minutes, and then put on some clean clothes. Your next job after that is to come back out here and clean the puke from inside the car. Have you got that, Michael?'

Michael almost crawled out of the car and just muttered two words, 'Yes dear.'

As he shuffled and stumbled into the house, Francis stood with arms crossed and shook her head. Then she slammed the car doors.

Michael stood in the shower for fully fifteen minutes. The hot water brought him back to life. He washed his hair, scrubbed himself, and got out with a small skip in his step, and then dried off. When he'd finished drying his hair, he looked in the mirror. Shocked, he took a step back and re-focussed—he looked like death warmed up, with his face a grey-white colour, bruises around one eye, and a cut on his chin.

That sickening feeling of remorse returned instantly, and he felt sure that Francis would make him pay for this. He retired to the bedroom, sprayed deodorant liberally all over, and put on a pair of jeans and a clean shirt. For some inexplicable reason, he felt as horny as hell. Of course, trying it on with Francis at the moment would be a big mistake. What he needed to do was to give her a large bouquet of flowers and a box of her favourite After Eight mints.

Dressed and desperate for a coffee, he decided to clean the car first before facing Francis in the kitchen. What a horrible job. He scooped up the vomit with inside-out plastic bags, and then opened the garage. He loved using the jet washer and gave the whole car a good valet. Soon, he stood in his welly boots, getting wet as he sprayed the car and cleaned it lovingly.

\*\*\*

Francis watched out of one of the upstairs windows as Michael pretended to be Luke Skywalker, fighting with a light sabre. She fought it for as long as she could but finally gave in and smiled. He was a complete rogue, but she loved him.

***

The car finished, and looking like it had just come out of the showroom, Michael stood and looked at it, gleaming black in the morning sunshine.

He turned when he heard the front door open.

'Breakfast is on the table. That is, if you're hungry?'

Michael smiled weakly and nodded like a little boy caught smoking in the school toilets. He walked into the kitchen to be met with the delicious smell of bacon and eggs. Starved, he sat in his normal seat and licked his lips in anticipation. Francis took a plate out of the oven and placed it on her side of the table. Michael looked at it: fried eggs, bacon, sausage, hash brown, and some beans—a veritable feast, and couldn't wait for his. Francis plonked a small side plate on his mat with a sorry-looking piece of dried toast. She sat down and tucked into her lovely cooked breakfast. Michael looked at her plate and then at his toast.

'I fully deserve this. I'm so sorry.'

'Are you, Michael? Are you really sure you're sorry? God, your behaviour has been extraordinary. Drunk, arrested, a night in the cells, you've ruined your best suit, and puking in the road and in the car, and worst of all ...' Her voice rose, and Michael waited for the next tortuous words. 'The worst thing of all was you farting in the packed train on the way home.' As soon as she said farting, she burst into laughter. 'You ever do this again, I swear, I will divorce you.'

Michael allowed the corners of his mouth to lift ever so slightly in a pathetic smile. Francis stood up, went to the oven, and brought out a second plate piled with bacon, eggs, and sausages, then she moved the plate with the toast on it and put the full plate down in front of Michael.

'You should have seen your face when I gave you that piece of toast. It was all worth it just for that moment.' Francis stopped smiling. 'No more feeling sorry for yourself. Okay?'

'Yes.'

'Now, stop talking and eat your food before it goes cold.'

Michael tucked in like he hadn't eaten for a week, washed it down with three cups of steaming coffee, and felt like he'd come back to life.

He spent the rest of the day making calls to recruiters with nothing positive to report at the end of it. Michael had gone to bed by nine p.m., and Francis crept in at ten-thirty and slid under the duvet, naked. Michael grabbed her hand and placed it on his huge erection. She climbed on top of him and lowered herself onto his hard cock.

The next day, things returned to nearly normal, with Michael spending hours in the office while Francis went shopping and did housework. She seemed pleased that Michael had calmed down and seemed to be getting stuck into finding a job. In truth, he looked but had decided it was a waste of time. No bank would give him a hundred-grand-a-year job—they just weren't available these days. He thought long and hard about what to do. Maybe he could do the same as Graham and get a job at thirty-odd K a year, but it didn't hold much appeal. He still had time to make his mark, to do something substantial; he had been successful once, and he could be again. It was just finding the opening. He had a feeling something would turn up, and it did on the following weekend.

Saturday morning, at eleven a.m., Michael sat in his office drinking coffee as usual and twiddling his thumbs. His mobile rang. He looked at the number and something about it seemed familiar.
'Hello, Michael Fletcher.'
'Michael, you don't know me. It's Sean King, from National Trust Bank. Are you able to talk for five minutes?'
'Sure, what can I do for you?'
Michael had retained all his accounts at the bank and assumed it was something to do with one of those.
'I'm involved in the investment arm, and I'm looking for some people who want to make shedloads of money. Does that sound like you?'
'Possibly, what sort of investment is it, exactly?'
'It's a property building investment in Kazakhstan. The bank's been working with the government over there for some months. We're putting in twenty million but want to offer some chunks out to preferential clients. Look, I know you left recently and have funds. It's got to be worth a ten-minute chat. What do you say?'

'So this is a National Trust Bank deal?'

'Absolutely. It's all kosher. I'm putting in three hundred thousand myself.'

'What's the return on investment and when?'

'Twenty-five percent after six months. It's an incredible deal.'

'Almost too good to be true,' Michael said, and he thought back to one of his sayings: If it sounds too good to be true it probably is. 'So this is definitely a National Trust Bank initiative?'

Michael then realised why he recognised the phone number; it was the National Trust Bank's head office.

'Absolutely, Michael. We're giving a presentation at the Landmark Hotel on Wednesday, so why don't you just come along and listen.'

Michael thought about Francis—she wouldn't like it. Then he decided she didn't need to know at this early stage.

'Okay, I'll come and listen. What time is it?'

'Ten a.m. A two-hour presentation followed by a spot of lunch. So, we look forward to seeing you then.'

'Yes, I'll be there, and thanks for the call.'

Michael sat back in his comfy swivel chair. It was a bank deal, so would be safe. He turned the figures over in his mind. If he invested two hundred grand, that would give him a return of fifty thousand—a nice sum of money. He wouldn't mention it to Francis, but would tell her he was going to see another recruiter. He spent the next day on the phone again, but couldn't stop thinking about the Kazakhstan deal, and looked forward to the elaborate and wow-factor presentation planned for the next morning.

Michael approached the glamorous Landmark Hotel in Marylebone Road and felt pleased. How typical of the bank to use a five-star hotel to promote an investment opportunity. He anticipated a nice lunch. A hotel concierge directed him to the Gold Suite, and he made his way there along the expensively-carpeted corridors. How many people would be present?

Another splendidly-dressed hotel concierge opened the door when he approached. He walked into the small room and did a quick headcount—about twenty-five people—and, as he scanned the room, he was surprised to see five-feet-five-and-round-balding Graham.

'What the hell are you doing here?' Michael asked him.

'Hello. Same as you, I guess. Come to hear how I can make some real money.'

'God, don't tell Audrey you saw me here. Francis thinks I'm at a recruiters.'

Graham laughed. 'Audrey thinks I'm at a banking conference.'

'Oh, we're both being sneaky then.' He joined in the laughter.

Michael had some coffee, and then he and Graham sat down and waited for the show to start. Four men entered the room and went to the front. One of them was Tony Morgan.

Michael turned to Graham. 'I see that bastard, Tony Morgan's here.'

72

Graham looked up. 'I had been slightly worried, but now he's here, that confirms the bank is running the show.'

Tony Morgan clapped his hands, and the room went quiet.

'Good Morning, and welcome to the Landmark Hotel. I'm disappearing in a minute, but I wanted to introduce Sean King, who is acting on behalf of National Trust Bank.' Sean—a tall, good-looking, well-dressed man—looked smooth. He smiled and nodded at the audience.

'The other two gentlemen are representatives from the Kazakhstan Development Corporation. We see this as a great opportunity for National Trust, as it could be for selected clients.' He scanned the room and made eye contact with as many delegates as he could. 'So, listen carefully, enjoy the lunch, and I look forward to us working together in the coming months.'

A smattering of handclaps sounded while Tony exited the room through a side door. The lights went out, and a screen flicked into life. The opening credit said:

KAZAKHSTAN

THE OPPORTUNITY OF A LIFETIME.

The investment included a new Hotel complex with shops, apartments, spa, and pools situated in the coastal resort of Aqtau on the Caspian Sea. The total investment was one hundred million pounds, and National Trust were putting in about twenty to twenty-five million. Other banks were involved and, of course, wealthy individuals were being given the opportunity to invest as well. Michael and Graham sat through the presentation without speaking. The resort looked fabulous, holiday numbers went up every year, and it was a prosperous, forward-thinking community. The presentation ended, and even Graham, usually ultra-cautious, thought it looked like an outstanding investment opportunity. Lunch turned out to be a delightful buffet, which Graham and Michael tucked into with fervour.

Graham went to the bathroom, and one of the Kazakhstan Development Representatives approached Michael.

'Good afternoon. You are Mr Michael Fletcher. I am Bekzat Abdulov. How do you do?'

'I'm very well, thank you. Nice lunch.'

'Good. What do you think of our little enterprise?'

'It all sounded terribly interesting. I'd like to know more.'

'Of course, and in that case, you must come out to Aqtau and take a look yourself at our expense.'

'I would like that very much. When is that likely to happen?'

'It is all arranged for August tenth. Speak to Sean and he will add you to the list. Most of the people here today will be joining you.'

'That's exciting. I expect we will meet in Aqtau, then.'

'Yes. I will be there, of course, as representative of the Kazakhstan government.'

Michael went to the buffet for a dessert, and Graham reappeared. The two of them then found Sean King and put themselves on the list for the visit to Aqtau.

'A free bloody holiday, all expenses paid, in a five-star hotel. Can't wait.'

Graham laughed. 'It's only three days, but yes, it should be fun.'

'I hope that bastard Morgan's not going. Sitting and being pleasant with him would stick in my throat more than a bit.'

They had two desserts each and left quietly. Michael wanted to get home early and stone-cold sober. Francis had made him promise that he would not go for even one drink, under any circumstances. The state he was in at the moment meant that one would lead to a second, and then goodness knows where.

Although he had promised to come straight home, she would still worry about him. At exactly three p.m., he opened the front door walked in, as sober as a judge. Francis just smiled at him and asked how the interview went. He replied that it looked promising, but that you could never really tell. Francis seemed happy with his good spirits.

# CHAPTER 6

Life had returned to just about normal for Freddie and Anne Rogers. They had gotten back into their strict weekly routine and desperately attempted to forget the attack and rape of Anne by the Serbian thugs. The local council had reinforced the front door and also attached a safety chain and cut out a peephole. DI Karen Foster had gone the extra mile and demanded a panic button be installed, and they had situated one inside a small bedside cupboard in the bedroom. The extra security measures had been welcome.

The worst moment, post-attack, for Freddie and Anne came when the police officer stationed outside the bungalow got whisked off to other duties. They had felt so safe with him there, and as soon as he left, they once again felt frightened and abandoned. There had been a family get-together to discuss what else could be done to offer Freddie and Anne peace of mind. Without someone actually moving into the bungalow, it was difficult to see what could be done. For a start, even if someone could be found, they only had one bedroom.

In the end, the family agreed to set up a rota, and members of the family and friends would take it in turns to visit. This wouldn't safeguard every minute of every day, but it would be an extra measure, and one that delighted Freddie and Anne. Karen Foster had also placed the address on the watch list, which meant that police cars would drive past and check the property whenever in the area, and particularly at night.

It would, however, take much longer for Freddie to get over the attack than even Anne. He thought of himself as a coward, an excuse for a man, who couldn't and didn't even try to protect his wife from that filthy animal. He couldn't see well, but still he could have done something. He'd known what was going on in the kitchen that day, and it haunted him every waking moment. He told his best friend, Phil, that he wanted to get a gun. Phil told him that if he'd had one, he would most likely have shot Anne and probably himself in the process of trying to shoot the assailant. Freddie said he would have been happy to take a bullet if he had shot that dirty, bastard, no good thug. Every so often, he would go to the bathroom and just cry. Anne understood but loved Freddie just the way he was—quiet, caring, and thoughtful to her needs.

The daily and nightly visits from family and friends became a nuisance more than a support, what with the long, tedious conversations, and making endless cups of tea with biscuits. In the end, they told the family it had to stop, that they couldn't take anymore, and it went to every other day, and then once during the week and once at the weekend.

Anne had moved on and felt delighted with the new security measures, and particularly the panic button in the bedroom, connected to Epsom Police Station. Freddie still went round checking the door and windows at least three times before they went to bed, and insisted on having his old cricket bat on the floor by his side of the double bed.

# CHAPTER 7

'I'm hardly going to get up to mischief with Graham in tow; you know what he's like.'

As soon as Michael said he was off to Kazakhstan for three days, the alarm bells had gone off for Francis, and she sat him down in the lounge and interrogated him for a full hour. As soon as she heard Graham Hawkins was going, she relaxed a little, but got straight on the phone to Mary, Graham's wife, to confirm the details of the visit. Michael and Graham had come up with what they thought was a sound story—that they were being paid to go out to Kazakhstan to help the Government with their banking systems. It was all being arranged by National Trust Bank, and the pair were lucky to be asked. Tony Morgan, no less, had invited them on behalf of the bank. Francis didn't like it, but they needed the money, so she tried to relax; after all, they were going on the Friday lunchtime and would be back Sunday night. How much trouble could they get into in such a short time?

'Just make sure you concentrate on the work and nothing else.'

'Scouts honour, Dib, Dib, Dob, Dob,' Michael said with a smile, holding up his fingers in the Scout salute.

'Very funny. Just make sure there's no repetition of the other day. I doubt the Kazakhstan police force are as friendly and amenable as our boys in blue. I won't be coming out to Kazakhstan to rescue you.'

'Don't worry, I'm not going down that road again, God forbid.'

Michael spent the next few days in the office, not doing a great deal of anything. He was now going to be an investor in multi-million-pound deals all over the world, and Kazakhstan was just the beginning. Friday the tenth finally arrived. Graham picked Michael up from his house, and they headed straight to Gatwick to catch the twelve-thirty flight to Aqtau.

At Gatwick, they met up with the group of potential investors, which numbered about sixteen. Sean King stood there, chatting to Bekzat Abdulov, and thank God, no Tony Morgan. Then they got the surprise of their lives, as they had fully expected to be flying economy on BA or Virgin but, no, they would fly in a private BAC 1-11 chartered private jet. Neither Michael nor Graham had ever flown in a private plane, and what an eye opener to see how the other half lived.

They went through a basic and quick passport control and soon sat in thick leather seats, drinking champagne and scoffing canapés. The air hostesses looked like Playboy centrefold models. Obviously, it would be five-star all the way, and Michael and Graham weren't about to protest. Cold salmon with hollandaise sauce came next, with new potatoes and broccoli, and Michael fell in love. The hostess looked slim, and had pert breasts and legs that went on forever, she also had his favourite long blonde hair tied back, and a pretty face. Her name was Ainalayin. He tried to chat with her, but she just smiled and said, 'No English, sorry.' Michael sat in shock, he couldn't take his eyes off her, and then Bekzat appeared.

'Hello, Michael and Graham.'

Michael always seemed to speak first, 'Good afternoon, Bekzat, how are you?'

Bekzat glanced to his left and right. 'How could I be anything other than fine in this superb private jet? I see you like Ainalayin.' He eyeballed Michael.

'All the girls are beautiful and ...' He wasn't sure how to pronounce it. 'Ainalayin is delightful.'

'You pronounced that almost perfectly, and yes, all the girls are handpicked by me to provide every comfort for our friends.'

Michael thought there could be a hidden message in that statement but wasn't sure.

'It's a shame she doesn't speak English. I would like to have spoken to her.'

Bekzat smiled. 'There are many comforts and pleasures that do not require conversation, are there not, Gentlemen?'

'I guess there are,' Michael said, almost certain that Bekzat was intimating that his girls might be proffering more than Salmon and Potatoes.

'I must go, and—I think you say—mingle; a strange word, indeed. If I do not see you again, I will see you at dinner tonight.' He turned to go but stopped. 'After dinner, we have some entertainment that I think you will appreciate very much.' He smiled and went to join a group at the front of the luxurious cabin.

After all the drinks and superb food, Michael and Graham both nodded off and enjoyed a sound sleep. The flight took six and a half hours, and was due in at Aqtau at seven p.m. They'd been booked into the five-star Riviera Grand Palace Hotel.

The BAC 1-11 flew through the skies, and they landed ahead of schedule at six-forty-two p.m. Neither Michael nor Graham had ever been to Kazakhstan, so felt excited and slightly anxious at the same time. The group filed off the plane and soon occupied a private VIP lounge, having coffee and cake. The absence of passport control flabbergasted Michael, but he felt sure that Bekzat and Sean King must have arranged everything well in advance. They left the small modern airport in a Mercedes mini-bus and soon got sight of a beautiful clear blue sea with long sandy beaches. They drove along the seafront, past several hotels, until they pulled into the largest of them all, the Riviera Grand Palace. As soon as they pulled up, staff swarmed over the bus, collecting luggage and escorting the group into reception—all black marble and luxury. Michael and Graham smiled at each other.

'This is going to be a wonderful trip. I can feel it.' Michael caught sight of Ainalayin striding to the reception desk. His look lingered on her long legs. God, how he would like to suck those toes, and then move up her legs with his tongue. He shook his head to try and focus on something else, but she was obviously staying in the hotel, which could only be a bonus. Ainalayin knew Michael was looking at her, and she flicked her long blonde hair from side to side and ran her hand through it sexily. Although a little old for her, he was handsome enough. She picked a key up off the desk and turned towards a group of lifts, then turned slowly towards Michael and gave him a lovely warm smile.

'Graham, did you see that she likes me? Oh God, I've got to have her, please, please, let me have her.'

'You're dreaming, chum, and you're a married man.'

'Yes, of course, I'll forget that idea. Yes, you're right.' Michael would make a play for the girl, but he would definitely not tell Graham anything. The hotel gave the group room key-cards, and staff escorted them to the third floor, where the entire group would stay. When Michael left the lift, what could only be described as a man-mountain of a man stood next to a desk, which surprised him.

Michael turned to Graham and whispered, 'Guards? That's a bit creepy.'

The guard eyeballed Michael, and then turned to Graham. He smiled in surprise and stretched out his hand. Graham shook hands with him and continued walking.

'Strange fellow. He must have mistaken me for someone else. I think a lot of these hotels have problems with prostitutes wandering around trying to find clients. I expect that's why he's here.'

Michael was surprised Graham knew that, but it seemed like a plausible reason.

'Have you stayed here before then?' Michael asked in a playful voice.

Graham replied in an uptight manner, 'No, I have not.'

'All right, keep your hair on.' Michael paused to deliver the killer line, 'What you've got left anyway.'

'Ha Ha,' Graham said. 'Very funny. See you later.'

Dinner would be at eight-thirty in the private Platinum suite of rooms. Michael loved his room—huge, with a massive double bed. He stripped off and soon luxuriated under a cascade of hot water, which rejuvenated his tired limbs. Dress code was smart casual, so Michael picked a pair of cream chinos, matched with a stripy, blue Ted Baker shirt. He hoped that Ainalayin would be at the dinner. At eight-fifteen, he made his way to the Platinum Suite. Security seemed tight, as he entered a small reception area and gave his name to a beautiful, young brunette, sitting behind an expensive antique desk.

'Please, go through, Mr Fletcher.'

Where did they find all these gorgeous girls? He pushed the next door open, and a stunningly-decorated room met him. Marble and statues were predominant and, in the middle, sat the most beautiful dinner table he had ever seen. Masses of brightly coloured flowers in huge vases made the room even more stunning.

'Michael, welcome to the Gold Suite. What do you think?'

'Stunning, Bekzat, absolutely fabulous.'

'You see, we like to take care of our business partners. Come, let me introduce you to some of the other investors.'

Fifteen minutes later, a loud gong sounded, and everyone fell silent.

A toast master announced, 'Gentlemen, dinner is served.'

Michael moved towards the magnificent table to sit down, and then noticed the name cards. He moved around the table and, finally, saw his name. With relief, he pulled the chair out and sat down. He then looked for Graham and spotted him at the other end of the table. All the men had seated themselves, and an empty chair remained to the left of each of the guests. Another loud gong sounded, and a pair of double doors opened at the far end of the room. A line of beautiful young women strutted into the room. All the men sat in shock and couldn't take their eyes off the beauties. Michael looked desperately for Ainalayin but couldn't see her. The girls filled the empty chairs.

Michael glanced over to Graham, who had a beautiful, slim, slightly tanned woman next to him. Then Michael jumped when the empty chair next to him got pulled back. He looked up to see Ainalayin smiling down at him. The sheer fabric of her dress revealed her nipples, which excited him beyond belief. He stood up and helped with the chair.

'Good eening, Mr Hlecher.' Ainalayin tried so hard to get it right.

Michael laughed. 'That was perfect, Ainalayin. I'm so pleased to see you.' He held her arm gently and didn't want to let go. He could imagine what she was like underneath the flimsy dress. Dinner began with a small cup of something white. Michael looked at the menu, which was in both languages.

Kumiss—a drink made from mare's milk. He took a sip, thinking it would be awful, but was pleasantly surprised. Next, came platters of mutton snacks called Khazi, Zhal, and Karta. The main course arrived on platters, and Michael had never seen such huge pieces of meat; massive boiled mutton shanks, served with slices of boiled pastry. Delicious wine accompanied every course, and Michael enjoyed himself immensely. He would occasionally lean over and whisper something in

Ainalayin's ear. She almost certainly didn't know what he was saying, but he drank in the smell of her scent and perfume. Towards the end of the meal, Ainalayin leant over and put her hand on the back of Michael's neck, then tousled his hair and whispered to him.

'You happe?'

Michael responded with a kiss to her cheek. 'Very happy, thank you.'

The meal ended, and the men passed cheese and vintage port round the table. The gong sounded and, immediately, all the women stood and walked back towards the double doors and disappeared. Michael felt sad for a moment—no goodbye, no see you later. He knocked back some more port, sure that he would see her again. The gong sounded once more, and Bekzat got to his feet.

'Gentlemen, I hope you enjoyed the traditional Kazakhstan dinner.' Shouts of 'bravo' came from around the table, and 'delicious,' and 'wonderful.'

'So, we now move into the entertainment for the evening. Kazakhstan is famous for its dancing, so we have prepared something special for you.' Bekzat clapped his hands. The double doors opened, and two tall, slim, beautiful women walked in and stopped. The men couldn't take their eyes off them, and then the music started, and the women danced around the table.

The dancing entranced Michael. When they swayed to the music, their breasts were revealed in all their glory; nipples hard and standing out. Then Michael received yet another shock when the women danced faster and faster, and then lifted their flimsy skirts to reveal naked buttocks and more. Mesmerised, Michael glanced around the table. No one could take their eyes off the two dancers. The music came to a crescendo, and the women collapsed onto the floor. The group burst into spontaneous roaring. They clapped, cheered, and shouted for more. Bekzat smiled at Sean King and nodded in satisfaction. After a fair time, Bekzat stood again, and silence reigned.

'I felt sure you would like our traditional dancers.'

One of the more drunk investors shouted out, 'Yeah, but we want more.' Everybody laughed.

Everyone at the table was now drunk or nearly there. New bottles of quality French wine appeared as if by magic, and soon, five-star Brandy was being quaffed. Michael joined in with the excess, enjoying every minute of it.

Bekzat, a good judge of character, looked at the group and decided to change the entertainment. He disappeared for two minutes but soon came back.

He stood again. 'Please, be kind enough to vacate the tables for a few minutes while we rearrange the room. It will not take long.'

Hotel workers entered and cleared the dinner table, then dismantled it and removed it from the room. They brought in six round tables and placed them at the sides of the room. Women entered and threw many soft cushions into the centre of the room, then invited the investors to sit at the tables. More drinks arrived with snacks.

The doors closed and the lights over the tables dimmed. The centre of the room was brightly lit, and all the investors waited for something to happen. And then it did. The door at the far end opened, and a single woman entered. Just like the others, she looked young and beautiful. Quiet background music came to life, and she strolled to the centre of the room. Absently, she picked up and threw cushions back onto the floor, and then sat down cross-legged. Nobody knew what would happen next. The atmosphere felt electric. Then the door opened again, and three large, muscular men entered, chatting and laughing. Michael's heart rose to his mouth. The anticipation felt incredible. The music got louder. The three men noticed the woman and stopped. All fell quiet. They whispered between them, and two of the men moved to either side of the room. The woman seemed oblivious to the men as if daydreaming. A man moved, and she turned and looked directly at him, then eased to her feet, and then turned and ran for the side. The second man appeared, and she stopped. Then she turned again and made for the other side, but the third man appeared, and she stopped again. She turned every way, looking for a possible escape route, to no avail. The three men closed in on their prey.

Michael felt excited beyond belief. He knew what would happen, but that didn't diminish the anticipation. He could hardly breathe, as he gulped some brandy down, not taking his eyes off the action. Suddenly, the three men and the woman froze. The door at the end reopened, and a group of women entered. Michael looked closely. They seemed different to the women at dinner. Ainalayin was not among them. They dispersed around the room and joined the men at the tables. Two women sat at Michael and Graham's table.

The action started again. The three men leapt on the woman, grabbing at her clothes and ripping off her dress. The woman fought back, but they were too strong for her, and soon she knelt naked. The atmosphere felt intense while the men kissed and groped at the woman, feeling her breasts and between her legs. Then it went quiet, and the three men stood back. The woman had accepted her fate—she could not get away. They dropped their robes to the floor to reveal massive erections, the woman gyrated and lifted her bottom. Then she opened her legs wide and swung her hips from side to side, teasing the men.

Still entranced, Michael felt a hand slip over his crotch and squeeze his hard cock. On instinct, he jerked back and then relaxed. He looked over and saw that the other woman had done exactly the same to Graham. So much for his holier than thou attitude of earlier.

Across the room, the three men grabbed at the woman, and she stayed compliant. One of them turned her over and climbed underneath her, then moved her knees to either side of him, which automatically lifted her bottom into the air. One man pushed his cock into her mouth while the man underneath entered her pussy, and the final man stood behind her and thrust into her back passage. The woman gasped, as did some of the men watching. The women at the tables were all over the men, and some were almost naked. The smell of sex permeated the air, as the music once again increased in volume.

The three men fucked the woman in unison, in and out, in and out. The woman gasped, moaned, and screamed, and then—unbelievably—they all came together with grunts and shouts. The woman reached orgasm and screamed for the last time, and they all collapsed to their knees. Michael and the others cheered and clapped. The entertainment had been a huge success.

The woman with Michael had nearly masturbated him to come but hadn't had time. He removed her hand, took another drink, and relaxed.

'The entertainment is good, no?' Bekzat shouted.

More cheering and clapping.

'Gentlemen, please give your warm appreciation to the troupe who, believe me, enjoyed it as much as you.'

The three men and the woman were all smiles as they stood and bowed before their audience. They seemed to have enjoyed it, but Michael did wonder if the woman really had.

'So, the evening has come to an end.' One or two boos sounded. 'Having said that, we are all adults here, so if you wish to spend some time with the ladies, please take them to your rooms and play chess or whatever.'

A man shouted, 'The whatever sounds much more interesting.' More cheers and laughter came.

'So, I bid you good night and look forward to seeing you at breakfast in here, which closes at ten-thirty. We are visiting the proposed building site tomorrow, which I know you are all looking forward to.'

Some of the men got up straightaway and went towards the door, holding hands with a woman. Michael looked at the woman next to him. She seemed attractive. Michael thought these were working girls, and he didn't want her, he wanted Ainalayin. He got up and looked at Graham. 'You coming?'

'Hopefully, very soon, yes.' He put his arm round the other woman, and they left the room together.

It seemed Michael was the only one who wasn't taking up the offer of some company. He looked at the woman and felt sorry for her. Then he had an idea and held his hand out. She smiled and took it, and they left together as well. They got to Michael's room and, to his delight, he found out the woman spoke some English.

He smiled as he asked her, 'You are working?'

'Yes, of course, I get paid a lot extra if I stay the night with you.'

'Do you know the other women? Do you know Ainalayin?'

'No, we are kept separate. The other girls are not prostitutes.'

'Okay, so you can stay here tonight, but you can get a good night's sleep instead of you know ...'

The woman looked shocked. 'I no understand.'

'You stay here, sleep, then tomorrow morning, you go.'

'What, no jig jig?'

'Exactly, no jig jig.'

The woman pulled the straps off her dress, and it fell to the floor, and then she climbed on one side of the bed, covered herself, and fell asleep within two minutes. Michael climbed in beside her, and soon, he too snored away.

The prostitute left Michael's room at seven a.m., and Michael took his time getting up, then strolled down to breakfast just after nine-thirty. He sat next to Graham, who had a smile on his face from ear to ear.

'I hope your night was as good as mine. What a woman. Hell, she knew more tricks than Paul Daniels.'

Michael said, 'I hope you had protection, mate?'

Graham froze. 'Jesus, the last time. Oh shit, if she's given me anything, I'll fucking kill someone.'

'Don't worry, it's too late now, anyway. Bekzat is so thorough that I'm sure the girls were tested and passed with flying colours.'

'Yes, I'm sure they were.' Graham didn't look so sure, though. 'I'm not going to give it another thought. So, we're off to the site today. Should be interesting.'

'Yeah, I can't wait. I'm getting some food.' Michael made for the breakfast buffet, which looked incredible.

Hungry, he stuffed his face with sausages, fried potatoes, scrambled eggs, and bacon. At twelve o'clock, they all met in the foyer and were escorted out to the Mercedes mini-bus. The day was hot, and Michael felt glad of the air conditioning when he climbed onto the bus. Soon, they motored down the coast road. Michael took everything in. The roads seemed good and had obviously been redone recently. The beaches looked sandy, and people lay sunbathing. It all looked good, and then the mini-bus slowed and turned off the road, then stopped. They parked thirty yards from the road and about two hundred yards from the sea. Bekzat and Sean King gathered the group together.

'So, gentlemen, we have arrived. This is the beautiful location we are planning to develop. The Kazakhstan government have recognised tourism as a key area for growth in the coming years, and that is one reason why they are supporting this project with finance of five million pounds. The National Trust Bank and others will make up a significant part of the balance, and private investors will have the opportunity to buy in with any amount they wish, as long as it is in one hundred thousand pound sums.'

The driver set up tables and laid out cold drinks. Also, a separate table held some rolled up paper scrolls.

'It is hot. Please, avail yourself of cold refreshments, and in ten-minutes time, I am going to show you the draft plans for the building. I know you will be impressed with the quality of the facilities.'

The group meandered over to the drinks table. Michael watched the driver pin out a huge drawing, which covered an entire table. He felt desperate to get a look, and then saw the driver nod at Bekzat.

'Please, come to the drawing table, and I will explain exactly what we are proposing, and then you can study the drawing at your leisure. Do not hesitate to ask me if you have any queries. The land you see between the four red flags is the designated plot.'

The area looked huge.

'The hotel will be central to the construction and will be a four-star establishment. Four star here is equivalent to five stars in most western European countries. Within the hotel will be a Spa, an indoor pool, restaurants, and designer shops. Outside, will be a further two pools, tennis courts, mini golf, and a children's playground area. No expense will be spared in the construction of this superb, must-visit location. Not forgetting it will be relatively cheap. Our wages are fifty percent lower than any major developed country.' Bekzat looked around, and most of the group nodded in enthusiasm. He smiled. 'And now, please, come and look at the plans. When we get back to the hotel, we have another surprise for you.'

One of the first to study the plans, Michael felt impressed at how professionally drawn they were, and the immense detail. He drew away from the crowd and looked at the huge piece of land, and then the blue sea. Yes, a good location, and he could imagine crowds flocking to the hotel.

Thirty minutes later, they pulled up back at the hotel. Staff escorted them to the Silver Suite, where they surrounded a huge table in the middle of the room, covered by a sort of tarpaulin with a rope hanging from the ceiling. Michael guessed what it was but still felt anticipation and excitement when the tarpaulin got raised. An incredible model of the new hotel complex filled the table. The detail was sublime, with miniature figures in swimsuits by the pool, and cars on the lifelike roads. With a sudden a swish, the curtains closed automatically across the windows. They closed tightly, and the room plunged into darkness. No one moved. Then the model lit up. Internal lights lit all the tiny windows, all the lamplights on the roads shone brightly, and floodlights played onto the swimming pools. It looked magnificent, and a burst of applause rang out through the room. Bekzat beamed and raised his arms.

'It is beautiful, is it not? And, within eighteen months, you will see this glorious complex rising at the location we visited earlier. I can assure you that no one is more excited than me about this project.' The group again burst into spontaneous clapping.

Michael looked at the model. This was it—the opportunity he had been waiting for. A chance to make some real money and maybe, just as importantly, good connections for the future. He looked at Graham, and they smiled at each other. Michael knew he was thinking exactly the same thing.

They had a buffet lunch and were then left to their own devices for the afternoon. Michael went to his room, sat at the desk, and worked out some figures. When he had finished, he put the pen down, leant back, and smiled. He felt pleased with himself. He then lay on the huge double bed and fell asleep. At four in the afternoon, he awoke and stepped onto his balcony. When he looked out at the shimmering sea, he thought of private jets and five-star hotels. This would be his future. And, on reflection, leaving the bank was the best thing that had ever happened to him.

# CHAPTER 8

Stanislav and Cedomir Kasan's money had nearly run out. They had to pay rent in advance for their room and a share of the bills. Just adding credit on their mobiles cost a fortune, so they decided to stop ringing home so often. Occasionally, they picked up a bit of casual work, but the gang bosses knew they were illegals and only paid them five pounds an hour cash. The trouble-free spoils from the elderly had dried up, and they became desperate.

They had tried to take more money out of the cashpoint with Freddie's card, but the machine had swallowed it, and the message was to contact the bank, which obviously, they didn't do. Stanislav was all for going back to Freddy and Anne's bungalow, but Cedomir had persuaded him it would be too dangerous. They were too afraid to walk around Leatherhead, Ashtead, or Epsom town centres too much, as the police were clearly looking for them. Luckily, Surrey police didn't have officers on the beat anymore; only mobile units driving all over the county at high speed and answering 999 calls. It was a stressful time for them both, and then Cedomir dropped the bombshell that he wanted to go home, that he was sick of life in the UK, and thought he could do better at home. Stanislav begged him to stay a short time longer, and then they would both go together. Cedomir agreed, and Stanislav persuaded him they could have a weekend of making money, ending with a revisit to the bungalow for one more pay day.

***

DI Karen Foster holidayed in Cannes, lapping up the sunshine and the chilled white wine in equally copious quantities. She had the time of her life, sunbathing on the beach for hours, eating superb freshly-caught fish in the restaurant every night, and if that wasn't enough, then followed by making passionate love with Esme in every position imaginable in the small cosy room above the restaurant.

Esme had asked Karen to consider moving to Cannes permanently. Mama and Papa were aging, and Esme felt—at last—ready to take over the restaurant. She said that Karen could help her run it, and that life would be perfect. Karen felt so tempted but said she would have to give it long and serious consideration. Karen had one or two major issues to think about. She didn't speak French, and thought that however hard she tried, she would never pick it up. There was her police career to consider and her pension. She cherished her work and would miss it dreadfully. Then, of course, there were her family and friends. Esme said that living in Cannes would be like being down the road from London, but Karen didn't quite see it like that. And lastly, what exactly was she going to do in the restaurant? She couldn't cook, and how could she work serving without some knowledge of the language? The attractions were easy to see: glorious sunshine every day, fabulous food, and a supposed great lifestyle, but was working every night 'til two in a hot, sweaty environment what she really wanted to do?

Karen would go back after the holiday and give it a lot of thought, and Esme would stay in Cannes, working with her Mama and Papa, taking more responsibility over the next few weeks, until Mama and Papa finally retired for good. It would be Karen's decision, and hers alone, whether she returned to Cannes to start a new life. Only a couple of days remained of the holiday, and Karen made the most of it, swimming, sunbathing, drinking, and eating.

The dreaded Sunday arrived, and Esme drove Karen to the airport. They didn't speak in the car, but Karen touched Esme's arm on occasion. She didn't want to go but felt confused: she looked forward to walking back into Epsom nick—her second home—and it would be tough to decide what to do. They parked up, and the tears started. Esme was the first, and as soon as she started, Karen followed. Esme spluttered that she would never see Karen again and begged her to come back as soon as possible. Karen cried because she thought this could possibly be the end of their relationship. Karen rushed through passport control, sat down, and pulled herself together. She'd already decided what she would do.

Karen touched down at Heathrow at four in the afternoon, got straight on the tube, and headed for London Bridge. She had to wait twenty minutes, but then caught the fast train to Epsom. She strolled into Epsom nick at seven p.m., mainly to get a heads up for what she could expect in the morning. It was deathly quiet, and a typical Sunday. She spoke to Constable Christopher Edwards at reception, the only officer on duty apart from the custody team, who had no visitors in the cells.

'So, Chris, anything exciting happened while I've been away?'

'Well, Boss, I'm obviously not privy to all that's going on, but I think I can safely say there've been no major incidents while you've been away. Having said, that some kids smashed up one of the swings at the playground in Roseberry Park.'

Karen just looked at him and shook her head.

'Sorry, Boss, but that's it. What do you want me to say?'

'Nothing. I'm off home. Call me a cab. Please.' She sat on one of the blue reception chairs and contemplated life.

***

Meanwhile, Stanislav and Cedomir made their plans.

'Next Friday, we will begin a weekend of making money, and once we have sold everything, we will leave this fucking country and go home. You are right, Cedomir, we do much better at home.'

'I'm glad you agree. So, what plans for next weekend?'

'We will create mayhem in local areas and make us rich at same time. Listen carefully ...'

# CHAPTER 9

Bekzat spoke to the assembled group, 'So, tomorrow you will all depart back to the UK. We, unfortunately, have to continue working as we welcome a group of investors from Germany and Austria. Of course, we all now live in a global society. Once you are back in the UK, Sean King from National Trust Bank will be in contact with you. You will then have the opportunity to join our party or not. If you wish to walk away from this incredible opportunity, plenty of investors are queuing to take your places.'

For just a second, Michael felt worried. He could lose out. Perhaps they wouldn't need all the investors. Some of them may increase their investment. He would have a quiet word with Sean before they left on Sunday.

'Tonight is the last opportunity for us to get to know each other even more and to, I think you would say, *let your hair down.*' Everybody laughed and one or two people shouted, *now you're talking.* 'So, at eight o'clock, we are going back in the mini-bus to a special club, where we will have a superb meal and, of course, marvellous entertainment.'

Michael smiled, as did all the group, sure the entertainment would be something exceptional. He went back to his room and again worked and checked on his figures; they were sound. After all, he had been in banking for twenty-eight years. Michael relaxed with a glass of wine from the fridge, took a shower, and then dressed in white Chinos and a loose, cream tee shirt. He made his way to the foyer, where he met up with Graham.

Graham leant over and whispered, 'What do you think?'

'I think I'm going to have a word with Sean so we don't lose out.'

Graham looked concerned. 'I'll come with you; stronger together, wouldn't you say?'

Michael laughed. 'Yes, Graham, of course.'

The group, all in attendance, got onto the mini-bus. They had stayed on the coast for the entire trip, but this time they headed inland to the town centre of Aqtau. Michael loved the smells, the heat, the dust, and the noise of local people talking, and felt like he was living his own Casablanca. They drove through the town centre and stopped at a restaurant at the northern edge of the town—called the Kuzakh Kyrgyz. It seemed a little rundown and the car park had not been paved or tarmacked. Just as Michael thought that it looked like a strange choice, Bekzat spoke.

'Do not be alarmed. You will see why we are here when you enter the restaurant. It will be an experience you will never forget.'

The group jumped off the mini-bus and made their way to the entrance, where they entered into a foyer and were asked to wait. Michael could hear loud music, and then the large wooden doors swung open and a group of clapping, cheering women entered, grabbed the hands of the investors and pulled them into the interior. Michael looked at the women. More beautiful young girls dressed in skimpy outfits. It was an amazing sight that greeted them. Rich tapestries covered the walls, hundreds of brightly coloured cushions littered the floor, and low wooden tables held food and bottles of expensive French wine, five-star brandy, and vintage port. Loud music, provided by a band seemingly playing traditional dance music, accompanied numerous belly dancers, who gyrated around the tables.

Hostesses directed the group to specific tables and they sat crossed leg watching the remarkably sexy belly dancers. A gong sounded, the dancers disappeared, and the music lowered to a subdued background noise. Michael helped himself to a glass of wine, and just then another, quieter, gong sounded. He looked to the door, and a line of women snaked into the room, and he saw Ainalayin with the huge, stunning eyes and delicious body. He prayed she would come to his table, but on this occasion, he was to be disappointed. She moved gracefully like a big cat and sat between two men at the table next to Michael's. He felt more than disappointed; he was totally gutted. He couldn't take his eyes off her, and what made it worse was that she appeared not even to know he existed.

Michael hit the wine big time and soon felt the effects. Incense burned at various locations throughout the vast room, which added to the intense atmosphere, and he was back in his Casablanca. The food seemed never-ending, and as soon as a bottle of wine was emptied, another appeared as if by magic. Michael continually looked over at Ainalayin, and she seemed to be having the time of her life. The two men looked entranced by her, as he had been and still remained. It was a heady evening and certainly a meal they would all never forget. It got to ten o'clock and staff passed the brandy and port round the tables. Michael had become drunk and didn't care. He reached for his glass, then felt a hand on his shoulder and heard a voice in his ear.

'Follow me.'

He turned to look. Ainalayin sashayed away to where he knew the bathrooms were. After a wait of ten seconds, which seemed like a lifetime, he glanced around, and then followed her. When he pushed open the door, there she stood, leaning seductively against the wall. His eyes zeroed in on the split in her gold dress and her long, slim, tanned legs waiting for his hands. He moved towards her, she smiled, and he knew this was the moment. Then he stopped close to her and called her name. She whispered back to him.

'Michael, I meese you.'

He looked at her lips and then into her eyes. Yes, she wanted him to kiss her. He closed in and felt her warm lips. With eyes shut, he kissed her full on with tenderness and strength at the same time. He held her in his arms and his erection hardened. She stroked his hair and her hand wandered to his cock, where she touched him playfully, and he went to another world. Then he pushed his hands down the back of her dress and felt her arse, and got so excited, but then she moved away from him.

'Later, Michael.' She smiled and kissed him on the cheek, and then returned to the festivities. Michael did likewise, now so happy he could have screamed. She wanted him. She was his. The most beautiful woman in the world, and Michael Fletcher, the unemployed banker, had pulled her.

He poured himself a large port and smiled, content. The meal seemed to go on for hours. The ladies at the tables left and new dancers appeared. They moved around the tables, seemingly floating, and gradually they undressed to nakedness. Breasts swayed and legs gyrated. The music grew louder, and the dancers faster. It was mesmeric, and the men couldn't take their eyes off the beautiful flesh dancing right in front of them.

What happened next, shocked Michael. One of the dancers took an investor by the hand—the man looked drunk—and she took him to a pile of nearby cushions where she took off his clothes until he, too, lay naked with his cock standing at attention. She lay on the cushions and pulled him down onto her, and soon the pair fucked right in the middle of the room. Other dancers took men and did the same in small, private spaces throughout the restaurant. It had turned into a full-fledged orgy. A dancer approached Michael. This tall, lithe, and tanned beauty sashayed toward him. He licked his lips and swallowed. She smiled and took his hand. Unable to refuse, he let her lead him to a space in the corner, where she pulled him to the floor. Her hands fumbled at his trouser belt, and he thought of Ainalayin. He grabbed her hand and smiled at her, shaking his head gently. She looked into his eyes, pleading, but he smiled and gently but firmly held her hand. 'No.'

Back on his feet, Michael walked to his table and hoped that later he wouldn't regret not fucking her brains out. Bekzat certainly knew how to throw a party, that was for sure. Naked couples writhed on the floor of cushions in all sorts of positions. The watching was almost as much fun as taking part.

Gradually, the evening came to an end. The men, spent, returned to their tables and drank greedily to quench their thirst. Michael's thoughts returned to Ainalayin; she had said *later*. Might she come to him? But they would leave the next day, so this was his last chance. He considered talking to Bekzat but didn't want to get Ainalayin in trouble, so dismissed that idea. Besides, he had no idea where she was, so couldn't set out to find her. It lay in her hands, and he could do nothing but hope and pray. The music stopped, and Bekzat ushered everyone to the door.

'A truly wonderful evening, my friends. Let us make our way to the bus, and we will be back at the hotel in no time at all.'

The return journey passed in a flash, and soon the group dispersed to their rooms. Michael made his way to his room, seriously considering whether to leave Francis and make a new life with Ainalayin. He opened his room door and turned on the light. The happiest he had ever been in his life, he thanked God: Ainalayin lay in his bed, and as she smiled at him, she lowered the single white sheet to reveal her nakedness.

'Michael, hat last you are herr.' He laughed at her English, and she lifted the sheet playfully and pretended to sleep. Michael stripped off and pulled the cover off the bed. Ainalayin looked beautiful with her light tan and smooth-in-all-the-right-places body. He had been right to refuse the other woman. At her feet, he licked and kissed her toes, and made his way up to her womanhood. She gave back in kind, sucking his erection 'til he could stand no more. Near his limit, he climbed on top of her and they joined together as one. It was over quickly, as Michael had been so excited. They got no sleep that night, and they must have made love six times, as they enjoyed each other's bodies.

Morning came, and Michael awoke feeling like he'd gotten about an hour's sleep. Ainalayin had gone, and he felt sad and upset beyond belief. Had it all been a dream? No, definitely not. His memory of the night of passion felt too vivid, and he could still smell her presence. What a woman. His head crashed back onto the pillow, he rested there for a few minutes, and then decided to go down and have some coffee—he didn't think he could manage to eat anything.

After he'd showered, it surprised him that he didn't feel too bad, considering how much he had drunk. Once out of his room, he took the lift, and then walked into the Gold Suite. Besides him, only one other person occupied the vast room. They said good morning, and Michael grabbed a cup of coffee and sat down. Hostesses stood ready to serve food, and Michael got up to see what was available. As usual, the choice looked magnificent. He took some sausages and eggs, as he had suddenly developed a hunger. Seated again, he tucked into the steaming-hot food. A hostess hovered nearby, and then brushed past him, dropping an envelope onto his plate. What was it? Michael picked it up and took out the single sheet of paper.

*(Michael, my name is Milania. I am writing this on behalf of Ainalayin.)*

*Michael, Michael, such a handsome English man. You are a very kind and lovely man, and I will miss you when you leave today. I wonder if we will ever meet again, and that is really up to you, not me. I expect you are married with a family. I wish things could be different. I am single and live in Aqtau, and I do jobs for Bekzat when he needs girls. Last night was so wonderful. I wish you were staying forever. Life is hard here. We have to do whatever we can to earn money. I hope you understand. If you come back to Aqtau, look me up. Ask any of the girls at the hotel. They know me. Goodbye, my love. Ainalayin XXX*

Michael turned to the hostess who had given him the note, and smiled at her, then read the note once more and tucked it into his pocket. With haste, he finished his breakfast and rushed back to his room, where he took a piece of the hotel paper and wrote:

*Ainalayin, my love, it is with great sadness that I leave today. I am so happy to have met you but distressed at having to leave you here. Yes, I am married, with two boys. What the future holds at the moment, I am not sure. All I do know is that I will return to Aqtau and see you again. When that will be, I do not know, maybe in a couple of months, we will see. Take care of yourself. Love, Michael XXX*

Michael folded the letter, placed it in an envelope, and sealed it, then wrote 'Ainalayin' on the front and headed back to breakfast. He saw the hostess immediately and gave her the envelope.

'Please, make sure Ainalayin receives this, and thank you so much.'

'Do not worry. I will make sure Ainalayin receives it very quickly.'

Michael returned to his room. The flight was at midday, and they had to be ready in reception at ten. He felt depressed but excited. The project had turned out to be more than he had hoped for, an opportunity not to be missed, and he wanted to revisit Aqtau as soon as possible to see Ainalayin again. His mind worked overtime. Perhaps he could set Ainalayin up in a house here and come out every month for a couple of weeks. The flying, jet lag, parties, and food and drink had taken their toll, and he needed a week off to get over the trip.

He looked at his watch: ten to ten, and then he grabbed his case, checked the room once more to make sure he hadn't left anything behind, and then left. He got to the lifts, one soon arrived, and he got in and recognised two of the other investors. They, too, looked despondent, and Michael tried smiling, but managed only a feeble effort. They got to the foyer and joined the rest of the group. Soon, they raced back down the coast road towards the airport.

As before, everything had been organised so well. Passport control was taken care of and they were ready to move airside. Bekzat rose once more to address the group.

'My friends, I hope you have enjoyed our hospitality and your stay in Kazakhstan. We have enjoyed your company and wish you a safe and speedy return to your homes in the UK. Sean, from National Trust, will contact you soon to discuss the investment.' He looked at everybody in turn. 'Bon Voyage.' Then he turned and walked towards the terminal entrance.

Staff escorted the group through to gate eighteen, where they waited for boarding instructions. The group remained quiet—it had been one hell of a party, and soon it would be back to reality. Michael sat next to Graham and they caught up. It transpired that Graham had also fallen in love with one of the girls, and also felt desperate to return to Aqtau as soon as he could. Michael had a second of indecision and thoughtfulness, but then slapped Graham on the back. Who wouldn't fall in love with the girls? They were all beautiful.

Food was served and the drinks soon began to flow. It seemed the party wouldn't finish until they touched down at Gatwick. After eating and imbibing a couple of drinks, Michael felt tired, and when he looked around, it seemed that everybody felt exactly the same way. Five minutes later, he was away with the fairies in a deep sleep, dreaming about Ainalayin.

The plane touched down at seven p.m., and Michael was pleased to be back. However much everybody complained about Britain, it always felt good to have the earth beneath his feet at Gatwick. Michael rang his local Kingswood minicab office, who told him it would be a half hour wait, but he didn't mind because they charged only a third of the cost of a Gatwick cab.

The minicab duly arrived, and Michael embarked on his way home. In a sober, reflective mood, he mused that he had been in another world—as far removed from life in Kingswood, Surrey, as he could possibly have been. He wasn't sure he wanted to be back, wasn't sure he wanted to be with boring, good old Francis, and wanted to live life, not just exist in it. To do that well, he needed money and contacts. This investment would start his new life; a life of five-star travel, five-star hotels, food and wine, and of course, not forgetting five-star Ainalayin. As they pulled into the smart driveway, he did feel quite pleased to be home. The boys came out to see him and helped carry his bags.

'How was it, Dad?' Harry shouted, all excited.

'Yes, very interesting, but very hard work. I'm completely pooped.'

'Hi, darling.'

Michael looked up. 'Francis, so pleased to be home.' He held out his arms, she came to him, and they embraced. He would have to make love to her that night or she would think he had been up to no good. When he looked at her figure and thought it wouldn't be too much of a hardship, he had to laugh at himself. She didn't have on a bra, and he could see her hard nipples through the cream tee shirt she wore. The boys disappeared upstairs, and Michael and Francis went into the kitchen, where Francis put on the kettle.

'I tell you what, I'll have a cuppa and then a shower, and then I think we should have an early night. I've been thinking about you for three days, and really want to fuck that nice pussy of yours.'

'Language. The boys might hear.' But she smiled.

The evening went just as planned, and Michael gave Francis a good fuck. What she couldn't know was that during the whole time, he had his eyes closed and thought of Ainalayin. As soon as he had come, he rolled over and fell asleep.

The next morning, Michael got up early, had some coffee, and shut himself away in the office at seven-thirty. At ten-thirty, Francis knocked on the door and told him that bacon and eggs were ready. He clicked off the porn site he had been watching, rubbed his hands together, and went to have his cooked breakfast.

# CHAPTER 10

On Friday, as seemed usual, clouds hugged the sky, and the wind blew in rough gusts. At three p.m., Stanislav and Cedomir stood by the Co-op in Epsom town centre and watched the cash points at the HSBC bank across the road. They had been there only ten minutes when an elderly lady approached the machine. Only one thing interested Stanislav—money.

'Stay here.' He crossed the road and stood behind the woman, and watched her put her card into the machine. He got even closer while she keyed in her pin number: four-four-four-nine. She collected some notes, put them into her chunky purse, turned towards the station, and set off at a slow pace.

Stanislav stayed right behind her while she strolled under the railway bridge, and he kept looking around to see who was on the street. Just past the bridge, an overgrown alley led off on the right-hand side. With another scan of the area, his heart raced. The lady reached the entrance. It was time. He struck. With two quick steps, he grabbed her by the arm and dragged her into the alley.

Taken by surprise, she didn't have time to scream. He pushed her to the floor and kicked her hard on the side of her head just once. Then he seized her bag and tipped the contents onto the gravel. Her purse fell out, he grabbed it, and took the cash and the bank card. He looked up—still in the clear—then he walked at speed back out of the alley, under the bridge, and to the cash points. With the card in the machine once more, he put in the pin number and, five seconds later, two hundred and fifty pounds clicked out and he slipped it into his pocket. As he crossed the road and eyeballed Cedomir, he tried to act casual.

'Let's go, hurry.' They strode the twenty paces to the nearby cab office and, two minutes later, were on their way to West Ewell.

Elaine Martin never recovered consciousness. The second his heavy boot had smashed into the soft part of her head, just next to her ear, she had died. This marked the beginning of a weekend of mayhem in the local area.

***

'Boss, a murder in Epsom town centre—an elderly lady robbed and killed near the station—see you in the car park.'

DI Karen Foster put the phone down and grimaced. Only back a week and it had started already. She got up, clutched her coat, and almost ran to the stairs. Although she hated to think it, she felt a little glad that something terrible had happened, as it would take her mind off Esme. Distracted, she hurtled down the stairs two at a time, and then ran for the car park. Sergeant Mick Hill sat ready at the end of the path, engine running, and passenger door open. Karen climbed in, and they sped off.

'So, what's happening?'

'The descriptions fit the same two who raped Anne Rogers. A nasty mugging in an alleyway just under the bridge near the station. Lady's been killed, probably with a blow to the head.'

Karen looked at her watch. 'Jesus, at three-fifteen in broad daylight. Those animals must be desperate.'

'Bastards, that's what I call them, fucking bastards.'

They hit the town centre, totally blocked, as police had sealed off the roads.

'Put the siren on or we'll never get there.'

They just made it through as the whole town centre shut down.

Karen got out the car, pleased to see everything had been done professionally. The roads had been closed, tape had been extended round the whole scene, and officers escorted people away from the area. Karen never liked to see the bodies, but it was part of the job. Some print marks had been highlighted on the path, and Karen and Mick kept away from them when they approached the body, covered by a white sheet.

The forensics team were on the way, and Karen and Mick were as careful as possible. Karen reached the body first and pulled back the sheet. She just stopped and stared. A sweet-looking old lady, and already beginning to turn the ashen-grey of the dead. She dropped the sheet and turned. They walked back down the path to where an officer stood with a spotty, teenage boy in a hoodie, holding his bike.

'So, young man, did you come across the body?'

'Yes, Miss,' he said.

'What's your name?'

'David Swift, Miss.'

'Well, David, you've been very brave. Did you see anybody else in the alleyway?'

'No, Miss, there was no one. Can I go home now?'

'Yes, in a minute.' She turned to the officer. 'Get a statement, and his address and contact details. Might be just as well if someone takes him home, he's had a terrible shock, and it may hit him later.' Then the DI turned to Mick, 'See if you can find a name, address, anything, so we can inform relatives.'

'Yes, Boss.' He went back to the body and the scattered items from her handbag.

Karen looked around. How sad was this? The restaurant in Cannes began to look like a good option. The arrival of the forensics team and the police photographer interrupted her daydreaming.

Karen looked at the team in their white kit. 'Do a good job, boys. I want these bastards sooner than later.' Then she turned away to find out if there were any witnesses who'd seen anything or anybody. Officers had been sent to all the local shops and interviewed anyone walking in the area. They had two good leads: a man in the small stamp shop across the road from the alley happened to glance out the window and saw a young, scruffy man exit the alleyway at the approximate time of the murder. He also added that he was almost certainly a foreigner and not British. The second witness, a lady, had seen what she described as two young thugs walking quickly away from the Co-op just after the time of the murder.

'So, one man did the killing, and he went back to pick up his mate afterwards,' Karen said.

A constable approached her. 'Boss, you need to speak to this guy. He runs a cab business round the corner next to the kebab shop.'

'Hello. Your name, please?'

'Costas.' He spoke quickly, 'Two young men, scruffy, East Europeans, came into the office at three-ten-ish, wanting a taxi to West Ewell. They were lucky we had a car ready, and they left straight away. They paid the driver with a new, crisp twenty-pound note.'

Karen couldn't believe they'd been so lucky. 'Where exactly did he drop them?'

'At the pub, the Spring Tavern, London Road, Ewell.'

Karen sprang into action and shouted, 'Sergeant Hill, here now.' Mick came running and stood next to her in seconds. 'Yes, Boss?'

'We're on our way to the Spring Tavern, London Road. Get an armed response team there now, leave a couple of officers here, and the rest are to follow us. Let's move.'

Seconds later, they hurtled towards London Road, only five minutes away.

'Two East Europeans, well, foreigners, anyway. One of them was seen at the alleyway, then got a cab to the Spring Tavern. Keep your fingers crossed. We could have the bastards.'

Karen got on the radio. 'I want officers on all sides of the pub. Armed officers to be spread out so everybody has protection.' Then she clicked off the mic' and said to Mick, 'Please, God, let those bastards be standing at the bar, drinking.'

Mick slammed the brakes on, and they pulled up at the main entrance, ran for the door, and burst in—forgetting protocol as far as safety was concerned, they looked around the bar while armed officers came in from all directions. Karen said one word, 'Shit.'

The pub looked nearly empty, with just a couple of old boys sat at the bar with half a pint, a young couple by the window, all loved up, and that was it. Karen approached the bar and shouted, 'Hello? Police.'

A young, big-chested girl came out from the side and looked shocked to see so many police officers.

'Hello.'

'Have you been serving here for the past hour?'

'Yeah, started at nine, serving coffees when we opened. Do you want to speak to the landlord?'

'Maybe later. Two young men, scruffy, foreigners, anyone like that been in, in the last hour?'

'Well, there was two blokes in not long ago, had tears in their jeans. I suppose you would call them scruffy. They weren't English. They left about five minutes ago.'

Karen turned and spoke to the two old men and the couple at the window.

'We have reason to believe those two men are responsible for the murder of an elderly lady in Epsom not long ago, did anyone see which direction they went in when they left? Think, it is very important.'

The young man at the window stood and answered, 'I watched them leave. They headed towards the town centre.'

Karen looked at one of the constables. 'Statements from them all, addresses, contact details, you know the drill. Take descriptions of the two men and get that to me as a matter of urgency. Mick, I want every available

officer in Surrey in this area in the next ten minutes. Let's go.'
*\*\**

Stanislav and Cedomir had grabbed another taxi and had arrived back in Epsom, where they were dropped outside the joke shop next to the Odeon Cinema. They entered and bought Spiderman facemasks and left in double quick time. They sauntered to the Cinema entrance and strolled in. The busy establishment was what they wanted. They approached the ticket office, put their masks on, and then Cedomir jumped over the barrier and shouted, 'Open the till now.'

Stanislav shouted along with him, 'Everybody out. I will shoot anybody who doesn't move quickly.' He held his hand up as though he had a gun, and a stampede ensued. Girls screamed, and pandemonium broke out. Someone rushed into the theatres and shouted, 'Evacuate. There's a man with a gun!' Meanwhile, Cedomir had emptied the tills and now stood in front of the barrier again. The crowds from the theatres poured out into the foyer and charged for the main exit. Stanislav and Cedomir blended in with the young crowd and made their escape.
*\*\**

The radio crackled into life just as DI Karen Foster climbed out of the car.

'All units in the vicinity of Odeon Cinema, Epsom, respond. Armed robbery in progress, two suspects, East European description.'

She took one more step and stopped dead. 'What the fuck?' She stood stock still for a moment. 'We're being played here. They're probably already on their way somewhere else.' She looked at Mick, 'Leave some officers here, and let's get back to Epsom.'

Then Karen called Chief Inspector Philips at Guildford with a personal plea for more mobile units. 'Yes, Sir, they're stretching us all over the place. ... Thank you, Sir, that would be most helpful.'

Reinforcements were on the way.

Mick Hill pulled up outside the Odeon cinema six minutes later. Cars blocked the road outside, and hundreds of cinema goers continued to stream away from the scene. Karen sat shaking her head and then got out. After she'd fought her way into the foyer, she looked for someone in authority, then made towards a man in a suit who stood directing staff. 'Are you the manager?'

'Yes, Paul Green.'

'I'm DI Karen Foster, and this is Sergeant Mick Hill. What exactly has happened?'

Uniformed Officers calmed the crowds and tried to restore some sort of order.

'Two men, youngish, scruffy, looked like foreigners, robbed the tills. One of them shouted he had a gun, and this is what happened.' He motioned with his hand towards the chaos.

'Did anyone see the gun?'

'No idea. I saw him but didn't see any gun.'

'Presumably they are long gone?' she said, looking around.

'It's been chaos. I can only assume they left in the rush for the doors and are well gone by now.'

Karen shook her head—all she seemed to be doing this particular day. Then she turned to Mick. 'So, they're on the loose again, and which way they will go, we have no idea, so ...' She thought for a few seconds. 'Get the mobile patrols moving in circles around the towns of Epsom, Ashtead, Leatherhead, West and East Ewell, Kingston, Chessington, Esher, and Oxshott. Get plain clothes and uniformed officers into all the town centres. If you have to take officers off other jobs until these bastards are caught, then do it.'

Karen's personal radio once again crackled into life.

She listened and said, 'Shit.' Then made for the exit.

# CHAPTER 11

Michael entered the Savoy Hotel at ten to three. He had visited many times, and it was one of his favourite venues for dinner. When he asked one of the greeters for the Abraham Lincoln meeting room, the man escorted him to the reception desk. Michael deduced that others had asked exactly the same question. They took his name and asked him to sit in one of the comfy chairs in front of the beautiful fireplace. At five past, a man called his name. Sean King approached.

'Michael, how are you?'

'Fine thanks, Sean, and you?'

'Never better, old boy. Have you got over the trip yet?'

'I slept forever. What a weekend.'

Sean lowered his voice conspiratorially, 'My dear chap, I was useless for three days. So, come on then, let's go and have some coffee and see where we are.'

Sean led Michael to the Abraham Lincoln meeting room, a sumptuously decorated and smallish room. They sat at an antique wooden table, and coffee arrived two minutes later.

'I'm assuming, because you are here, that you wish to progress with the investment?'

This was the moment Michael had been waiting for, and it suddenly threw him; he had spent hours deliberating over how much to invest and, now that he sat here in front of Sean King, he felt scared. Still, he hadn't told Francis anything and wanted to surprise her when the profits rolled in, but the real reason he hadn't told her was because she would have stopped him.

'Yes, I am, and one of the main reasons I am is because of the bank's involvement. Why didn't we have this meeting at head office?'

Sean held his hands in the air. 'It's so ridiculous, it's crazy. Seriously, can you believe that there aren't enough meeting rooms available today? Remember, I've been seeing people all day—and, I would add, every person from the trip has gone forward with the project—so it just seemed sensible to move out for the day, and it's not a bad venue is it?'

'No, it's one of my favourite hotels. Okay, so how do we now take this to the next step?'

'Easy, Michael, you tell me how much you wish to invest, we draw up the papers, get them over to you—you would obviously want to have your own man check them—you agree, the deal pays you money, and you start counting the days 'til you see a more than satisfactory return on your investment.'

'Sounds straightforward enough.'

'You're a banker, and you know how it works.' Sean lowered his voice, 'We all look after each other. It's what we're used to. We are all part of the establishment, and we look after our own. Also, remember that the Kazakhstan government is guaranteeing the project.'

'As you say, we look after each other. Is Tony Morgan putting up some personal cash?'

'Michael, you know I can't answer that, but suffice to say, Tony doesn't like to miss out on golden opportunities to feather his nest like the rest of us.'

'Okay, so I'm in for seven hundred K.'

Sean King didn't blink, and just wrote the figure down on a piece of paper.

'We will progress on that figure and get the paperwork done, and of course, you're not fully committed until you sign the papers, which will be ready in about a week. Good, now, how are the family, old chap?'

'Fine. The two boys will soon be ...' while Michael spoke, he couldn't stop thinking about Francis and remembered her words: *Just promise me you will not do anything with the money without discussing it with me first.*

Ten minutes later, he walked outside in the sunshine, heading back to Charing Cross Station to catch the tube to London Bridge. He felt happy but still a little shaky. Seven hundred grand was a lot of money, and it would take all his redundancy payment, a three hundred thousand loan, using the house as collateral, and two hundred K from his pension pot. If, for whatever reason, it went pear-shaped, then he would be finished, and Francis would likely shoot him, but if it went according to plan, then he would make a cool one hundred and seventy-five grand clear profit. And, if he paid it into an offshore account in Jersey or the Cayman Islands, there would be no tax. That thought cheered him up, and he might just have a swift pint to celebrate. Francis flashed into his head, and he changed his mind—homeward bound it was. He got a good connection at London Bridge and made it home by five-fifteen. He opened the front door and smelt one of his favourite dinners—Lasagne.

'I could smell that Lasagne down the road. All the neighbours will be knocking on the door,' Michael said, as he walked into the hall. Francis laughed heartily from the kitchen.

'Well, they won't get anything. It's ready. We're having an early dinner.'

'Oh, okay, I'll just get changed.'

Michael zipped upstairs, wondered why they were having an early dinner, but thought no more of it. They ate dinner, scraped the Lasagne bowl clean, and the delicious salad and French dressing accompaniment went down a treat.

Francis said, 'I'll clear up. Go and put your feet up.'

'Well, if you insist, darling.' He filled his glass with red, picked up the mail, and went to the lounge. Francis came in fifteen minutes later with a pile of what looked like bills. Michael put his paper down. 'What do we have here then?'

Francis smiled. 'Just a couple of bills, but I thought you ought to see them so that you're up to date with what things are actually costing us.'

Michael had no idea; Francis paid all the bills.

'So, first of all, the Gas bill—eight hundred and twenty-six pounds.' She stopped and looked at Michael, who was in shock.

He didn't speak at first, then shouted, 'Over eight hundred quid a month? You're not serious?'

'No, that's for three months, but it is still a lot of money.'

'Damn right, it's a lot of money. Turn everything off. What the hell's gas, anyway?'

'The cooker and central heating.'

'Well, central heating's not on now, we're in summer.'

'The cost is spread over the year.'

'Well, I'm going to email Chris Bailey. He needs to get his finger out and do something. How the hell do families on low income survive? Not to mention pensioners.' Chris Bailey was the local Conservative MP, and whenever Michael felt something was wrong with the country, he would email him.

'Electricity nearly as bad—seven hundred and fifty-nine pounds.'

Michael stood up and walked to the bottom of the stairs.

'Boys?' He waited. 'Boys?'

'Yes, Dad?'

'From now on, when you are not using them, turn off computers, printers, Xbox, stereo systems, televisions, and DVD players.' He took a breath. Had he forgotten anything? Then he remembered: 'And the lights. You two leave lights on all over the bloody house.'

'Okay, Dad, but what's the issue?'

'The issue is seven and eight hundred pound bills. We're on an economy drive.' And with that he marched back into the lounge.

'What's next?'

'BT—one hundred and sixty-three pounds.'

He stared at his wife. 'Let me tell you something. I never use the landline, my mobile is on contract, and I never use my full free amount, so it's those two, isn't it? They run out of credit and use the home phone. Can we put a lock on it?'

'We can, actually, but what if there were an emergency?'

'Hmm, well, it's unacceptable. I'm fed up shouting at them. I suggest you try the sit-down-and-reason-with-them approach.'

'I'll try and remember. They'll both be gone soon, which will save us a good bit of money.'

'Anything else?'

'No, but just so you know, we get through about three thousand pounds a month before we spend a penny on food, clothes, petrol, car tax, restaurants, stamps, and all the other stuff. If you add it all up, we're spending five thousand a month just to live here.'

'So, you're going back to the downsize plan?'

'No, not at all, you just need to find a job that, after tax, nets you five and a half grand a month.' And she left it just like that. 'Now, another glass of wine?'

Francis had just told him to get a job at about ninety grand a year, if he wanted to continue the lifestyle they had at the moment, or otherwise do something else. Well, he already had, and once the money from the Kazakhstan investment came in, she'd soon change her tune. Michael went to his office and picked up the phone.

'Graham, how are you?'

'Good thanks, Michael. You?'

'The same. Quick call—are you going ahead with your investment in the Kazakhstan deal?' Michael was desperate to know if safe-old-Graham was in or out. If he opted out, then Michael would pull out too.

'Papers are being drawn up now. In for four hundred K. Impressive operation.'

That made Michael happy, and he had just one more question.

'Have you told Mary about the investment?'

'Good God, no, she'd go crazy.'

'So, look, I haven't told Francis, either. Best we both keep it like that so neither of them can talk to the other.'

'Sounds good to me.'

They chatted for five minutes about the trip to Aqtau, about the price of gold, and whether Greece would leave or get kicked out of the European Union.

Michael sat back. Graham had gone in for a substantial sum. Sean King and Tony Morgan had put money in, National Trust Bank were putting in millions, and the Kazakhstan Government would guarantee the whole deal. He took a sip of wine. No going back now, as far he was concerned. He couldn't wait to sign the papers.

# CHAPTER 12

The staff had become complacent. Becky Adams pressed the button to open the security door to let Mandy Raven into the till area. As soon as Stanislav heard it click open, he rushed the door and smashed it fully open with his arms and pushed Mandy to the floor at the same time. Becky stretched to press the panic button but didn't quite make it as the thug grabbed her round the throat, pulled her away, and slammed her up against the back wall. Cedomir followed Stanislav in and had Mandy by the hair, dragging her along the floor. Stanislav shouted in Becky's face, 'You have three seconds to open the till before I cut your throat.' Becky didn't need asking twice and nodded. Stanislav let go of her, and she opened the two tills. Stanislav beamed; notes packed both tills—mostly twenties. He bundled the money into a carrier bag, and then grabbed Cedomir by the collar.

'Let's go.' He marched towards the front door. Just before they got there, it swung open, and an old man with a roll up fag hanging out of his mouth entered. He saw the two thugs leaving and smiled at them.

'Any luck, boys?'

The brothers laughed. 'Yes, excellent day for us.'

'Lovely,' the old man said, as he sat at one of the tables and picked up the Sporting Life.

Becky shook all over but managed at last to press the panic button, and then she collapsed on the floor next to a terrified Mandy. It had all been over in two minutes, and the Ladbrokes betting shop in Green Street, just outside Epsom town centre, had lost three thousand and forty pounds. Ecstatic, the two thugs got back to their room in Leatherhead in no time.

They threw the piles of cash onto the bed, and it looked like a lot. Next, came the counting—two fifty from the cashpoint, fifty cash from the purse, one thousand two hundred from the cinema, and—the biggest of them all—three thousand and forty from the bookies. A grand total of four thousand five hundred and forty pounds. Stanislav and Cedomir hugged and danced around the room, singing a song from home. It had been a day to remember, and Saturday promised to be even better.

\*\*\*

DI Karen Foster stood in the bookies, interviewing Becky and Mandy. There was no doubt it was the same two bastards that had raped Anne Rogers, robbed the cinema, and killed poor old Elaine Martin. Had they finished for the night? Or, in a few minutes time, would there be another call? She suspected they had gone to ground. They must have gotten a substantial amount from their day's work, and were probably sitting back right now, whisky in hand. Substitute Russian Vodka in place of the whisky and Karen would have been right.

Karen Foster stayed up for a further six hours while she dealt with the three serious crimes that had stretched their resources to the full. She got back to her flat at two-thirty in the morning and went straight to bed.

Karen awoke at seven and felt exhausted. She dragged herself out of bed and stumbled to the bathroom. Hopefully, a hot shower would reinvigorate her. It certainly helped. The hot water cascaded over her body and brought it back to life. While she soaped herself, she thought of Esme and missed her. After the shower, Karen had a delicious, hot cup of coffee and some toast with Lime Marmalade—her favourite. At seven-forty-five, her mobile rang.

'It's Mick. They're off again. A newsagents in Banstead. Descriptions are perfect. It's definitely our two friends.'

'Shit. The question is, where will they go next?'

Mick kept quiet.

'What do you think, Mick?'

'Wherever it is, it will be local, and we have to smother the area: mobiles circling, officers in the town centres, and as many men as we can get.'

'I agree. I'll speak to Guildford. Anybody hurt at the shop?'

'No. A lady on her own—they terrified her, and she just gave them the money. Oh, and they took vodka and hundreds of fags.'

'You deal with it. I'll be at Epsom nick in ten minutes.'

Karen felt angry. A couple of bloody young thugs taking the piss out of Surrey Police. It couldn't go on much longer, and once the papers got hold of it, they would be a laughing stock. She grabbed her keys and rushed towards the car; she had to speak with the Chief Super as soon as possible to get more men. For once, nobody high up worried about the overtime, and every available officer and some borrowed from the Met swamped the local towns, and mobile units were taken off the M25 to help.

On the way to the station, she stopped to get some papers. The local headline read: CRIME WAVE HITS SURREY. Thank goodness the nationals hadn't got hold of it yet, but it wouldn't be long. Karen arrived at Epsom nick and soon sat in her office, coffee in hand, looking at the huge map of the local area on the wall. She pinned the four crimes so far, but it didn't mean anything. They were mobile but obviously didn't have their own car, which was why they used minicabs. So, how many minicab firms were there? She grabbed the phone and rang down to CID.

'Ted, find out how many minicab offices there are in Epsom, Ashtead, Leatherhead, and Ewell. I need to know yesterday.'

Ted came back ten minutes later. The local council said there were twenty-three licensed minicab offices in those four towns, which pleased Karen.

'I want an armed plainclothes officer in all those cab offices within the next two hours. You got that?'

'Consider it done, Boss.'

\*\*\*

Although good thinking, Stanislav was ahead of her. He knew they couldn't keep taking cabs and early that morning they had stolen a blue Mondeo in Leatherhead town centre. They had then driven up to Banstead and robbed a newsagents at the end of the high street. He had also sussed that they needed to change their clothes, and at nine a.m., they went into separate shops and purchased chinos and good quality shirts. Next, they got a good haircut and were set for the day ahead.

When they drove back to Ashtead, they looked like a well-to-do pair of young bankers, driving around on a Saturday morning, shopping. They hit the Shell petrol station in Ashtead next. Cedomir drove into the quiet Shell station and made sure he stayed well away from the CCTV cameras.

Stanislav jumped out of the car and made his way into the shop. He looked around, waiting for the right moment to strike, and watched the forecourt to see if new customers drove in. The Asian lady behind the till never gave him a glance as he looked in the chilled cabinets at the soft drinks. The way clear, Stanislav hurtled over the half-door and, before the woman could scream, struck her on the head with a small steel baton. When her skull caved in, he felt and heard the crack, and she collapsed in a heap on the floor. He grabbed all the notes from the tills, took an empty shopping basket, and filled it with cigarettes and three bottles of vodka. Then he smashed the CCTV camera into pieces and calmly walked out of the shop. After he'd jumped in through the open passenger door, Cedomir accelerated out of the car park and towards the high street. They both jumped slightly when they turned the corner, past the Leg of Mutton and Cauliflower pub, as a police car cruised past them, going in the opposite direction. The police car disappeared, and the two boys burst out laughing.

'If only they fucking knew,' Stanislav said, hardly able to speak as he was laughing so much.

\*\*\*

The police car drove past the petrol station, only to return four minutes later at close on a hundred miles per hour, on hearing that a robbery and murder had taken place. By then, Stanislav and Cedomir were heading towards Epsom Downs and their next target.

\*\*\*

Karen Foster got to the petrol station ten minutes later, demented with feeling so inept. She looked at the body and walked back out of the shop, away from the mayhem, and placed a call on her mobile.

'Yes, Sir, that's what I said. I wish to be relieved of command. The bodies are piling up, and I don't know which way to turn. There must be another officer. Someone with more experience. Someone—'

'Listen to me, Karen, you are a first-class officer with more experience than most. Who the hell can I replace you with? Request denied. Get on with finding those two bastards as quickly as you can.' The phone went dead.

Karen felt bloody sorry for herself. When she looked around her, none of the officers had a clue what to do and looked to her for leadership—she had to get a grip on it and fast.

'Mick, they're not in a cab anymore. Get a list of every reported stolen car in the area in the past twenty-four hours, and get the outside CCTV checked, just in case they made a mistake. Take the mobile units away from Ashtead, concentrate on Epsom and Ewell, and set up random roadblocks at major arterial roads. I don't care who complains, just get it done, now, even if you have to block every fucking road in the County.'

Mick rushed off to carry out his orders. Karen again stopped and put herself in the thug's shoes. They wanted money and, it would seem, as much as possible as quickly as possible. So they must be going on a trip soon. Maybe back home. This must be their last payday, the way they'd upped their game. With a grim face, she rang Ted at Epsom CID.

'Alert all the airports, ferries, stations, and Eurostar. We believe the two thugs are on a last payday prior to possibly leaving the country. Send out the ekit as soon as possible.' At last, she felt like she had gotten a small grip and had made some progress.

\*\*\*

Stanislav and Cedomir had arrived on Epsom Downs, and they parked outside the sandwich bar next to the Co-op at Tattenham Corner. They bought bacon rolls and coffees to take away, then drove two hundred yards and parked up in the public car park across the road from Tattenham Corner Station. Still early, not many cars were about. The brothers felt happy; a further six hundred pounds from the Shell petrol station, which made the bacon rolls and coffee taste even better.

They had been in the Co-op before. It had five tills, and all could be manned during busy periods. A typical morning would see two tills open, manned by young girls. The Tattenham Corner parade of shops had no CCTV.

The two thugs finished their rolls and coffee and mentally prepared for the Co-op gig. The shop always had people in and, as usual, they would rely on terrorising staff and customers alike to create chaos. Cedomir pulled out of the car park and turned right, and then he pulled into the shopping parade and motored slowly towards the Co-op. Outside the shop, Stanislav opened the passenger door and jumped out, took one step and saw two police officers coming out of the sandwich bar next door. *Shit.* He kept walking towards the supermarket entrance. The two policemen crossed his path, and one of them gave him a look, and then turned away as his colleague said something to him. Stanislav kept calm, even though his heart pounded, and walked into the Co-op, where he browsed the shelves. Sweat covered him head to toe; being near the coppers had been a terrifying experience.

\*\*\*

Cedomir turned the corner, looking for a parking space, and the police car sat there, right in front of his eyes. He looked inside and saw it empty. Where were they?

He drove on slowly, and then glanced in the mirror. Two policemen walked towards their car. Shit, what to do? Stanislav must have almost bumped into them. Cedomir drove on, pulled out of the parade, crossed the road, and parked in front of the small library. When he looked back, Stanislav walked out of the Co-op with a newspaper tucked under his arm.

Stanislav scanned the area and stiffened when he saw the police car and the two coppers getting into it. He remained like ice and strolled towards the library. He looked once more at the police car, as did Cedomir, and the two officers ate sandwiches. The driver glanced around as he ate, and then stopped as though to listen, maybe to his radio. The officer went back to eating, and Stanislav had nearly reached the car.

An engine started, and both men glanced back once again. The police vehicle moved forward, and both policemen looked at Stanislav and the car. He broke into a sprint as the police car roared out of the shopping parade. When he reached Cedomir and the vehicle, he jumped into the car, and Cedomir—ready—floored the accelerator. Dust and grit flew up from the back of the car as they hurtled back onto the road and headed back to the Downs. The police officers pursued at high speed. Cedomir swerved onto the racecourse road and soon drove at eighty miles per hour. The siren of the police car wailed behind them.

Cedomir hit the first mini roundabout doing ninety, he clipped the kerb, and almost spun out of control. Then he slammed the pedal down as hard as he could, increased speed to a hundred, and got on the straight road towards the racecourse grandstand.

Cedomir screeched round the roundabout in front of the main grandstand entrance, and then hurtled down past the cemetery and towards Epsom. Another mini roundabout loomed ahead. Stanislav's eyes popped out of his head when a police car came speeding up the hill towards them. Cedomir wiped sweat off his forehead and shouted, 'What do we do?'

'Keep going. Don't fucking stop.'

Cedomir had almost reached the roundabout. The police car swerved and blocked the road. It all happened so quickly it was incredible. Another police car came from the right of the roundabout and crashed into the side of the one blocking the road. Windscreens shattered, the blocking car shunted onto the pavement, and bedlam ensued.

Stanislav shouted above the noise of crashing and screeching metal on metal. 'Take right. Right.'

Cedomir whipped the steering wheel to the right and lost control of the back of the car. He braked, adjusted, and roared on.

'Right again.'

Headed back up to the Downs, the cemetery now lay on their right-hand side. They had to change the car, or they were done for. They sped up the hill, crashing over the speed bumps, and then Stanislav pointed.

'Turn into that big house. In the drive, a BMW, hurry.'

Cedomir pulled in and slammed on the brakes.

\*\*\*

Karen Foster screamed at Sergeant Mick Hill, 'They're on Epsom Downs. Let's go, get everyone moving, seal off every exit, and get the chopper up. I want them. No mistakes.' They roared out of the petrol station and headed for the Downs, located about five minutes away.

The police officers drove like madmen to get to the Downs. This was their chance, their opportunity to get the two murdering thugs and put them away where they belonged.

Karen and Mick charged up the hill. Ahead, lay the carnage: Two police cars smashed and stuck together, with steam rising from the engines.

'Shit,' Karen shouted. 'Stop. We have to help them. There could be a fire.' Karen got on the radio and called for the fire brigade and ambulances. Mick rushed to see what he could do for the officers. Blood had splattered everywhere in the first car—the two officers must have taken their seatbelts off for a quick exit, and they hung through the broken windscreen with blood-covered faces. Both lay unconscious, and possibly dead. In the other car, the driver moaned and held his shoulder. The passenger-side officer sat slumped in his seat, unconscious.

\*\*\*

Stanislav jumped out of the car and rushed to the front door. He pushed the doorbell, hard, but had a hunch no one was in. No answer. He ran to the side of the house, smashed a large window, climbed in, and went straight to the hall. He laughed to himself; hanging on a nice key holder was a stocky, black BMW car key fob. Stanislav grabbed it and ran back outside in seconds. He shouted at Cedomir.

'Hide the car round the back.'

Ten seconds later, they pulled out of the driveway in a nearly new, sleek, blue five series BMW.

Cedomir turned right and soon reached the grandstand roundabout again. He took the first left, first right, and then headed down to Epsom College. Stanislav ducked out of sight when a police car hurtled past the other way. They got to the traffic lights by the college and went straight ahead. Stanislav looked in the wing mirror, and two police cars arrived at the junction behind and started sealing off the roads.

'Drive slowly. We don't want to exceed the speed limit.' He took a deep breath. 'I think we may have got away, but stay alert.'

They went round the houses and, an hour later, got back to Leatherhead. They loved the car, but it was far too conspicuous to keep, so they dumped it in a secluded wood two miles from where they were staying. One final, easy payday remained, and then they would be finished.

# CHAPTER 13

The week went by quickly, and on Thursday, 5$^{th}$ September, the weather cooled down a little. Tomorrow, Michael would sign the papers for the Kazakhstan investment. The loans had all been agreed by the bank, and everything put in place. Stephen Coker had checked the papers and had come back to Michael saying that the papers were in order but he, of course, could not comment on the investment. Michael was already planning his next trip to Kazakhstan to see Ainalayin.

This time, Sean King had invited Michael to the head office of the National Trust Bank. Michael felt happy about that; it gave him some extra reassurance, and he arrived early at ten a.m. for a ten-thirty appointment. At ten-fifteen, Sean King came into reception and collected Michael, and then they went to a meeting room on the first floor. Michael felt tense; he had never signed a document and handed over seven hundred thousand pounds of his personal money before.

'So, the time has come, Michael, coffee?'
'Yes, thanks, that would be good.'
Coffee arrived two minutes later. Sean took a stack of papers out of a folder and adjusted them into a neat pile. He passed them to Michael.
'Okay, so we need you to initial every page and sign and date the last page where appropriate.'
Michael had sat in front of hundreds of people who signed for loans, and now it was his turn. Excitement accelerated his heart rate, and nerves made his palms

sweat. He went through the pages quickly and signed in the margins. When he came to the last page, he didn't know why he said it but looked up at Sean, 'Has Graham been in yet?'

Sean smiled. 'Later this afternoon.'

Michael went back to the document, signed and dated it twice, and the deal was done.

'Congratulations, Michael.' The two men shook hands. Two glasses of champagne arrived, and they toasted to a successful investment and many more to come. Michael had done it, and there was no going back now. The money lodged with his solicitor would be winging its way electronically to the Kazakhstan investment account at National Trust Bank within the hour.

Sean accompanied Michael to the main entrance, where they shook hands again, and Michael left the building. He thought of Ainalayin while he walked down the road in a slight daze. Two hours later, back home, he saw Francis and imagined what she would say if he told her he had just committed them to a seven hundred thousand pound investment. It was a strange feeling at dinner that night. The boys had left that morning, and Francis found it difficult to adjust. Michael felt happy they had gone. They had to find their way, as he had done, and as millions of other teenagers would do this September.

The next few days were tricky. Francis still cooked meals for four, and Michael piled on the weight, as he didn't like to see good food go to waste. She also fretted constantly about the boys and, of course, boys being boys, they never rang home. Meal times were the worst. They would sit opposite each other and eat mostly in silence. An email arrived on the fifteenth of the month from the Kazakhstan Investment Group, saying that the required capital had been raised for the project and that they were moving to phase two. Thank God. It would be all right. He opened one of his best bottles of red wine and called Francis to the lounge.

When she entered, he handed her a glass of St Emilion—one of his favourites. Francis smiled and said, 'That's very agreeable. What's the occasion then?'

'No occasion, just thought you might like a glass of decent wine.'

Francis laughed. 'You mean you wanted a glass of good stuff and knew that if you opened it you would have to share it with me.'

Michael gave her his lost boy look, and she laughed again. He put his glass on the coffee table and took Francis in his arms.

She looked into his eyes. 'You should open a bottle of St Emilion more often.'

They kissed and tore at each other's clothes. Such raw lust didn't happen often, but when it did, they were like animals. He ripped at her blouse and jeans like a madman, and she behaved almost the same, yanking at his belt and pulling his trousers off. Desperate to get to his cock, she finally got hold of it and sucked it for all she was worth. He had his fingers in all her holes and pushed his cock down her throat. All at once, they stopped. She got on all fours, and he rammed her from behind.

'Fuck me, Michael. Hard. Harder. Oh yes, good.' Francis thrust back as he pushed. 'Yessss.' She collapsed forward, shaking with pleasure. Michael masturbated and shot his load over her peach-shaped arse. She shook her bum, and his cum dribbled down her crack. Michael's breathing came heavily.

'You need to do some exercise. You sound like you're having a heart attack.'

'Wow, that was ...' He couldn't think of the right word.

'Spontaneous, and I loved it.' She turned slightly, wiped some of him up with her finger, and licked it off. 'Hmm, I feel like being filthy. What about you?'

'Same. What's next?'

'I've got a new toy for you to play with.' She jumped up, ran to the dressing room, and came back with a shoe box.

He raised his eyebrows. 'What's this?'

She opened the box, took something out, and threw it to Michael. An eight-inch black dildo landed in his lap.

'Oh my God.'

'And, after you've used it on me, I'm going to stick it right up your arse.'

Michael's eyes bulged. 'We'd better get started then.' With eager hands, he pushed his wife onto the sofa.

They had incredible sex. Francis could still surprise Michael even after all these years. Although madly in love with his wife again, it would only last a few days at the most.

# CHAPTER 14

At eleven p.m., Stanislav and Cedomir stood thirty yards from Freddie and Anne's Bungalow. They had checked earlier and seen them turn the lights off and move to the bedroom.

Stanislav laughed. 'They will have new phones by now. New bank cards. Talk about easy money. Are you ready?'

'Of course. How are we getting in?'

Stanislav thought for a moment. 'What you do in their place? After last time.'

'Make front door more secure. Put in alarm system. Do they have police panic buttons here?'

'Yes, so we will go to back of property. That will be bedroom. By the way, if you want, you can have woman first.'

'No thanks, she's not my type. I'll wait 'til get home.'

'Please yourself. I am going to have again.'

\*\*\*

In bed, the couple lay watching the late night horror film on the television, which sat on a table at the end of the bed. They sipped hot chocolate and looked relaxed. Freddie had locked the windows, but Anne had reopened them half an inch to let in some fresh air.

\*\*\*

The two thugs worked their way silently to the back of the property. Heavy beige curtains covered the windows. They could hear the television blaring. Stanislav took hold of the frame and pulled gradually. He had half opened it when it made a shocking squeak, so he stopped dead and prayed. The television continued to blare. He breathed out—they hadn't heard him. With the window open as far as it would go, they were ready. The plan was for Stanislav to go in first and scare them. In bed would be a good, secure place to keep them, plus he could fuck the woman in comfort.

Stanislav took out his small but sharp knife and prepared to leap in. He placed both hands on the window ledge and leapt. His knee caught on a sharp nail sticking out of the frame, and he almost screamed, then he made it through the window and rolled onto the floor. Despite his knee pain, he jumped up and brandished the knife.

'Hello. Look who is back.'

Anne screamed. Stanislav smashed her face with his fist, and she went quiet. Freddie panicked. Cedomir came through the window, and Stanislav told him to search for mobiles, bank cards, and anything else of value that would be transportable.

'What do you bastards want?' Freddie cried.

'Same as before—money, mobiles, ... you understand.'

'I understand you are nothing more than cowards. You are the scum of the earth.'

'Be extremely careful. I will only take so much, even from retard like you.'

*** 

That hit Freddie hard. He had promised himself that if they were ever attacked again he would fight back whatever the cost. He repositioned his arm to the side of the bed and felt for the old cricket bat. When his hand came into contact with the handle, he smiled.

'What's the bank pin number?' Stanislav asked.

Freddie got a bit of his own back, 'Anne's the only one who knows the pin, and you've knocked her out. That was clever.'

Freddie felt more confident this time, and he didn't care what happened to him. As long as Anne stayed safe, he would gladly die, but he wanted to injure these two men, particularly the one left in the room.

Stanislav took a step towards Freddie and hit his face with the handle of the knife, but it came as more of a shock than actually hurting much.

'That's last warning. Open fucking mouth again and I'll cut your wrists, and you'll bleed to death slow-slow.'

Cedomir came back from ransacking the bungalow; he had found thirty pounds cash, two debit cards, and two brand new iPhones.

Freddie sat as still as he could, with his hand on the bat.

'So wake bitch up. She has pin number.' Cedomir shook her, and she stirred.

'Get some water,' Stanislav said.

Cedomir went to the kitchen and came back with a pan full of cold water, which he threw over Anne's head. She gasped—now awake.

Stanislav leaned close to her face and raised her chin. 'I want pin number for bank card.'

'No,' just the one word, said with such force and finality that Stanislav was shocked into a moment's silence.

'I like to give people second chance. Remember what happened to you last time? Now, what is pin number?'

Anne lifted her face and looked him in the eye. 'Do whatever you want, but I won't tell you.'

Stanislav's face flushed with fury, and he attacked Anne, pummelling her body and face with his fists. Freddie attempted to get out of the bed, but Cedomir pushed him back.

Stanislav stopped at last. Freddie, in shock again, managed to collect his thoughts and waited for the right moment.

Stanislav leant over Anne once more. 'This last time I ask you. If you do not tell me pin number, I slit his wrists, and he will bleed to death.'

'No.'

Stanislav took a step back. Freddie could see that he wanted to kill her, but then he would never get the number.

\*\*\*

Karen Foster had been at home pampering herself and knocking back a bottle of Prosecco. She had luxuriated in the bath, enjoyed a facial, and then did her nails. At eleven-thirty, she took the last sip of the wine. She had to wait for her nails to dry, and then she would go to bed. With a sigh, she leant back on the sofa and tried desperately to relax. But it proved almost impossible, as turning off from work was difficult at the best of times, and with the two thugs on the loose it was far from that.

She closed her eyes. They had been so close, and now two officers had been killed in the crash, and two seriously wounded—what a fucking disaster. Those two bastards had a lot to answer for. They would catch them. It was just a matter of time, as long as they had enough of that vital ingredient. Karen yawned and finally headed towards the bedroom, where she pulled back the covers and lay on the bed—the night too hot for a duvet. Soon, she nodded off and slipped into a dream, and then she sat bolt upright. She didn't know why but she felt worried about the couple at the bungalow. Freddie and Anne—something was wrong; she had to be certain.

'This is DI Foster. I would like a car to check the bungalow where Freddie and Anne Rogers live. The address is on the watch list. When can that be done, please?'

'It's a busy night. Maybe within the hour.'

'Okay, make sure it's done as soon as possible.'

The called finished with, she lay down again but couldn't sleep. With a sigh, she grabbed the phone again.

'Mick, I know it's late, but I need your help.'

'What's happening?'

'I need to go and check on the Rogers bungalow ... just something ... I'm worried.'

'Okay, no need for both of us to go. I'll be there in twenty minutes. You go back to bed.'

'No, I want to come but I've had a couple of glasses of wine. Please, pick me up.'

'Sure, I'm leaving in five minutes.'

Karen got out of bed and dressed in jeans and a jumper.

***

Cedomir took a step and whispered in Stanislav's ear. The side of the hard, wooden cricket bat hit him full on the back of his head, and his skull smashed. Freddie grinned, and then lifted the bat again and went to strike Stanislav, but he never stood a chance. Stanislav ducked down and whipped his knife across Freddie's throat. The cut went deep, and blood spurted into the air like a fountain. Freddie swayed, dropped the bat, and fell forward onto the bed, where he bled to death.

Stanislav took a breath, and then Anne attacked him. The woman tore at his eyes with her nails. He fought her off, but she came back, demented and with the strength and courage of a lion. Stanislav tried to push her away again, but she scratched him badly down the side of his face. He held the knife tightly, slammed it into her stomach, and twisted and pulled up. Anne screamed when he ripped her from her stomach up to her chest. Blood poured out of her mouth, and then she gurgled, and it was over. The knife had pierced her heart.

Stanislav looked around. Blood and gore covered the bed, and the smell was horrific. He went to Cedomir, but he lay dead. He took the cash and the mobiles and left through the window. Outside, he stopped, and tears streamed down his face. Shocked and grieving, he looked back at the window.

'Goodbye, my brother. I will see you, maybe soon, maybe later, but I will join you again.' Then he jogged away.

***

Karen stood ready and waiting, and when Mick turned up, she dashed out to his car and jumped in the passenger seat. Without a word, Mick pulled away.

'Why are you so worried about the Rogers?'

'I don't know. I'll just feel happier when I know they're all right.'

'I'm sure they are, but let's go and check, and then we can all get some sleep.'

'Step on it then, slow coach.' They shared a chuckle.

They encountered barely any traffic and soon arrived at the bungalow. It looked dark, and Karen didn't feel happy.

'Don't they usually leave a light on?'

Mick didn't answer, and just headed towards the front entrance, where he positioned his ear to the door.

'Television's on.'

Mick rang the doorbell and waited. The chime sounded loud, and the couple should have heard it. Perhaps they felt too scared to answer the door at this late hour.

'You stay here, and I'll check the back,' Mick said.

Karen stayed by the front door, and Mick disappeared into the blackness. A minute later, the front door opened. Karen took one look at Mick and knew something terrible had happened. She rushed past him and headed to the bedroom. Mick got on his mobile and called in the murders. Before she got there, Karen could smell the slaughter. She slowed, and then pushed the bedroom door open wide.

Everything seemed to be in slow motion. The sight frightened her: Three bodies on a blood-covered bed and gore splattered up the walls. The unidentified stranger had to be one of the thugs. Freddie looked at peace and had obviously died fighting for his wife. Even Anne looked happy in death. Karen couldn't take it all in. The men had come back for some easy money, but Freddie and Anne must have fought back. With so much death, blood, and carnage in such a small space, Karen felt claustrophobic, and the smell alone overwhelmed her. She stumbled, and Mick caught her arm and helped her out the door. Karen had seen more death than most, but still the sheer futility of it all shocked her; so much death, pain, and suffering, and all for a couple of hundred quid.

'Are they on their way?'

'Yes, it'll take a bit longer than usual but they'll all be here as soon as possible.'

Half an hour later, the photographer turned up, followed by the crime team ten minutes after that. They sealed off the area, and the forensic examination of the scene began. The three bodies lay intertwined on the bed, and the room being so small made it a difficult job. The photographer had to take a break after having only been in the bedroom for a couple of minutes. No one alive had seen more dead bodies than him, but he found these murders harder to bear than most.

The team had nothing to report that couldn't be deduced from looking in the room. Freddie and Anne Rogers had been murdered by two thugs, one of whom had been beaten with a cricket bat and killed. They had entered the property through the back window, and the one that left by the window was bleeding, and that could be partly explained by the amount of skin and blood underneath Anne's fingernails.

Karen could feel nothing but compassion and fierce praise for Freddie and Anne. They had fought back against two mindless thugs intent on stealing from them and ultimately murdering them. They had stood up for themselves, but had it been worth it?

# CHAPTER 15

Life went brilliantly for a couple of days. The spontaneous sex had galvanised their relationship, and they did it four more times in two days—previously unheard of.

Michael had to be cunning, as Francis would see loan repayments start leaving their accounts in October. He told her he wanted to monitor the accounts and be right on top of the bills, and also to see where they could cut back. His last sentence had won the day: *'If you can't trust me with money, then who can you trust? After all, I've been a banker for twenty-eight years.'*

Michael felt back on top—he had Francis scampering around after him and was about to make a sizable profit on the Kazakhstan deal, but things would be tight. He'd worked out that they could survive 'til February, but would then be penniless.

Michael rang Graham to see how he was, but he didn't answer his mobile, so he rang the house number and, again, no one seemed to be at home. He made a mental note to phone him later.

Francis carried on her daily routine of cleaning, shopping, and cooking. Michael occupied all his time in his office, supposedly looking for a job but, for the most part, reading books online and watching porn. The outgoings had gone down considerably now that the boys had left; for a start, the continuous requests for cash had stopped, and the phone bills went down dramatically. When he told Francis that, she'd been delighted that he was right on top of the finances. Time flew by and the days became colder and colder. Winter soon fell upon them. Michael refused to put the heating on and sat in his office with a thick jumper on. October passed in a flash, Ainalayin faded to a distant memory—a dream that he'd had about a beautiful princess that wasn't real—and he had to focus to remember what she even looked like.

Today, seated in his office shivering, hands wrapped around a mug of steaming coffee that Francis had brought him, Michael had become aware that she wore thick blue tights and felt convinced it was because of the cold. He concluded that the time had come to put the heating on, and he would do it later as a surprise for her.

Michael got the number from the website, and he picked up his mobile and pressed the numbers.

'Good Morning, Riviera Grand Hotel, how may I help you?'

He pressed the red button. Shit. Images of Ainalayin flooded back to him. She could be at the hotel right now, this second, and he had to think of a way.

'Good Morning, Riviera Grand Hotel, how may I help you?'

'Good morning, I'm trying to locate someone I met in the hotel a week ago. Actually, I have a scarf of theirs and wanted to return it, and I've lost her mobile number.' Michael cursed the fact that Ainalayin had lost her mobile the day before he arrived in Kazakhstan. Then he thought that maybe she hadn't lost it in truth. Maybe she met people all the time. No, she had never asked him for anything, and if she were a player, then she would have asked him for money.

'Hello, are you there?'

'Oh, sorry, I was miles away.'

'What was the lady's name, please?'

'Ainalayin.'

'And her surname?'

Michael felt such a fool. 'Sounds ridiculous, but I can't remember.'

'I do not know the lady in question, and if I did, I could not give you her contact details. I'm sorry that I cannot be more helpful. Would you like to leave a message?'

Now Michael didn't know what to do.

'No, thank you. Oh, wait, do you know Milania?'

'Yes, everybody who works here knows Milania.'

'Is she there now? I need to speak with her.'

'I have not seen her this morning. She is probably coming in at two p.m.'

'Listen, it's important. Please, help me. I'll call at two o'clock. Please, ask her to be by the phone—tell her it is Michael from England—will you do that for me?'

Silence filled the long-distance connection. Then, 'Well, okay, on this occasion, I will ask her.'

'Thank you so much. What is your name?'

'Larissa.'

'Thank you, Larissa, goodbye.'

God, he felt excited. He looked at his watch—two hours to wait, and he prayed that Milania would be able to help. He jumped up because he had to do something, and went to the kitchen to make another coffee. On the way back, he turned the thermostat up to twenty-four degrees. Never before had Michael looked at his watch so much. Time had stopped. He couldn't help it, as every minute seemed like an hour.

The office got warmer, and when Michael put his hand on the radiator, its heat nearly scorched his hand, so he took his thick sweater off and felt better. He looked at his watch again—one-thirty—not long to go.

Transfixed, he stared down at his watch and could hardly breathe—two p.m.

He pressed the numbers.

'Good afternoon, Riviera Grand Hotel, how may I help you?'

# CHAPTER 16

Stanislav reeled. Cedomir, his kid brother, killed by that bastard with a bat. The younger brother he had sworn to protect, if needs be, with his life. He sat on the bed in his room and cried with his hands on his face, cursing Freddie, cursing the police, and cursing the world. At least they had paid in blood, those two bastard retards. If he could, he would have tortured them for hours. And the woman, she was crazy. Because of the cuts on his face from her nails, he wouldn't be able to go out until they healed. Fucking bitch. At least he now had enough money not to worry for a few weeks, and if he ran out and the supposed friendly guy he was staying with didn't like it, he would take care of him permanently. In a foul mood, he reached for the three-quarter-full bottle of vodka, opened it, and drank straight from the rim. He finished half of it, lay on the bed, and soon fell asleep.

***

Karen Foster sat in front of the new Chief Inspector of Surrey Police at Guildford.

'I was feeling sorry for myself. Won't happen again, Sir.'

'Karen, you're one of the finest police officers in Surrey. We're lucky to have you. Everybody has a blip now and then, so don't worry about it. Now, what is your next move to catch this other thug?'

'Well, it's all gone quiet. Losing his partner must have hit him hard and, judging by the skin and blood under Anne Rogers's nails, I suspect his face could be messy, so

I don't think we'll hear from him for a few more days. He may well decide to try and leave the country and, if so, I don't want him getting away.'

'I couldn't agree more. Unfortunately, criminals seem to be able to go back and forth as they wish, and we're an Island. I despair sometimes.'

'We'll be doing everything possible to catch this man, and I mean everything. We had them on the Downs but—'

'Nobody's perfect. Police officers make mistakes like everybody else. Those drivers were so intent on catching the thugs that they forgot the basics. It gives a salutary lesson to all of us and, sadly, they paid with their lives.'

'Yes, Sir. A terrible tragedy, indeed.'

'Okay, so get to it. The only advice I have for you is this: Don't go running around like a headless chicken. Take your time, stay out of the chaos, and look at it from outside. That is the only way, okay?'

'Good advice, Sir. I do like to get involved.'

They laughed.

'Let me know how you get on.'

They shook hands and Karen left.

On the drive back to the station, Karen stopped at the Grapes pub just outside Epsom and had a steak with salad and a large red wine. She felt like staying in the pub the rest of the day and getting pissed. For weeks, she had been off the booze and well behaved, but now Esme had gone back to Cannes, the compulsion to drink heavily returned. Karen had also been well behaved sexually, although she had thought about contacting Friday again but hadn't as yet.

Back in her office by three, Karen asked Mick Hill and other senior officers to join her for a progress meeting on the case designated as *Flyer*. She thought the thug they were after would try and skip the country, which gave her the name of Flyer.

Karen recapped and went back over the individual cases they felt the two men had been involved in. First, the rape of Anne Rogers and attack on her husband Freddie, then the murder of Elaine Martin in Epsom, the robbery and murder at the petrol station, the bookies and the newsagents, the return to murder Anne and Freddie Rogers, and finally, Karen added the two dead officers from the car crash, although they couldn't be charged with any offence concerning that event.

'So, our man has gone to ground, and we need to flush him out. Any ideas?'

A wall of blank faces met Karen until Paul Stewart, a young officer who had come down from Glasgow, spoke up.

'We have a good ekit. Let's put it on the front page of every local and national paper in the country.'

Karen smiled. 'Thank you, Paul. I think that's a good idea. Let's make it so. He's scared to show his face in public. Come on, chaps, please, let's chuck ideas in—doesn't matter how crazy they are.'

Mick spoke, 'He's a young foreigner, maybe here illegally, and he definitely won't own a property, which means he's either renting something or staying with someone. So, we make sure all the estate agents get the ekit. My guess is that he's in a flat and that it could be in a run-down, cheaper area, so let's pinpoint some targets in Epsom, Leatherhead, and Ewell, and do some house to house, or in this case, flat to flat.'

Karen nodded to Mick. 'I like that. If he hears we're doing house, sorry, flat to flat, he'll be shitting himself. Anyone else?'

Carla Westburgh, an up-and-coming officer marked out for quick promotion, spoke hesitantly, 'What about a reward for information leading to his arrest? Also, have we paid off snitches to put the word out?'

'Jesus, basic stuff and we haven't even mentioned it. Carla, you and I will look at this area after the meeting. Well done. Good input.' Karen smiled at her team.

'Okay, so we have work to do. Mick, Carla, stay behind. We reconvene in one hour when responsibilities will be confirmed. Keep thinking of ideas.'

Karen ordered coffee. 'So, Carla, I want you to organise a reward. Speak to the Chief Inspector's PA at Guildford, and she'll sort it and then get back to you with the date. Always say you're calling on my behalf. After that, get numbers of snitches from all the team, and let's hand out some money and see if it leads us anywhere. Mick, you will organise the flat-to-flat search.' She raised her eyebrows at this new terminology. 'When you've done that, brief Guildford and get them to organise the newspaper images. Okay, I'm happy. Anything else? Good. So, let's enjoy the coffee break, and then get to it.'

They did enjoy their coffee and Karen talked about anything other than work for fully five minutes. They finished their drinks and went to administrate the actions. Later, the meeting reconvened, and Karen put officers into teams, and then it was over for the shift. The day's work pleased Karen. Now they just had to catch the bastard.

# CHAPTER 17

Michael drummed his fingers on his desk. 'Is that Larissa?'

'Yes, and you are Michael. Hang on, please.'

Francis shouted from downstairs, 'Do you want another coffee?'

He held the phone behind his back. 'No thanks.'

'Michael, it's Melania.'

'Thank you so much, Melania. How is Ainalayin?'

'She is very well, of course, and trying hard to learn English.'

'Does she have a new mobile phone?'

'Yes, the number is 4437205612.' Michael grabbed a pen. 'Repeat that, please.'

He took the number down.

'You can write to my email. I will make sure Ainalayin sees it straight away. My email address is melania2@hotmail.kz.com.'

'Is she in today?'

Silence fell for a second, and then a new voice spoke on the phone—her.

'Michael, Michael, thank you for calling. I meese you.'

'Ainalayin, I am always thinking of you. I send you big kisses and love.'

Ainalayin didn't understand 'big kisses' but did know the word 'love'.

'I love you, Michael, bye.'

Melania came back on the line.

'We have to go to work. Send email.' The line disconnected.

Michael put his mobile on his desk and took a deep breath. He felt so happy that he had spoken to her, and wanted to go back and see her. Doubts surfaced. Was she playing him? She still hadn't asked for money for her sick mother or sister, though. No, she might think he was rich, but he saw nothing wrong with that. Whatever happened, he would see her again and see if she was for real.

Miserable for the rest of the day, Michael wanted to be somewhere else, but the last thing in the world he wanted to do was hurt Francis. He would have his time. When the money rolled in, he would travel. He might even setup a new home with Ainalayin in Kazakhstan, and property was dirt-cheap out there, so they could get something fabulous with a pool. Francis shouted dinner was ready, which interrupted his daydream and reality crashed back. He got up and headed to the kitchen. As he ate his homemade shepherd's pie, he thought about what to write in his first email to Ainalayin, which he would send later that night.

He finished the message at ten.
*My darling Ainalayin,*
*It was so good to hear your voice this afternoon.*
*I have missed you more than you could know, and my heart aches to see you.*
*If all goes well, I will be able to come and see you soon. I am investing in Kazakhstan and will be able to travel often. I wish I could see you sooner.*
*I cannot forget the wonderful night we had together. You are a beautiful woman.*

*I will be in touch soon. Take care.*
*All my Love*
*Michael XXX*

\*\*\*

Melania rose from her chair, strode to the printer, picked up the piece of paper, and went back to her desk. The large room was sectioned off into four distinct areas, easy to see, as all the chairs were either grey, blue, black, or white. Melania sat in the blue area, which had a business-like atmosphere, with about sixteen women and four men scattered at the desks, working at computers. Melania spoke to the five other women in her section, and they crowded round her desk like a group of teenagers. Ainalayin, dressed in casual jeans and tee shirt, stood among them.

'Shhhh. Stop talking,' Melania said with a raised voice.

'Listen, you will like this.' The cluster of women were all ears.

*'I have missed you more than you could know, and my heart aches to see you.'*

The women doubled up, laughing hysterically.

'I never knew Englishmen could be so romantic. The French, yes, and oh my God, the Italians, the Italians.'

The women joked and laughed, but then fell silent and returned to their desks.

'Are we working or playing the fool?' Bekzat had walked in.

He went to a huge desk on a raised plinth at the far end of the room. At the side, on the wall, hung clocks with names underneath: London, Berlin, Paris, Rome,

New York, Sydney, Moscow, Warsaw, Dublin, and Copenhagen. Bekzat pressed a button on a phone pad, it lit green, and he picked it up.

'Sean, how are you?'

'Fine, are we ready?'

'Of course, we always keep to schedule, do we not?'

'Yes, Bekzat, you do.' Sean chuckled.

'A successful operation for us all.'

'Yes, of course. We will meet again when you are next in London.'

'I look forward to it.'

He clicked off and pressed another button, which went green.

'Bonjour Sava?'

It was akin to a military operation or a large multinational business. The colour codes signified a group of countries, and a team managed each. The room sat in the basement of the Riviera Grand Palace Hotel. Bekzat paid a fortune to the hotel owners and, as he was one of the partners, he paid himself. He had set up a one-off scam that, if all went according to plan, would net him personally—after all the expenses—at least twenty million dollars. He would then move onto something even bigger and more intricate. Bekzat loved the money but he also loved the deal, the intrigue, and the craft of the scam. The more complicated, the more he loved the machinations of it all.

***

Michael woke early, had a shower, dressed, and went downstairs. He loved the smell of the freshly made coffee and warm croissants permeating up the stairs. Francis stood in her fluffy, pink dressing gown, and the front kept opening every time she moved. Michael noticed she wasn't wearing any knickers and felt a stirring in his groin. He gave her a look and opened his mouth to speak.

'Don't even think about it. I am not in the mood.'

He closed his mouth in slow motion and smiled.

She moved her right leg forward and the dressing gown opened to reveal her most intimate place.

'But I might very well be in the mood later.' She placed the coffee and croissants onto the kitchen table.

'That would be agreeable. As dirty as last time?'

Francis leaned across the table. 'In fact, I think I might let you fuck me up the you-know-where.'

Michael stopped chewing the croissant, his eyes lit up, his nods got faster and faster, and he laughed.

'What are you doing today?'

'Town. It's nail day, and I'm having a coffee with Sophie Ricketts.'

'Okay. See you later.' Michael disappeared once again into his office.

Michael clicked on his computer. Would there be any message from Ainalayin? There wasn't, but he did have a message from a Carole Matthews, asking him if he'd like to fuck her, as she only lived two miles away. Although tempted to start a conversation, he felt he had enough on his plate with Francis and Ainalayin. He skipped through a few job sites without any real interest, and then his heart missed a beat. His whole body pounded, his hands shook, and he could hardly breathe. On the news feed was a headline: news from hell.

'KAZAKHSTAN PROPERTY PRICES COLLAPSE.'

He didn't want to read the rest of the article and sat back for a second and took some deep breaths. When he felt a little better, he looked at the screen.

*The newly installed Kazakhstan government today announced a devaluation of their currency. Property prices have crashed, and all building projects have been abandoned. The foreseeable future is bleak but, as before, the government will pull the country through a dark time in its history.*

Michael thought he would be sick, rushed to the downstairs bathroom, and threw up his croissants. He spat and blew his nose until he felt a little better. Then he staggered back to his office and collapsed into his chair. Sweat beaded on his forehead. *Pull yourself together. The deal is guaranteed by the Kazakhstan government. The investment is safe.*

He needed to find out more, so he tapped in 'BBC News' and found another article similar to the newsfeed, but the bit he really didn't like on this one was the caption:

'INVESTORS LOSE MILLIONS IN KAZAKHSTAN DEBACLE.'

He went to NBC and then FOX, and they all had the same story: Kazakhstan was in deep shit and people were losing their shirts. He had to call someone. Who to call first? His brain couldn't function properly.

He pressed speed dial and held the mobile to his ear, with his hand shaking.

A machine told him to leave a message.

'Sean, its Michael Fletcher. I need you to call me as soon as possible.'

He punched some more numbers into the phone.

'National Trust Bank, how may I help you?'

'Tony Morgan, please, its Michael Fletcher.'

'Mr Morgan is in conference and cannot be disturbed. Can anyone else help you?'

Michael didn't bother speaking, he just pressed 'end call'. Then he jumped. God, he must phone Graham. Graham wasn't available either, and the beads of sweat dripped down his face. He stood up and held the back of the chair tightly, but couldn't stop his hands shaking. Then he heard the front door open. Francis was home.

'Hi, darling, I'm home.'

Michael closed his eyes and prayed he was asleep and having a nightmare. The room swayed. He collapsed, hit his head on the side of the desk, and lay on the floor out cold.

\*\*\*

Francis was hanging her coat up when she heard the crash.

'Michael? Are you there?'

She took tentative steps to the office. 'Michael? Are you all right?'

She quickened her pace and pushed open the door.

Michael lay on his back. A massive egg-sized bruise appeared on his forehead. 'Jesus, Michael. Michael.' She bent down and pulled his eyelid up. He was unconscious. Then she rang 999 on her mobile. 'Ambulance, please.'

She turned him on his side the best she could, but it was incredible how difficult it was to move a man without any cooperation.

The ambulance duly arrived eight minutes later and took Michael to the local Epsom General Hospital's Accident and Emergency department. Francis followed in the car, and they got there in exactly nine minutes.

Doctors examined Michael thoroughly, and came to the conclusion that he had fainted and hit his head. Hopefully, he would wake up within a couple of hours and, if not, they would investigate further. Francis sat at his bedside for an hour, and then he started babbling. It was all incoherent rubbish at first, but then:

'Money's lost, no, no, no, no, bank's involved, money's safe. Money, must be safe, go back see Ainalayin, love Ainalayin. Love Francis, always rock in storm. Need money. Call Bekzat?'

Francis at first felt hurt, and then she got angry. Who the hell was Ainalayin? Oh yes, probably some fucking prostitute tart he met in Kazakhstan. And then the money—something had gone wrong. Wait 'til Michael woke up. He had some explaining to do.

A further two hours passed before he came round properly. There didn't seem to be any complications but they kept him in overnight for observation. You could never tell with head injuries.

Francis went home and stewed, had a few glasses of wine, and stewed some more. She would wait 'til he was sat down at home, and then a serious interrogation would start.

\*\*\*

The next day, Francis picked him up at ten. The doctors had been happy to let him go with the proviso that if he had as much as a small headache, he should go back to A and E. Michael just felt glad to get out of the hospital and couldn't wait to get home. He would change that particular tune quickly. They arrived home and Francis made Michael comfortable in the lounge on the sofa. After she'd made tea, she started on him.

'You said quite a lot while you were waking up.'

Michael froze but tried to act calm. 'People talk all sorts of rubbish when they're semi-conscious.' He laughed, then continued, 'So, what's new then? How was your coffee with, erm, oh yes, Sophie?'

'What's happened to the money, Michael?' Straight and to the point.

'Nothing. What the hell are you going on about? You're like the bloody Gestapo, for Christ sakes. I'm ill.'

'Who the fuck is Ainalayin then? You bastard. Quick shag in Kazakhstan was it? I hope she gave you a fucking dose, you low life bastard.'

'Nothing happened. We sat together at dinner one night. She was a hostess, for goodness sakes.'

'Hostess with the fucking mostess no doubt. Let's go back to the money. Have you spent money on something expensive?'

'No.'

'So you're telling me the money we have in the bank is intact, and that everything is all right? Is that what you are telling me, Michael?'

'I've got a headache coming on. Leave me alone. Not now, please.' He buried his face in his hands.

'No. We're going to get to the bottom of this right now, or you won't get any peace.'

'Please, Francis.'

'The money?'

Michael took his hands away from his face. His wife would find out eventually. He prayed it was retrievable but had serious doubts.

'The money—it's gone.'

Francis gasped. 'What did you say?'

Michael raised his voice, 'The money. It's gone, finished, kaput.'

Francis sat in shock. 'Nearly two hundred thousand. What the hell have you done with it?'

Michael started crying.

'What have you done with it?'

Michael spluttered. He wanted to get it all out in the open now. 'Not just that.'

'What do you mean? It couldn't be any worse, could it?'

'My pension money … all gone, and a loan on the house … all gone.'

Francis stood up. 'So how much have you lost?'

Michael looked her in the eye, and the tears flowed down his face.

'How much?'

'Seven.'

'Seven what?'

Michael said it slowly, 'Seven hundred thousand pounds.'

Francis grabbed the chair armrest. 'What? You madman. Where is it? Horses, I suppose, or the casino.'

'No. I was trying to help us, trying to get us back on our feet. It was the bank, National Trust, they approached me and asked did I want to invest in a building project in Kazakhstan. It all seemed kosher. They should give me the money back. I'm sure they will.'

'Bollocks, they will. You've been so fucking stupid. I can't believe it. We're ruined, penniless, and we'll be living rough on the streets.'

Francis broke down.

'Don't worry. We'll get through this.'

Francis looked up at him, her eyes blazing, then ran to the kitchen and grabbed a knife by the bread bin and rushed back. She got close to him.

'We'll get through this. Are you fucking demented? You fucking idiot.' She pulled her hand from behind her back, and it clenched the long, serrated-edged bread knife. Michael shrank back, fearing the worst. Francis waved the knife in front of his face.

'All the years of pain, the sweat, the hard work bringing up your kids, and then you do this.' She shook her head. 'You bloody fool.'

'I'm not the only fool. Graham has lost four hundred thousand.'

'What? Graham, of our friends, Graham and Mary, has chucked away four hundred thousand? I don't believe it. He's not that stupid.'

'Phone them. You'll see. I'm not the only idiot.'

Francis wiped her eyes. 'That's exactly what I'm going to do.'

She composed herself, picked up her mobile, and rang the number, putting the call on loudspeaker.

'Hi, Mary, it's me. How are you?'

'Great, thanks, Fran, and you?'

'Don't ask. Do you know about this investment in Kazakhstan? We've lost quite a lot of money. No, let me rephrase that, Michael has lost us a substantial sum of money.'

'Oh God, that's terrible. Yes, I know all about it. Graham told me all about it at the last moment, and I persuaded him not to go ahead. He was about to sign the papers, for God's sake. I hope you didn't lose too much?'

'No, we'll still be able to eat.' She laughed. 'Well, I'm busy cooking. We'll catch up soon.'

Francis turned to Michael, unable to speak, but didn't need to say a word. Michael's face said it all. He'd gone a deathly-whitish-grey colour, and looked like he would drop dead at any second.

Francis stumbled out of the lounge, climbed the stairs, and walked into her bedroom. With the door locked, she went to bed. Michael curled up on the sofa and shut his eyes, but he couldn't sleep, so eventually he got up and went to the cellar. The last bottle of St Emilion called to him. He took it, opened it, and sat sipping the nectar until he held an empty bottle. Michael eventually fell asleep on the sofa.

When he woke up at ten-thirty the next morning, he felt better. Francis knew everything, and the cat was out of the bag, so to speak. He made some coffee and thought about going up to see Francis, but then he remembered the knife and thought he would leave her 'til she was ready to come down. Instead, he sat in his office, sipping his steaming-hot coffee. Then he got angry. It had all been so easy, and now he and Francis and the boys would have to pay. He wasn't worried about James and Harry—they would make their own way in life. Francis would come round. Maybe they would end up living in a caravan somewhere, but that could be fun. He knew one thing: Today he would speak to Sean King and Tony Morgan and see if he could get any of his money back. He finished his coffee, took a shower, dressed in smart casuals, and went to it.

The first call was to Tony Morgan at the bank.
'Tony Morgan, please, it's Michael Fletcher.'
'I'm afraid Mr Morgan is in conference and cannot be disturbed, is there anyone else who could help you?'
'Listen carefully. Tell Tony that if he doesn't speak to me, his name will be in every newspaper in the country tomorrow morning, reference Kazakhstan.'
Ten seconds of silence ensued.
Tony's voice came on the line, 'Michael, no need to be rude to the girls, for Christ's sake. What's up?'
'What's up? Are you being intentionally obtuse? My fucking investment in Kazakhstan, that's what's up.'
'Terrible business. I had no idea you were involved. How much did you lose?'
'Seven hundred K.'
'You're not serious? Jesus, what on earth were you doing investing so much?'
'I only got involved because the bank was putting in millions. You must be gutted to lose so much?'
'We didn't lose anything. Where did you get that information from?'
'Your bloody employee, Sean King, told me, fact.'

'Sean King does not work for the bank. He's a financial consultant that we do some work with occasionally, but he's nothing to do with us.'

The bank didn't put any money in? Sean King didn't work for National Trust? Shit. It was getting worse.

'He told me that the bank were guaranteeing the deal for investors, so what about my seven hundred K? And he also told me you had invested a considerable sum personally.'

'I didn't invest a penny. The man's spinning yarns. Wait 'til I see him.'

'Tony, you fronted up the presentation at the Landmark Hotel. You gave your stamp of approval to the deal.'

'We've done some trivial business with the Kazakhstan Government through Bekzat Abdulov, and he asked me to introduce him to some possible investors. That was the sum total of my involvement. Listen, Michael, you made an investment, it went tits up, it happens, now move on and make money somewhere else.'

'Easy to say.'

'If I can I'll swing some deals your way, that's the best I can do.'

Michael wanted to call him a cunt and tell him to fuck off but instead he said, 'Tony, I appreciate that and thank you for your time.'

Michael clicked the phone off. He hadn't done his homework. He'd gotten carried away by the deal. His friend's words came back to haunt him:

*If it looks too good to be true, it probably is.*

He punched a speed dial and put loudspeaker on again, then he placed the phone on his desk and sat back, not expecting the person to answer.

'Sean King.'

Michael jolted to life. 'Sean, its Michael Fletcher. What the fuck has happened to my seven hundred K?'

'Jesus, Michael, I've been trying to get hold of you. It's a complete fuck. I've lost three hundred K of my own money. It's terrible. Terrible.'

'I feel for you. So, what is the situation?'

'The Kazakhstan Government has collapsed, and the new guys are not honouring the previous government's contracts and, basically, it's a pile of shit.'

'So you're telling me my money's gone?'

'I'm afraid that's the long and short of it.'

'I want to know exactly who has my seven hundred K, and what bank account is it in?'

'Honestly, I don't know. All the investment money was transferred from National Trust into the Kazakhstan development accounts at the Kazakhstan National Bank. I assume the new government has frozen the accounts, but I couldn't swear to it.'

'So I need to speak to Bekzat then?'

'He'll know more than me, that's for sure. Hell, I wish you all the best, Michael.'

'Thanks. I may speak to you again.'

The call would be a waste of time, nobody wanted to be associated with a sinking ship, and Kazakhstan was exactly that. Sean had most likely used the bank name and Tony Morgan to get investors on board—old-fashioned salesman's license—and he had fallen for it, lock, stock, and barrel. His seven hundred K was sitting in some account somewhere, and he meant to find it. Next on his list was Bekzat.

# CHAPTER 18

Nartay strolled into his local Co-op convenience store, picked up a Sun newspaper, went to the counter, ordered twenty Marlboro, and paid. He walked back out and put the cigarettes into his side jacket pocket, and then opened the back page of the paper to look at the headlines to see if there was any news of his team, Manchester United, but there wasn't. When he flipped the paper over to see what was on the front page, he gasped. There, right in the bottom right corner, was a quarter-page image of Stanislav with the caption:

*Dangerous criminal on the loose. Have you seen him?*

Quickly, he folded the paper in half and walked off at a brisk pace to get home. On the way, he planned what to do. He would have to go—it was as simple as that. To have him in the flat would be crazy, and he could go to prison for years as an accessory to God knows what sort of crimes he'd committed. He opened the paper again, turned to page five, and read: *Murder of an old-aged pensioner, murdered a handicapped couple in their home* … he couldn't read anymore. Stanislav was a dangerous, violent psychopath, and he would have to be careful how he played it.

***

Stanislav's wounds had healed enough not to be instantly recognisable. He felt sick of watching television and desperately wanted to get out of the flat, and even a ten-minute walk in the fresh air would have been wonderful. However, he was a wanted man. Not just wanted, but urgently wanted. Police officers had died, and they wouldn't rest until they'd caught him. He had to leave the country, but how? They would have surveillance at all the airports and ports, and it wouldn't be easy. Perhaps Nartay could help in some way. He made another one of the endless coffees he drank all day, and just then the front door open. Nartay entered the lounge and threw the paper on the tiny Formica table.

'You better look at the front page.'

Stanislav picked it up and looked. 'Fuck, it looks like me, bastards.'

'You have to get out of the country as soon as possible.'

'Yes, but how the fuck am I going to do that?'

'I have a friend, but it will cost you.'

'How much?'

'I don't know. Maybe a couple of grand.'

'How can he help?'

'You go by ferry to France in the boot of his car. They're not interested in who's leaving, so it would be easy.'

'Call him and get him to come round. The sooner we do it, the better.'

***

Nartay couldn't have agreed more; the sooner the lunatic got out of his life, the better.

The man turned up at ten the next night. No names were mentioned, as it stayed more secure that way. The man had done it before and was willing to help Stanislav for two and a half thousand. If he were unlucky and got stopped and searched, he would do a minimum of five years in prison. Stanislav agreed to the price and paid five hundred in advance as a goodwill gesture, and the remainder would be paid once they had landed in France. Everybody happy, they toasted a successful outcome with numerous shots of neat Russian vodka.

*** 

DI Karen Foster felt happier than she had been for some time. Patrols were out knocking on doors and had already arrested a known criminal, who opened his front door smiling, but that soon changed when he saw two policemen stood there. Pictures had gone out in the papers, and they were about to post a reward of twenty-five thousand pounds. Snitches had been given a bonus, so everybody was looking for the killer, and it was only a matter of time. And then a fish took the bait.

'Hello, Sir. I understand you wanted to speak to me in connection with the image on the front of the papers.'

'I know him, I know where he is, and I know how and when he is going to leave the country.'

'I'm more than interested, go on.'

The man sounded foreign, but where from, she couldn't tell. Although he sounded Russian to her.

'I am here illegally but have committed no crimes in this country, and for the record, nowhere else either. I am only interested in the money. If I hand him to you on a plate, I want to stay here. Can that be arranged?'

'Yes, you have my word.'

Karen didn't care what she promised; she wanted the bastard more than anything.

'Okay, so a car will take the ferry from Dover to Calais, and he will be in the boot. The reward is twenty-five thousand, yes? Once you give me the money, I will give you the make and registration of the vehicle, and the date they sail.'

'You haven't done this before; I can tell. You only get paid when he is arrested and convicted of his crimes, and you may have to give evidence in court, but you can do that in secret to hide your identity.'

He went quiet.

'That's the only way it can be done. Why don't you just tell us where he is now, and we can get it over and done with.'

'That's not possible. I don't want him to know it was me. He has some very unpleasant friends.'

'I'll bet he does. So, when will you let me know?'

'He wants to go as soon as possible, so I will call you soon. Just so you know it's me, should we have a password just for us?'

Karen laughed to herself. 'Okay, our password is "James Bond". I look forward to speaking with you soon.'

'Good.' He clicked off.

# CHAPTER 19

'Bekzat, it's Michael Fletcher. Where is my fucking seven hundred K?'

'Michael, please, unpleasant language will not help the state of affairs. As regards your investment, it has been confiscated by the new minister of commercial activity to prop up the economy. In short, my dear friend, it has gone, and I know it does not help, but I lost three hundred thousand myself.'

Michael could have screamed. Commercial fucking activity minister. 'Sorry, but you can imagine how I feel. So you're saying the money is irretrievable?'

'I'm sorry to say that this is the truth. I hope that it has not hit you too hard?'

Michael felt near to tears. 'I'll get by. If the situation should change, you will let me know.'

'Of course. I am praying daily that something good will happen.'

'Thank you, Bekzat. Goodbye.'

Michael put the phone down. He wouldn't see the money again, and his days as an international wheeler-dealer were over before they had even begun. Sick and tired of it all, he made for the kitchen to make coffee but stopped at the door—Francis sat in there.

'Hello, Francis. How are you?'

She didn't acknowledge him or the question. Without looking his way, she picked up her cup of tea and walked past Michael. A few seconds later, the bedroom door thumped shut, and once again, the key turned in the lock. Her appearance had stunned him. She looked like death warmed up. With a defeated shrug, he made coffee and told himself she would come round. Then he took the coffee to his office and sat down. He thought about the financial situation, the loan repayments, and his pension destroyed. God, what a mess. So awful. He turned off and read his latest book, Blood Money—a gangster thriller.

Later, Michael sent a final email to Ainalayin. He couldn't afford the bus fare to town, let alone an air ticket to Kazakhstan, so his flight of fancy with her had to be over. At least he had the memory of that one night, and what a night it had been.

*My dearest love, Ainalayin,*

*I am so sad today. My investment in Kazakhstan has been lost. I am a ruined man and have brought great suffering on my family. It was, of course, unintentional, but still, I have been a complete fool. My only memory of Kazakhstan will forever only be you. It is my dream that I see you again, but in truth, it is not likely to happen. I am penniless. Please, forget me.*

*I wish you a long and happy life. God bless you.*

*All my love*

*Michael XXX*

Michael sent the email, and then went up to the spare room. He felt mentally exhausted and soon fell into a deep sleep.

*\*\*\**

'I will kiss and suck your toes for hours. You will be my foot princess. Oh, how I long to hold your glorious feet in my hands once again.'

The group of women howled with laughter while Melania read the latest email from Luiggi, one of the Italian investors.

'Listen, we have a new email for Ainalayin from Michael Fletcher in England.' She skimmed through the email. 'Oh my God, you will like this.' She acted as though on a theatre stage in London's West End.

*My only memory of Kazakhstan will forever only be you. It is my dream that I see you again ...*

The women screamed with laughter again—some of them actually in pain through laughing so much. They all laughed, except one of the women who stood at the back. Although close to tears, she wouldn't dare let anyone see her reaction.

\*\*\*

Two days later, a letter arrived from National Trust Bank customer services. A direct debit to Sutton and East Banstead Water for five hundred and twenty-three pounds had gone unpaid due to lack of funds. The bank had charged the account a twelve pounds administration fee. Michael read in shock. How the hell could they have run out of money so damn quickly? He signed in to his online accounts and studied them. Money had been pouring out: bills, direct debits, car insurance—an endless list of payments with nothing in the credit column.

Michael made an instant decision. He took a storage box from a shelf and retrieved an envelope. Then he grabbed his car keys and shut the front door quietly when he left.

Three hours later, he arrived back home, having walked from the bus stop. He had sold the car to his local garage for fifteen thousand, and must have appeared desperate because it was well under the value. He didn't care. The money had been transferred directly into his account, so short-term, the crisis was over. He put the carrier bag onto the kitchen worktop and removed the contents: a bottle of South African rosé wine—three pounds ninety-nine from the Co-op, a Cornish pasty—reduced by fifty pence as it was going out of date, a small one-litre bottle of milk, and a packet of Jaffa Cakes for Francis.

While he emptied the bag, he thought of the song, *Hey big spender,* and he laughed. He planned to save the wine as a special treat for later but couldn't resist tasting it. After he'd got the corkscrew out, he realised it was a simple screw top. So, he undid it, took out an everyday drinking glass, and poured a half glass. He looked at it and thought it didn't look quite right. When he held it up to the light, it looked browner than rosé, and he didn't like the look of it at all. Next was to taste it. Michael looked at it again and grimaced; three ninety-nine—what do you expect? Then he took a sip, swished it around his mouth, and then swallowed. It was, to put it mildly, an unpleasant experience. He had never tasted wine like it in his life, and it tasted so bad that he considered pouring it down the sink. Beggars can't be choosers, though. He left the Jaffa Cakes on the unit in the hope that Francis would at least eat one or two. Then he made coffee and went to his favourite room in the house, his office.

The problems were so many and so complex, he felt overwhelmed by them. He thought back to work, where he had often been under intense pressure and working to strict deadlines. Prioritise your list of jobs. Start at number one and work your way through them until you finished. He took a piece of A4 paper and wrote one to ten down the left-hand side. Then he sat back. What was number one? For a couple of minutes, he thought about it and decided there could only be one, and that was cutting back and managing the little money they did have. He went through every account online, cancelling all the direct debits and standing orders. Then he decided what they could do without and cancelled numerous subscriptions, even cancelling the daily paper that was delivered, and the BBC licence fee monthly payment. The next day, he would open an eBay account and sell the television and other non-essentials like his golf clubs. He felt pleased; he'd made a start. Francis didn't come out of her room all day, and he got more and more concerned.

*** 

'But, Graham, I've been friends with Francis for years, for God's sake. They're in trouble.'

Graham shook his head at Mary. 'I'm sorry, but as far as we're concerned, they're history. That Michael is a loser, and I don't want us having anything to do with them, do you understand?'

'I just don't see why I should lose a good friend because—'

'I am *not* going to keep repeating myself. If they phone, do not answer. Cross them off the Christmas card list. Now, do you see how serious I am?'

'Yes, but—'

Graham raised his voice to almost shouting, 'Enough. The conversation is closed.'

\*\*\*

Francis eventually appeared at six p.m. She went to the kitchen, made a cup of tea, and went back to her room. Michael hadn't dared show his face, but he crept into the kitchen after he heard the key turn in the bedroom door. He opened the door, and shock hit him. Francis had opened the Jaffa Cakes and smashed them into bits all over the kitchen. Michael just stood and looked at them, then started to cry. Francis could well be having a nervous breakdown. God, he needed help for her. What could he do? He thought of Graham's wife, Mary. They'd been friends for twenty-five years. He went to the office and rang the home number.

Mary answered the phone in her usual cheerful manner.

'Hello, the Hawkins residence.'

'Mary, it's Michael. I need your help. It's Francis. I think she's having a nervous breakdown. She's shut herself away ...'

The phone went dead.

He looked at the phone and muttered, 'Bloody BT. Useless.'

He redialled the number.

'Hello, the Hawkins residence.'

'We got cut off. As I was saying—'

'Didn't you get the message, Michael? Do not phone us again, ever.'

Mary put the phone down.

Michael couldn't believe what he had just heard. Mary actually told him not to call them again. Unbelievable. Extraordinary. He collapsed back in his seat. Now he knew what it was to be a so-called loser, and had no doubt this would just be the beginning. He could imagine people crossing the road if they saw him. No one wants to be associated with a failure.

The weeks went on, and the money dwindled away. Francis got up more, but she didn't shower and spent her whole life in her dressing gown. She must have lost at least three stone, and looked painfully thin. Michael had, on occasions, nearly given up himself. How he kept going, he didn't know, and the temptation to walk out of the house and sleep rough in London was strong—no bills, no more worry, except where to get some food. In fact, he even contemplated committing a crime so he could get free board and lodgings, plus three square meals a day, as a guest at one of her majesty's prisons.

On Tuesday morning, banging on the front door woke him up. His watch showed the time at seven a.m. Jesus, who the hell could that be so early? He stuck on his dressing gown and stumbled downstairs to the front door. When he opened it, he saw two large gentlemen who looked like nightclub bouncers.

'Good Morning. Are you Mr Michael Fletcher?'

'Yes, I am. What can I do for you?'

'We're bailiffs, acting on behalf of Southwark Crown Court. We've come to collect monies owed, and if you don't pay now, we have a warrant to enter the property and confiscate goods to the value of three hundred and ten pounds.'

'What the hell is this? What's the bill?'

'A parking fine received in Sutton some six months ago. You've had numerous requests for payment and ignored them.'

'And now I owe over three hundred pounds? How did that happen?'

'Interest has accrued, Sir, and you have to pay for the bailiff service.'

'Bloody hell. Can't I pay it off monthly?'

'I'm afraid it's too late for that, Sir.'

'Can we step inside, please?' the second man said.

'No, you cannot. Just wait here while I get my card, and I'll pay you.' Michael pushed the door, leaving it open an inch, and went to the office to get his wallet. He returned to the front door and was shocked to see the two men standing in his hallway.

'What the hell are you doing in here? I told you I was coming to pay you, and you have no right to just walk in my house.'

'We have every right to enter the property, Sir. We have not forced entry. Can you pay now, please?' He took a card payment machine out of a bag.

'You can stand there all fucking day. Now you've come into my house without an invitation, I won't pay a penny, and in fact, I'm calling the police.' Michael dialled 999 and explained that two thugs were threatening him in his house. The bailiffs refused to leave, and Michael refused to pay. Stalemate.

***

On their way back to Epsom, DI Karen Foster and Sergeant Mick Hill stopped for fuel at the Shell petrol station in Burgh Heath. Just as they pulled out, the radio crackled and informed them of a disturbance at a house in Kingswood—a mile away. Karen turned on the siren, and Mick pushed the accelerator pedal down hard. They got there in one minute and thirty seconds. They parked in front of the property, noting a Ford Mondeo already on the property. Mick banged on the door, and a dishevelled man wearing a dressing gown opened up.

'Hello, officers. I'm Michael Fletcher. Please, come in.'

Michael held the door open, and Mick led Karen into the hall. They saw the two large men and asked who they were. They told Karen they were bailiffs from the court and that they were chasing a fine that had not been paid. Karen asked Michael if that was the case, and he agreed it was.

'So, Mr Fletcher, pay the money and then we can all get on.'

'I told these ...' He stopped for a second, and then continued, 'Gentlemen, that I was going to pay, and I went for my wallet. When I returned, they were standing in my hall. It's disgraceful behaviour, so I'm refusing to pay until they leave my house. Everybody hates bailiffs, and policemen are no different to anybody else.'

Karen looked at the bailiffs. 'You want to get paid, so step outside and he'll pay you.'

'No chance, we're not moving. He could shut the door.'

That pissed Karen off, and she spoke to them again. 'Easy. Sergeant Hill will hold the door so Mr Fletcher can't shut it.'

The senior bailiff didn't look impressed. 'We have a legal right to be in the property.'

Karen felt more pissed off by the second. What a waste of time was this? 'Can I have a word with you, please, Mr Fletcher?' She took his arm and escorted him into the adjoining dining room.

'Is this worth all the hassle? I could just leave and let you get on with it. Just pay.'

Michael shed a tear. 'Officer, my wife is upstairs having a nervous breakdown, I'm going to lose my house, and no doubt I will become a bankrupt, not forgetting also that we have little money for food or to pay the bills with. Those bastards pushed their way into my house. Do you understand?' Another tear dropped down his cheek.

'Do you own a Mondeo, Mr Fletcher?'
'No, why?'
'Well, there's one parked in your drive. Did they ask permission to park on your property?'
'No.'
'Leave this to me, Sir.'

Karen went back into the hall and fronted up close to the two bailiffs. 'A complaint has been made by the homeowner that you two are trespassing on his property. What do you say to that?'

'It's ridiculous. We're accredited bailiffs working for the court.'

'You may be, Sir, but is that your car parked outside?'

'Yes, it is.'

'And have you had permission from the homeowner that you may park on his property?'

Silence fell for a moment. 'Well, no, actually, we haven't but ...'

'In that case, I must ask you to leave the property immediately.'

'But we are—'

'If you do not leave the property in the next five seconds, my Sergeant, here, will arrest you.'

The two bailiffs looked at each other in shock, and then opened the door and left.

'Wait outside the property, please. I want to speak with you in a minute.'

Michael cried with happiness.

Karen and Mick both felt for Michael and wanted to try and sort it out before they left.

'Mr Fletcher, if you were to write a cheque, I could take it to them and then they wouldn't have to come back.'

'Yes, that's a good idea.' Michael went to the office wrote a cheque and gave it to Karen.

'Thank you, Sir. I hope things improve for you.' Just as she said that, Francis came shuffling down the stairs. Karen looked at her, and her eyes widened at the sight. The woman reminded her of when she had been at rock bottom, lying on her kitchen floor, drunk and covered in vomit. Francis slipped and nearly missed the next step.

Karen, Mick, and Michael all jumped forward. Karen got to her first and held her arm, which felt painfully thin.

'Who are you? And what are you doing in my house?'

'Mr Fletcher called us as there was an altercation with a bailiff, but it's all sorted now.' She smiled warmly at the wreck in front of her. 'Fancy a cup of tea? I could use one.'

Francis looked around at the three of them. 'Yes, thank you. Let's go to the kitchen.' She hobbled off to the kitchen, and Karen followed. Francis seemed to have taken to the policewoman. She sat at the table and told Karen where everything was, and she whipped up four lovely cups of Tetley. Five minutes later, Karen whispered to Mick that he should go back to work, and she would follow later, and that he was to cover her arse and let her know if anybody was chasing her.

'So, Francis—'

'My friends call me Fran,' she said while slurping the scalding hot tea.

'So, Fran, you look like shit, truly.' She said it with a smile and a laugh.

Francis laughed. 'I know. I've been ...' She stopped speaking for a moment, and a tear rolled down her cheek. 'I've been down. Things have happened. My husband, he's lost all our money, he went abroad on business, and fucked some bitch, and it's all gone wrong. Very fucking wrong.'

Karen could understand. 'I know. I've been where you are now, Fran. Let me help you. As soon as you've finished that tea, you're going under the shower. You smell like rotten cabbage.'

'Oh my God, lead the way.'

Karen followed Francis upstairs in case she fell backwards. The woman probably hadn't eaten a proper meal for days and looked weak. Karen walked into Francis's room. Shrouded in darkness, it smelled horrible. Karen pulled the curtains and opened the windows wide. Fresh air rushed in and soon replaced the dank, stagnant atmosphere in the room. Next, Karen pulled all the sheets off the bed and threw them outside onto the landing.

'Right, get undressed and follow me into the bathroom.' Karen went into the en-suite and turned the shower on, but couldn't get any hot water. She turned it off and went back into the bedroom, where Francis stood naked.

'Back in a second. Put on a dressing gown.'

Karen went down to the office where Michael sat hiding. She knocked and opened the door.

'Francis wants to take a shower, and there's no hot water?'

'I know, I turned the heating and the hot water off.'

'Do you have a bucket?'

'Yes. What do ... ?'

'Fine. Fill it with hot water and bring it upstairs. Then you'll need to refill it, okay?'

'Sure. How is she?'

'She's improving.'

'Thank you so much for your help.'

'I'll help as much as I can, but I have to go back to work soon.'

'Of course, I understand, I'll get on with the water.'

'As soon as possible, please.'

Karen went back upstairs and found Francis sitting on her bed. She had put on her dressing gown, which made her look normal size again.

'Michael's filling buckets, and he'll bring hot water in a jiffy.'

Francis just shook her head. 'That idiot has ruined our lives. Guess how much money he's lost for us.'

'I have no idea, how much?'

'Seven hundred thousand.' Her words hung in the air—such a huge sum.

'Fuck. That *is* a lot of money.' Karen felt shocked. How could you lose money like that? Michael must be a fool.

Francis stood up. 'You're right. It's a fuck of a lot of money.' She shrugged. 'I need a pee.' She entered the bathroom and shut the door behind her.

The hot water arrived, and Karen made Francis sit in the bath while she ladled hot water over her. Then she soaped and scrubbed every inch of her body and washed her hair. Francis got out of the bath, and Karen dried her. Although Francis was thin, she still had a good figure, and Karen couldn't stop admiring her firm breasts.

'Your tits are great. So much nicer than mine. How come they're still so pert?'

'Always wear a bra in bed; they last a lot longer that way before they head rapidly south.'

With a chuckle, Karen found her way to the airing cupboard, made the bed with clean sheets, and got Francis in a comfy sitting up position.

'Right, I'm going to knock up some food for you. Definitely won't be Jamie Oliver but hopefully edible.'

Francis smiled, and Karen felt pleased.

Downstairs, she asked, 'Michael, is there any food in the house at all?'

'You could do scrambled eggs and grilled tomatoes—she loves that.'

'Good, that will do nicely.' Karen got on with it, and ten minutes later, she carried a tray of piping-hot food up to the bedroom.

'That smells delicious. Karen, you've been so kind.'

Karen placed the tray on Francis's lap.

'Sit with me, please, just for five minutes.'

Karen sat next to her on the bed and looked at Francis. Wow, she looked so much better—a real transformation. Francis wolfed the food down, which didn't surprise Karen in the slightest, considering she hadn't eaten a proper meal for days.

Karen cleared the tray away and retook her seat on the bed. Francis leant her head on Karen's chest and held her hand. Karen stroked Francis's hair. Then she glanced at her watch. She had to fly.

'Francis, I must go, I have work to do.'

'I know.' She held out her arms.

Karen bent down to give her a cuddle, and Francis held her tight. Karen could feel her breasts through the flimsy nightie, and she so wanted to touch them. Then Francis kissed Karen on the neck and then the cheek, Karen reciprocated, and it just happened. Their lips and tongues met in a passionate kiss. Francis took Karen's hand and placed it on her breast, and it felt firm and delicious. Karen kissed the hard nipple, and then stood up quickly.

'God, I'm sorry ...'

'No need to be, Karen, it was lovely. Will you come and see me again? Say you will.'

'Yes, I will. I like you very much, and I want you to get better, and that means you have to eat your greens.' They shared a chuckle.

'Thanks, Karen.'

'My pleasure. See you soon.' She blew Francis a kiss, and then went downstairs to the office.

'Michael, I'm off. I'll pop back in a couple of days. Get some food in the house. Francis needs feeding up. I'll let myself out. See you soon.'

# CHAPTER 20

At six in the evening, Stanislav, seated on the old green sofa in the lounge, watched television. He couldn't wait to get back home. He felt sick of hiding, watching TV, and drinking vodka. Nartay stuck his head in the door.

'I'm just popping out. Do you want anything?'

'Yes, get me another bottle of vodka and some cigarettes.'

'Will do.'

Stanislav watched him leave, sensing he appeared to be a little nervous.

He listened to the front door close and waited a few seconds. Then he bounded up from the sofa and crossed the hall into the kitchen. Stood by the window, he watched the main entrance to the building. Nartay appeared a few seconds later; he seemed furtive and glanced up at the window, then took out his mobile. With another look around, he held the phone to his ear. Stanislav smelt something wrong. Nartay talked on his mobile and continued to look around him. Stanislav felt sure something was amiss. He could smell trouble, and Nartay smelled like rotten cheese. Stanislav went back and sat down. He had some thinking to do. Could he even trust the driver? He'd seen the reward offered in the Sun newspaper—twenty-five thousand pounds was a lot of money.

Nartay returned forty minutes later and gave Stanislav his vodka and cigarettes.

'Is everything all right with you?' Stanislav asked.

Nartay went quiet and didn't answer straight away. 'Well, you've noticed, so I'll tell you. I've split up with Sezim. She wants to get married, have kids, and I'm just not ready yet. She keeps calling me, and it's doing my head in.'

Stanislav felt satisfied. He had met Sezim, and Nartay would probably be better off without her. She was one of those women who clung. Always wanted to know where you were; a fucking pain in the arse. Stanislav opened his new bottle of vodka and lit up a Marlboro. Two days to go 'til Saturday. They would travel at peak time—ten a.m.—when staff would be under the most pressure. He couldn't wait.

***

Karen returned to Epsom police station by minicab and sought out Mick. Nothing had happened, although some idiot calling himself James Bond had wrung and would call back at four-thirty. Karen felt immediate excitement.

She spoke quietly to Mick, 'If James Bond calls, and I'm not around, find me. It is important.'

'Oh, okay.'

She never failed to surprise him, which felt fine by her. Karen's brain worked overtime. Hopefully, at four-thirty, she would have the date and time she wanted. Only an hour to wait. It would be a long hour. At exactly four-twenty-nine, her office phone rang. Switchboard said James Bond was on the phone and did she want them to put the call through or not? She said yes, and the man came on the line.

'I have the information you require. Where will you do it?'

'Just leave that to us. It's better you don't know.'

'I will be the driver. I expect to be arrested as well, and then immediately let go, yes?'

'Yes, he will think you have both been betrayed by someone else.'

'Good, so we are catching the ten a.m. ferry at Dover and travelling to Calais. I will arrive at the Dover terminal at about eight-thirty. I am driving a silver Volvo estate, registration NTO3 GVR. Is there anything else you need?'

'No, that's fine, thank you.'

The call over, Karen alerted the Port Authority Police and Kent Constabulary, who would be assisting in the arrest. She felt tempted to go herself but wanted to see Francis on Saturday and, anyway, it should be an easy take. She would send Mick to monitor the operation.

\*\*\*

Stanislav fretted. Could he trust the driver? In reality, he had no choice. You have to trust somebody some of the time. This was his moment. The driver would pick him up at five a.m. on Saturday morning. The moment he had been waiting for.

\*\*\*

On Friday, Karen rang Michael to see how Francis was and told him she would visit on Saturday morning at about eleven. Then she toured the nick, saying hello to people she seldom saw in a normal working day, which made the time a little more interesting. By four o'clock, she felt so fed up that she left early and went home. The Francis Fletcher woman had muddied the water further.

What had she been thinking? They'd only just met, for God's sake. And Karen had been on duty. The woman could easily have made a complaint of sexual harassment against Karen.

\*\*\*

Mick had also left work early, to travel down to Dover. He would stay in a hotel close to the ferry terminal.

The next day, Mick awoke at four a.m. and arrived at the terminal at quarter past, and then he sat in on the briefing. Barry Gunn, the senior commander in charge of the operation, said it would be a textbook take. Four cars with armed officers in would be used, and the manager's office in the terminal building would be the command post, as it gave a clear view of all the car lanes, and officers could spot the Volvo entering and communicate that to all officers. The driver should be arrested but released as soon as the man in the boot had been taken from the scene. They went over it five times. Mick felt no worries, and hot coffees got passed round prior to the officers going to station. Mick would stay in the command post and, hopefully, observe a textbook operation.

\*\*\*

The Volvo parked up outside the flats, and the driver flashed his lights. One minute later, Stanislav came out of the flats, put his bag in the back, and sat in the front passenger seat.

'Good morning. All is satisfactory. Did you sleep well?'
'I am fine. When do I transfer to the back?'

'We will stop five miles from the port, and we will then hide you as best as we can.'

'Good. Let's go. I can smell the French women from here.'

The driver laughed, and they pulled away. The roads held hardly any traffic, and they made good time. The driver had brought a flask of hot coffee with him, which they shared, and which meant they didn't have to stop. They were soon only seven miles from the port. Two minutes later, he pulled off the main road and into a wooded area that he had used before. It was all done quickly, and five minutes later, the car pulled out of the woods and sped towards the ferry terminal.

***

With miles of lights and a few cars, the ferry terminal looked lit up like a Christmas tree. They came early: it was only seven-thirty. Staff directed the car to lane four, where it took the first slot in that lane. Mick watched the car from the office in the terminal. Parking attendants directed one of the patrol cars to lane four, and it parked directly behind the Volvo. They repeated this action, and a further unmarked police car drove to lane three, then stopped right at the front next to the Volvo. The third police car went to lane five, and parked at the front as well, next to the Volvo.

Mick watched and felt impressed. If it had been the Met, there would have been screeching tyres, guns everywhere, and loud-hailers. He smiled. One or two of the plainclothes policemen and women got out their cars, supposedly to stretch their legs after long journeys.

They should have been on the London stage. Mick sat transfixed when it turned serious all of a sudden.

A Port Authority van drove across the front of the Volvo, and then two officers got out and pointed handguns at the driver. The other officers came to life and assumed positions around the vehicle, aiming their weapons. The driver's door opened, they dragged him out, and threw him to the concrete floor. Then they opened the hatchback door at the rear, pushed cases out of the way, and dragged a man from the boot of the car. Officers pulled his arms roughly behind his back and handcuffed him. A police van pulled up alongside the target, and the officers locked him in a cage at the back, then the van took off at high speed with two police escort vehicles—one in front and one behind. They would take the package to Dover Police Station for the morning, ready for a lunchtime transfer up to Guildford in Surrey. A minute later, officers allowed the driver back in the Volvo, and he pulled away and headed back out of the port.

'Sir. Congratulations on a job well done. It was a superb snatch. No theatrics. Good, solid, controlled police work.'

'Thank you, Sergeant. Yes, it went well. You know the police saying, *planning and preparation is everything.* I suggest you get back to your hotel, and we'll see you later at Dover nick.'

'Just got to phone the boss. She said it didn't matter what time it was, so ...'

Mick pressed the contact image on his phone.

A sleepy Karen Foster answered the phone.

'Boss, it's Mick. Job done. He's in custody. Went like clockwork.'

'Brilliant, Mick. Thank them all for me, and see you lunchtime.'

\*\*\*

The police van entered Dover police station, and officers dragged the package out from the cage and took him to the custody suite. He seemed unable to walk properly without assistance and hadn't said a word since they'd grabbed him. Perplexed, they took him to a cell, gave him a plastic cup of tea, and shut the door. Then they called the duty doctor, and he arrived twenty minutes later. He went straight to the prisoner to assess his health. The doctor came back from the cell and said the man had a large bruise on his head, but other than that he looked fine and had said a few words.

'Can we book him in, then?'

'I don't see why not. Give him half an hour, and I expect he'll be feeling a lot better. He asked me to tell you he was James Bond. These people.' He shook his head and laughed, as did the custody suite Sergeant.

\*\*\*

Mick arrived at Dover Police Station at eleven-thirty and went straight to the custody suite to check on Stanislav. The Desk Sergeant said that the man was well, and everything was fine, except that the man had no ID on him and had refused to give his real name. Mick thought about that for a second, and then asked, 'If he's not giving his real name, what name is he using?'

'You won't believe this. Says he's Bond, James Bond.'

The custody suite Sergeant expected Mick to laugh or at least smile, but he did neither. Instead, he stared at the Sergeant with a blank, expressionless face, and then he put his hands over his face and muttered five words, 'I. Don't. Fucking. Believe. This.'

After a few seconds, Mick gathered his thoughts. 'Take me to see him, right now.'

Mick spent five minutes with the man in the cell. He repeated he was James Bond and that he had agreed the code word with DI Karen Foster. He also told Mick that when they pulled into the woods to hide Stanislav in the boot, he got hit on the head and didn't remember a single thing until he woke up properly in the cell. Mick couldn't believe what he heard. The operation may have gone like clockwork, but they forgot one major, golden rule, and that was to establish without any shadow of a doubt that they had the right man in custody. Now he would have to phone Karen and tell her. Fuck, he didn't look forward to that. He informed James Bond he had some admin to do, and then he would be released.

'I'm sorry, Karen, I can't believe it either.'

'I knew I should have fucking well come down there and done it myself. Fucking bunch of fucking amateurs. A fucking multiple murderer and we let him drive away while we're smiling and waving at him. I'll tell you the truth, Mick, I've a good mind to make a serious complaint about this. It's just fucking unbelievable.' The phone went dead with an almighty crash. Mick phoned Commander Barry Gunn and, surprise, surprise, he wasn't taking calls. Mick decided not to hang around. Soon, he sat in his car and sped back to Epsom.

# CHAPTER 21

'Hello, Francis. How are you?' Karen kissed her on the cheek. She'd hoped to see a big improvement, but there had been hardly any. It would take time. If you don't eat for days on end, the body takes time to recuperate and get back to full strength. She sat on the side of the bed and held her hand.

'Have you eaten this morning?'

'Not yet. I didn't feel like it.'

'Has Michael done some shopping?'

'Yes, miracles. He went out and bought loads of my favourite things.'

'So now I'm here, what do you fancy?'

'Now, there's a question.' Francis went all schoolgirlish and pretended to blush and be embarrassed.

Karen laughed. 'You, you're impossible.' Then she looked at Francis, and with care and meaning in her words, said, 'I like you so much. I don't say that often, so it means a lot, believe me. You need to get better. You have to eat, sleep, and not worry.'

'So, if I eat a meal, will you give me a prize for being a good girl?'

'Yes, yes, yes. I will. What would madam like as a treat?'

'I want you to get undressed and get in bed with me.'

Karen just looked at her. She so wanted to.

'Yes, I would love to, but you have to eat all your greens, or it ain't gonna happen.'

'I can't eat greens for brunch, yuk.'

'Okay, no greens. I'll go and cook.'

'I'll have a shower and put perfume in all the right places.'

'Sounds good. See you in a few minutes.'

Karen's emotions were in turmoil. She kept thinking of Esme, but Esme was hundreds of miles away, and Karen needed warmth, love, passion, and raw sex. In the kitchen, she cooked up a feast of scrambled eggs, grilled tomatoes, sausage, mushrooms, and Francis's favourite: fried black pudding.

Francis ate with gusto. Although she'd felt starved at times, she hadn't had the desire or energy to cook for herself. Karen felt pleased as she watched Francis wolf the food down and all but lick the plate clean.

'Wow. I needed that. I—' A knock on the door interrupted her.

'It's Michael. Can I come in?'

Francis jerked and screamed, 'Go away, you fucking bastard. Fuck off, you cunt. You, who lost everything, you piece of shit. You come in here, I promise I will kill you, you bastard.' She collapsed on the bed, spitting hatred at Michael.

Karen opened the door a tiny bit.

'Go away. I'll look after her.'

Karen felt shocked at the aggressive outburst. She sat on the bed and tried to comfort Francis, who lay down, breathing hard. She looked worried and fretful and sweated—still swearing at Michael but quietly.

The whole thing upset Karen. 'Francis, don't be upset, please, my darling.' She stroked her hair. Karen then made a decision and stripped off and got in the double bed, as naked as the day she was born. She lay on her back, and without any communication, Francis cuddled up to her, and Karen brought her in close, feeling her breasts push against hers. Francis's legs came over Karen's, and they lay together. Karen loved the feel and smell of a woman naked and close to her. Before she knew it, they both fell asleep and didn't let go of each other until they awoke in the middle of the afternoon.

'Hmm, that was so nice. You smell lovely.'

Karen chuckled. 'And I was just thinking the same thing about you.'

Francis rested her breasts on Karen's and kissed her full on the lips. Karen responded, and soon they were stuck together in a passionate embrace. They spent the next hour exploring each other's bodies. For someone unwell, Francis was insatiable. She licked, sucked, and slurped on every inch of Karen's body, and she loved it. Karen gave Francis an incentive to get better. As soon as she was strong enough, Karen would take her out for dinner, and then she could stay at her flat for the night.

'I would love to see where you live. You promise?'

'Yes. Maybe next weekend. What do you think?'

'I'll be ready. Count on it.'

'Good. Now, I have to go. I'll call you.'

They kissed, and then Karen left.

\*\*\*

Michael had gone back to the office and stayed there while Karen was in the house. This time, Karen left without saying goodbye, and he had the feeling something was going on between her and Francis, but he wasn't sure what.

He'd spent an hour going over the bank statements. He didn't trust the bank, and they made mistakes all the time. He would visit his local branch of National Trust on Monday, and saw no point hiding. He needed to renegotiate loan payments and discuss how they were going to move forward, and at all costs, he wanted to save the house if he could. He was friendly with the manager, Christopher John, and felt sure he would help.

The weekend flew by. Francis stayed in her room mostly but did come out to cook herself some meals, which was a good sign.

Michael arrived at the branch at nine-thirty.

He approached one of the greeters, who he recognised. 'Good morning. Can I see Chris John, please?'

'Good morning, Mr Fletcher. Chris left us three months ago. We have a new manager now, a Miss Andrea Houlihan.' She raised her eyebrows, which Michael took as a warning sign.

'Okay, do you think she could spare me a few minutes. It's important.'

'I'll see what I can do.'

Two minutes later, she came back and said Miss Houlihan would see him at ten, and she also whispered that she was checking on all his accounts before they met. Michael could feel the cold wind of change as he sat down to wait, and could guarantee the woman was a career banker who had ambitions to get to head office as soon as possible. At exactly one minute to ten, a smartly dressed thirty-something-year-old woman came through the security door. He knew straight away it was her.

'Mr Fletcher. Follow me, please.'

Hardly a friendly welcome. He followed her into one of the small meeting rooms.

'So, what can we do for you today?'

Michael instantly hated this woman. No, 'I see you used to work for the bank', no smiles; a ghastly, horrible woman.

'I need to discuss my financial status and agree a plan to get over the current blip in our situation.'

Miss Houlihan looked at the papers in front of her.

'Well, I had a quick look at your accounts, and I'm glad I did. You seem to have been given some special dispensations in the past, presumably because you worked for the bank.'

'Twenty-eight years—a long time.'

'Yes, well, that will all stop now. Your accounts are haemorrhaging money and, before long, you will default on payments. For an ex-banker, you appear to be in a complete financial mess.'

'Bad investment in Kazakhstan, happens.'

'Well, only if you're ...' She left that hanging, but he knew she meant stupid.

'So, what do you propose to do, Mr Fletcher?'

'Please, call me Michael, it's much friendlier.'

'I don't do friendly, Mr Fletcher. I manage money for people, and you may like to consider moving your accounts to another bank who might be able to offer you a service more suited to your needs.'

'Look, you snotty cow, I've been at this branch nearly all my life. I am not taking my business elsewhere and, to be quite frank, your whole attitude stinks. You are here to help me, and that is exactly what I expect you to do.'

'Times are changing, Mr Fletcher. We don't want liabilities. My job is to make this branch as profitable as possible and, by hook or by crook, that is exactly what I intend to do. So why don't you write out a plan and come back and see me again, and oh, make an appointment this time.' She got up, the meeting over.

'Next time I speak to Tony Morgan, I'll put a good word in for you.'

However tough the cow was, Michael expected her to change her tune slightly at the mention of the Director's name.

'You won't get the opportunity, Mr Fletcher. Tony Morgan was fired last week. Good day to you.'

Michael couldn't move, he was in so much shock. Tony Morgan gone. As the bitch said, times were changing. Michael left the bank in a foul mood. Any trace of goodwill that he'd still felt towards National Trust had evaporated. What a bitch. He laughed out loud. If anybody were going to get screwed because of his financial situation, it would be National Trust. How ironic is that?

He went straight home. Francis had been cooking but, as usual just lately, hadn't cooked for him. He disappeared into the office and immersed himself in job hunting.

Tuesday morning, Michael rang the jobcentre. If he wanted to register as unemployed, he could do that on the phone, but he had to visit the jobcentre in Epsom for an interview and to get any payments that may be applicable. A cancellation had come in for that afternoon, so if he could make it at short notice, it was available.

The last thing in the world Michael wanted to do was visit the jobcentre, but needs must, and so he confirmed that he would attend the interview at three p.m. with Mrs Catherine Jones. He also had to get the bus or train, which meant an expense, and it would be time-consuming. For lunch, he had a cheap plastic cheese sandwich, and then set off. Fifty minutes later, he reached Epsom town centre and walked from the clock tower down the high street, under the railway bridge, into East Street, and opened the jobcentre door at two minutes to three.

'Yes, Sir. Can I help you?' a cross between a guard and a greeter asked.

'Good afternoon. I have an appointment with Mrs Catherine Jones.'

'First floor, thank you, Sir.'

Michael soon found himself seated on a blue chair, alongside three other men, waiting for their names to be called. The three men talked, and they obviously knew each other. None of them sounded English. One of the desks stood right in front of where he sat, and he heard every word said. He hoped the woman interviewer wasn't Mrs Jones. The woman stood up, shook hands with the man, and said, 'See you same time next week.' Then she sat down, shuffled through some papers, and looked up.

'Mr Fletcher?'

Great. The whole world would be able to hear their conversation. They said good afternoon to each other, and he sat down.

'So, you have just registered, and this is your first visit to us?'

'Yes.'

She looked at him, and he looked at her.

'So, what brings you here today?'

'I was made redundant in August, so was advised to visit.'

'Oh, I'm sorry to hear that. Right, well, I'll skip through a set of questions, and then we'll see where we are.' She smiled. 'Who did you work for?'

'National Trust Bank.'

'Length of service?'

'Twenty-eight years.'

Mrs Jones nodded as though she'd heard it all before a hundred times.

'Did you get a redundancy payment?'

'Yes.'

'What was your salary? And how much redundancy did you get?'

Michael leant forward a little. 'Salary was a hundred and twenty thousand a year, and the redundancy package was three hundred thousand.'

Mrs Jones took a while to speak. 'Really? That much?'

'Yes.'

'Did they give you any other benefits?'

'Well, they gave me a BMW.'

Mrs Jones looked dumbfounded. 'Value?'

'I sold it for fifteen thousand.'

She made another note on her form.

'I see. Well, what do you want here, then?'

Michael leant further forward. 'I'm broke and in serious financial difficulties. Is there any help available?'

Mrs Jones now looked more than shocked. 'How can you be broke in such a short time?'

'It's a long story, but in a nutshell, I made a property investment in Kazakhstan and it went tits up. Sorry, I lost all my money.'

'How much did you lose?'

'Seven hundred thousand.'

Someone in the front stalls whistled and shouted, 'Yo, that's a lot of dough to lose.'

'Who's been a silly boy then?' Mrs Jones just couldn't help herself.

'My wife says something slightly different to that.'

'I'll bet she does, Mr Fletcher. So, look, I need dates. We'll finish the form, and then process it and see where we go from there. But, I can tell you now, you have wasted your redundancy and, because of that, I suspect you will not qualify for any help for months, if ever. So, shall we carry on?'

She picked up her pen and sat ready to ask the next question.

Michael spoke before she could say anything, 'Actually, I tell you what, thank you for seeing me, but I'm withdrawing my claim.' He got up. 'Goodbye, Mrs Jones.' Then he marched out the door.

Back at home, he hid himself away in the office again. He checked his to-do list, and the next item was for him to phone the council. He didn't want to do it, as he knew what the outcome would be, but did it anyway. The conversation went similar to the jobcentre interview, and they informed him that he could apply for benefits online, but it was unlikely he would receive any. He had to laugh when the woman told him that if they became homeless, they should contact the council. And they would probably be able to find a Bed and Breakfast for them at short notice, but it would probably be in Croydon, which was where they were now sending people. The woman had also told him he could try for Tax Credits, but Michael couldn't face another bout of questions, so he just gave up. He thought there was one positive outcome from the Jobcentre and Council conversations, and that was that at least now he knew he was on his own. No one would help and, in truth, why should they after he had been so damn bloody stupid?

In the past, Michael had never seen the postman and had never given him a second thought. Now, the postman terrified him, and if he happened to catch sight of him, he almost shook with fright. The post would arrive like clockwork at nine-thirty-six or seven every day. He was the deliverer from hell, and what seemed like a never-ending mountain of bills would suddenly appear on the carpet by the front door. Michael now called the postman a disciple of the devil himself. Never any good news, but just a constant stream of bills. And then it got considerably worse. The bank cancelled his credit and debit cards. He had maxed them all, and the total owed amounted to eighteen thousand. And then the letters about the mortgage began, friendly at first: 'If you are experiencing short-term difficulties, please get in touch so we can help.' Whenever he got a letter from the bank, he felt sure that that bitch Andrea Houlihan had something to do with it. The letters progressed to quite threatening, and then the first arrived that said they were instigating legal proceedings to take the house. It would take months, but they were on the slippery slope to losing his most treasured possession. Although, in truth, the bank already owned most of it.

The phone had been key to Michael maintaining communication with the outside world. He used BT Broadband for his internet, which meant he had prioritised phone bills for payment above everything else. It was a two-edged sword, as the phone rang all day, with people chasing payments—never-ending, and Michael avoided answering it these days. He had gotten some cash when he'd been able to and hidden it in the office for a rainy day. He started paying the phone bill at the post office with it.

Any debt letters that came into the house, he put in a box in the office. He didn't want Francis to read any of them. A little better, she ate well and had put on weight. He had said hello to her one morning when she came into the kitchen, but she blanked him as though he didn't exist.

# CHAPTER 22

Nartay felt happy that at last Stanislav had left, even though it was so early in the morning. The minute he saw the Volvo drive off, he poured himself a whisky, sat down, and relaxed. What an absolute joy to get his place back without worrying about anybody else, especially a lunatic like Stanislav. He climbed back into bed for a few hours and finally got up at eleven.

He made himself two fried eggs on toast and a cup of Maxwell House instant coffee. Then sat down and flicked through the TV channels, trying to find something remotely interesting to watch. A loud knock came at the door. He wasn't expecting anybody, so it must be someone selling something. Ready to tell them to go away, he opened the door. Stanislav stood there.

Before he could speak, Stanislav punched him square on the jaw and sent him flying back into the hall. Then he stormed in and shut the door behind him. Next, he grabbed Nartay by the arm and dragged him into the lounge, where he deposited him on the rug in the middle of the room.

'What was your share? You bastard.'

Nartay still felt groggy and muttered a reply.

'Speak up. I don't hear.'

'I said I have no clue what you're talking about. What the fuck are you doing back here?'

'Police all over ferry port. Was setup. Just managed to get away.'

'What happened to the driver?'

'Got nicked. I was lucky, he set me up, and maybe you helped?'

'I had nothing to do with it, I promise you. How did you get back?'

'I took off in Volvo. You were in partnership with driver for reward?'

'I swear to you on my mother's grave, I was not involved.'

For some reason, Stanislav believed him.

'If find out you lie, you will regret.'

'I'm not lying.' Now he felt worried. 'Where's the Volvo now?'

'Don't worry. I dumped it miles away and got tube. Will find car eventually, but I'll be gone soon.'

'How are you going to get away?'

'I'm going to Liverpool. Will get boat over to Ireland and stay there for bit, and then move on.'

***

He stayed true to his word, and the very next day, he left and got on the first train to London to take a coach from Victoria. That evening, he booked into a cheap Bed and Breakfast close to the port. He would make contact with someone in one of the local port pubs, and it wouldn't be difficult to hitch a ride to Ireland when he had plenty of cash in his pockets.

***

Karen went to pick Francis up at ten-forty-five. She'd had the bad news from Mick but felt determined not to let it ruin her weekend. She knocked on the door, and Michael opened it.

'Come in, come in.'

'Is she ready?'

'I have no idea. I'll call her.'

He went to the bottom of the stairs.

'Francis. Your visitor is here.'

The bedroom door opened, and Francis came down the stairs. Michael stood out of the way, not wishing to get shouted at or abused. She got to the bottom of the stairs, and both Michael and Karen stood still, shocked.

Francis must have spent some time getting ready, and she looked stunning. With perfect makeup, she wore tight blue jeans and a flimsy, see-through, sky-blue blouse that showed off her dark-blue bra underneath. She had some gold jewellery around her wrists and looked a picture.

'Wow, you look fantastic,' Karen said with a huge grin.

'Yes, I have to agree, I've ...' Michael trailed off, as Francis turned to him with a look that could kill at five paces.

Rather than cause trouble, Michael retreated to his den—the office.

'You look rather nice as well,' she said to Karen. 'So, are we ready?'

Karen smiled again. 'Definitely. Got everything?'

'Yep, all ready.'

The two of them left and soon headed towards Epsom town centre, where Karen planned to treat Francis to some shopping and a hearty lunch.

# CHAPTER 23

Michael's job hunting became a nightmare, and as usual, he now sat in his office sipping coffee. Francis had gone out with the copper, so he had the house to himself. He had come to the conclusion that he wouldn't get another exceptionally well-paid job—if he got a job at all—so what to do was the question. Maybe Graham hadn't been so foolish to take the council job at thirty K a year. If he'd kept all his money, then they could have survived on that salary. But the problem was, he didn't want to survive, he wanted to live comfortably and have a good lifestyle.

No question, he'd been stark raving mad to invest in the project in Kazakhstan, and what had possessed him, he didn't know. He could start out on his own as a financial advisor, that would be feasible, but he needed to get some extra qualifications, which would take time. He could rob a bank. No, of course, that was out of the question, and he would get caught and spend the rest of his life in prison. For sure, though, if he did nothing, nothing would change, and it would all end in total disaster.

For a mid-afternoon snack, he cooked up some cheap beef sausages and made a sandwich with brown sauce. Then he slept for an hour and, feeling re-invigorated, went back on his computer at four. He checked his email inbox and found six emails, mostly rubbish, but one stirred his curiosity. It bore the heading: *Kazakhstan*. He opened it, and it had no text but did have a photo attached, which he opened. He stared at the image, not knowing where it had been taken or the person in it, and then he looked much closer and nearly fell off his chair. He said out loud, 'What the fuck?' When he enlarged the size to full screen, he could see as clear as day. He couldn't take his eyes off the image while he tried to make sense of it. The one thing he did notice straight away was the date down in the left-hand corner. He stood up and paced around the tiny office, with his mind racing. 'What the fuck?' He couldn't stop himself from repeating it over and over again.

He still felt completely mystified when, a full minute later, his mobile rang. He didn't recognise the number.

'Michael Fletcher.'

Michael listened and answered after the other person had spoken.

'Yes, I got it.'

...

'I'm beginning to understand.'

...

'My God, I don't know what to say, I, I'm in shock, say thank you, it's a miracle.'

...

'Yes, goodbye.'

Michael couldn't believe what had happened. It seemed nothing short of incredible. He wouldn't tell Francis anything, as he didn't want to upset her any more and would only speak to her when and if something developed. But what a hell of a shock, and he could only guess at where it could possibly lead.

Francis arrived back on Sunday night, proceeded straight to her room, and he heard the key turn in the door once again.

The financial problems piled up. The fucking bitch Houlihan from the local National Trust bank had started phoning herself. And it pleased him that she must be pulling her hair out, agonising what to do about his debts to her branch of the bank.

The problems had become so serious and complicated that he couldn't care less. All the letters that arrived from insurance companies, the bank, utility companies, and many others he put in a cream-coloured plastic washing basket on the floor of the office. The box he had been using had long since filled up.

On Monday morning, he got up early, as he needed to think. He had the photo but what could he do? To unclutter his mind, he would do some walking in the local area, and then pick up some bits at Asda in Burgh Heath. The fresh air felt invigorating and helped to unblock his overburdened brain. Despite enjoying the walk, he felt that he needed some wheels. After the walk, he caught the bus to Ewell and visited a well-known scrap metal dealer who sold old bangers on the side.

*** 

Francis heard him exit the house. She'd had the most enjoyable weekend of her life with Karen shopping, having meals out, and sex—what more could a woman possibly want? Downstairs in the kitchen, she made a cuppa, then mooched around the house for five minutes. What was Michael up to?

Back upstairs, she pushed the office door open and entered his den. She looked around. It hadn't changed except for one of her washing baskets, full of letters, sitting on the floor. She picked up some of the loose papers and scanned through them. Bills, hundreds of bills, unpaid bills, Electric, Gas, Water, Mortgage, Bank, Loans, and even from the local newsagents who hadn't been paid. Shakes overtook her. There must be thousands of pounds unpaid. She grabbed letter after letter, and they all wanted the same: *County Court action after County Court action*. And then she unsealed the one that finally pushed her over the edge.

*The Bank has no alternative other than to apply through the courts for the repossession of your property.*

Francis crumpled the letter up in her hand, went a deathly white, and could hardly breathe. She didn't cry, but just turned around and made her way slowly back up to her bedroom.

\*\*\*

Michael, tall, thin, and worn-out-looking, pulled into the Asda car park in Burgh Heath. He wore a pair of food-stained, old, grey trousers and an expensive white shirt that had extremely frayed cuffs and shirt collar. The exhaust rattled, and smoke poured out from the fifteen-year-old pale grey Ford Fiesta. He parked up as far away from other cars as he could. How embarrassing to drive a car like this. The thought of meeting someone he knew terrified him.

Driving the old car depressed him and he felt absolutely dreadful. He checked in the ashtray to see if it held any loose coins, and almost laughed when he found none. Of course there weren't any. What did he expect? He grabbed hold of his empty Wilkinson carrier bag and made for the front entrance, without bothering to lock the car. It had nothing of value inside, and who the hell would want to steal an old banger like his Fiesta?

While he strolled to the entrance, he remembered that he hadn't insured or taxed the vehicle. Then he laughed. The car had no MOT, so he couldn't have done them even if he had wanted to. The car had cost him fifty quid from someone at the scrap yard. Then he thought of his beautiful company car—the sleek, black, seven series BMW with all the extras. God, how times had changed.

He got to the entrance and picked up one of the green baskets. First port of call, as usual, was the paper stand, where he selected the Daily Mail and skimmed through it, reading anything that caught his eye. He finished off at the sports pages, frantically reading as fast as possible. Only the week before, a member of the security team had asked him if he was buying the paper, as they weren't a library. Paper finished, he went straight to the section where they sold short-dated products cheap. Two women stood chatting and looking at products at the same time. He surreptitiously pushed in near the side of the cabinet, and one of the women turned when he brushed her shoulder, so he smiled at her and leant across to see what was available. In these dire straits, he couldn't afford to miss any bargains.

He scanned the shelves, and then he saw them, two individual, single-portion shepherd's pie ready-meals. Oh, the joy. When he reached out and grabbed them, he almost knocked the woman nearest to him over in the process. He looked at the price, reduced from one pound to sixty pence—a real bargain. That was one meal taken care of. He saw nothing else of interest and dashed to the chilled meat aisle to see what was on special offer there. He strolled down the aisle looking at the legs of Lamb for eighteen pounds, picked one up to feel the weight of it, and imagined thick slices with homemade mint sauce. Those were the days when money was no object and Francis would just pick up whatever she wanted, not bothering about the cost.

Then he picked up a beef joint and looked at the price: Twelve pounds for a tiny piece of meat that would feed two at the most. Chickens seemed to be reasonable value, but even that was beyond him today, and he ended up where he nearly always did and picked up a six-ounce-tray of cheap minced beef—more boring spaghetti Bolognaise—and that meant two meals done.

Only wearing the light shirt, he shivered when the cold from the chillers crept into his bones. He strolled down the pasta and cooking sauces aisle and picked up a small bag of Asda brand pasta at fifty-nine pence—three meals done. The only reason he was doing the shop was because Francis had been so unwell. He wanted to cheer her up and bought two packets of Asda Jaffa Cakes on special offer. After those, he bought a few more items, mostly cheap Asda branded and decided to call it a day.

At the fast self-service exit, he put the basket down next to the scanner, scanned the first item, and heard the beep. Then he passed the pasta, and again it beeped. He then moved the minced beef past the scanner and placed it in the bag—no beep—he stopped. This had happened before, and the machine usually said there was an unidentified object in packing and would stop, but this time it said nothing, so he passed the next item, and it beeped.

When he looked around, he saw one girl checking on ten scanners, and she seemed to be rushed off her feet. When he finished the scanning, the amount to pay came up: nine pounds and thirty pence. He paid with the only money he had on him, a ten-pound note, then picked up his change and the two bags and strolled to the exit. The security desk stood unmanned, and he went through the automatic double doors and stood back outside. He had got a free meal, the minced beef, and felt so happy—every little helped. Wait 'til he told the missus. Then he shook his head. How fucking sad to get excited about saving a few pence. It showed how far they had sunk into the misery of debt and almost-bankruptcy.

Back in the car, he started her up, and clouds of smoke poured out from the exhaust. He could have cried. With a deep breath, he pulled himself together, pulled out of the car park, and headed for home. They had been served the final papers that confirmed the house would be repossessed unless monthly payments re-commenced and drew up a plan to pay off the thousands of pounds of arrears. This desperate situation could only end badly. How he had kept going, he did not know, and he felt deeply concerned about his wife. Had she thrown in the towel?

Outside their four-bedroomed detached house, just a five-minute drive from the supermarket, he pulled up close. Then he opened the boot and grabbed the two bags of shopping. He had to be upbeat and tried to be as cheerful as he could as he turned the key and entered the hall.

'I'm home,' he shouted up the stairs. When he heard no reply, he thought she may have nodded off, so he went to the kitchen and unloaded the shopping, packing everything neatly into the appropriate cupboard. Next, he filled up the kettle and turned it on, and then decided to check on Francis to make sure she was all right. Back out in the hall, he ascended the shabby, blue-carpeted stairs on tip-toe, as he didn't want to wake her if she had fallen asleep.

At last, he got to the top and shuffled quietly along the landing. Finally, he reached the door to their bedroom, which stood shut. He grasped the handle and turned it slowly. He got to the point where he couldn't turn it any further and eased the door open just wide enough to stick his head through.

Nothing could have prepared anyone for the sight that greeted him that day. With a gasp, he almost stopped breathing, and his hands shook uncontrollably. Ready to pass out, he pushed the door open fully and screamed her name as he ran to her. From the open window, a slight breeze made her swing to and fro, and the noise of the rope moving made him feel sick. His wife hung by a rope from a beam across the ceiling. Her face had gone a ghostly grey colour, and her dark purple tongue protruded from her mouth. Her face had twisted in a frightening grimace. Numb, he grabbed hold of her legs and looked up, but he was wasting his time—she was, without question, dead, and he could do nothing.

Distraught, he let go, and then the smell hit him—excrement covered her legs and had slipped down them to form a mess on the beige carpet floor; he also smelt urine and saw her nightie was soaking wet. Weak-kneed, he collapsed to the floor in a flood of tears.

'Why could you not stop her? She has been a faithful servant to you all her life. You are no God. You do not exist, you bastard,' he screamed out to the heavens.

His breathing became difficult, and his breaths came quicker and shallower. He had to gasp for breath, and the noise sounded more animal than human. Was he dying? Soon, he would be unable to breath at all. Then he remembered his last visit to the GP. He'd said something. Yes—hyperventilating—that's what was happening to him now. Even if only for a few seconds, he had to control himself. He dragged himself to the bathroom and pulled open a drawer, scattering the contents onto the green tiled floor. He saw and grabbed a brown paper bag, put it over his mouth, and tried to breathe. It felt miraculous, how quickly his breathing came under control. And, although he felt weak, he could feel himself getting back under control. Slumped on the floor, he felt like this was it, the end, and thought of joining his wife. He didn't have anything else. He couldn't fight any more. He'd lost. With tears streaming down his face, he took out his mobile and pressed 999.

'Ambulance and Police,' he said through sobs. 'My wife. She has ...' He stopped. He couldn't say it. He pulled himself together. 'My wife, she has hung herself, she is dead, my address, yes, it is ...'

Leant against the wall, he took a few deep breaths and sat still, thinking. His mind wandered. Someone would pay for this. In fact, quite a few people would pay for this. They'd as good as killed her. He needed to write a list. A list of the bastards who had done it. Loud banging on the front door roused him. Why didn't they ring the bell? Then he answered his question himself: they couldn't take the chance of a doorbell not working. Which was just as well, as he hadn't bought any batteries for months. Near hysteria, he stirred. It would be either the police or ambulance or both. He grabbed hold of the small white radiator and pulled himself to his feet and headed towards the stairs.

***

Karen heard about the death on her mobile in Marks and Spencer, where she'd been buying some new underwear for the next time she saw Francis. She couldn't take it in and had to sit down on one of the makeup chairs. All she could think about was the fact she was cursed when it came to partners. She'd felt attached to Francis but not like Chau and Esme. After all, they'd only just met, but even so, it hit her hard. Thirty minutes later, she pulled up outside the house. Everything seemed quiet. Suicides always had a certain feel about them. People had to be so depressed, so desperate, to commit such a terrible act. Karen found Michael.

'What the hell happened? I left her in a great frame of mind.'

'I don't know, but she'd been in the office reading letters. Bills, and letters from the bank, stuff like that.' Face in his hands, the tears flowed.

'It was all your fault, you bastard. Chucking away all that money.'

'It wasn't—'

'Don't you dare tell me it wasn't your fault. It's all your fault. You may as well have killed her yourself.' As soon as she stopped, she regretted saying that.

'Michael, I'm sorry.'

'No, you're right. I accept that it was me. All down to me.' He hesitated. 'I want you to come back another day. There are things …' He paused and took a breath. 'There are things I want—need—to tell you, but I can't do it now.'

When they eventually brought the body down in a black, zipped up body bag, neither Michael nor Karen could look. The police crime scene team didn't like suicides either. It just seemed to be more upsetting than a murder, unless, of course, children were involved, which was the worst of all by a clear mile. Karen had kept her emotions under control. Due to her job, she had a part of herself where she could put away work and turn her emotions off. No human being could cope with continually seeing harrowing scenes without being affected, unless they found a way to manage it.

\*\*\*

Michael felt lost. Not that long ago they'd been gloriously happy on holiday in Portugal. Oh God, the boys, he hadn't even given them a thought. He must contact them as soon as possible. They wouldn't have any money, and he couldn't give them any, and worst of all, how in God's name was he going to pay for a decent funeral? Then his mind flashed back to the incredible phone call he had received not long ago. Everything done that needed to be done for now, once again the house stood empty and quiet. Michael lay on his bed, crying and begging God for forgiveness. He shut his eyes. First, he would try and get hold of the boys by phone, and if not, would email them with a message to call him as soon as possible.

\*\*\*

The next morning, Michael couldn't get hold of either of the boys and emailed them. At ten o'clock, he left the house, and then sat in the car thinking about the image, the phone call, and the instructions that had arrived by email. He reached Epsom and parked in the Ashley Centre multi-storey. Excited beyond belief, he walked the two hundred yards round the corner and saw the Western Union shop. He smiled to himself. Hopefully, it would be worthwhile. All the email had said was a sum of money. He pushed open the door and looked around; he had never been in a Western Union money shop—it looked a bit like a tiny bank with one till operator behind a security screen. He approached the desk and said, 'Good morning. I believe there is a payment for me?'

'The code number and identification, please, Sir.'

Michael had written the code on a piece of paper and placed it on the counter with his passport. The woman took both and keyed the number into her computer.

'Thank you, Sir. What denominations would you like that in?'

'How much is it exactly, please?'

'After costs, the exchange value is eight thousand pounds.'

Michael just stood there in complete shock, and couldn't believe the amount. A fortune.

'How would you like that, Sir?'

'As many twenties as possible, and the balance in tens and fives, thank you.'

The clerk counted out the money, placed it in a large, brown parcel envelope, and handed it across the counter. Michael took it and didn't know whether to cry or scream with happiness. The one thing he did know was that he would put it to good use, and that meant he would use it wisely to get back as much of the lost money as he could. He left the Western Union and scanned around him to make sure no one followed him. When he walked back past the clock tower, he saw a man selling the Big Issue at the Ashley Centre entrance and gave him all his change, which amounted to three pounds. Then he walked into the recently opened Metro Bank on the corner next to Starbucks.

A tall, handsome, uniformed greeter stood in the centre of the bank floor.

'Good morning, Sir. How can we help you today?'

'I would like to open an account, please.'

The greeter beamed with delight.

'Very good, Sir. Let me call one of the staff, who will be able to assist you.'

He turned and raised his eyebrows at one of the blue-uniformed hostesses to his right, and she came forward.

The greeter turned to Michael, 'And your name, Sir?'

'Michael Fletcher.'

He turned to the hostess when she arrived at his side.

'Mr Fletcher would like to open an account with us.'

The hostess smiled. 'Good morning, Mr Fletcher. My name is Carole. Would you follow me, please, Sir, and would you like a cup of coffee?'

Michael felt like crying; he was being treated like a human being again.

'Coffee sounds wonderful, thank you, Carole.'

Carole looked shocked when she asked him how much he wanted to open the account with. He put the brown envelope on the table and tipped the notes out, which had been tied by an elastic band in one-thousand-pound amounts. He gave Carole seven bundles, took the elastic band from around the eighth, took a hundred pounds, and gave Carole the balance.

'Seven thousand, nine hundred pounds, I know you will want to check it.'

'I'll just take this to the cashier. Top up for your coffee, Mr Fletcher?'

'Yes, thank you.'

He left the bank, feeling like a million dollars. He'd come back, and a desire for retribution burned away at the back of his mind. They would pay, one way or the other. But, before he did anything, he crossed the road and entered Café Rouge, where he ordered a bottle of the Cotes Du Rhone red wine and a medium-rare Sirloin steak with all the trimmings. The wine arrived, and the waiter poured for him to taste. He enjoyed the bouquet, took a sip, swished it around his mouth, and savoured every drop as it slipped smoothly down his throat.

'Fine, thank you.'

Seated at one of the outside tables, Michael enjoyed his wine and steak while people-watching as shoppers went about their business. Steak and fries had never tasted so good, and the wine was delicious. A police car came round the corner of the one-way system and stopped directly in front of the café. The passenger door opened, and Karen Foster stepped out of the car.

Karen looked at the steak and wine. 'Michael, I see things have improved somewhat. I thought you were broke?'

Michael wasn't about to start explaining. 'Please, Karen, it's a long story, but allow me one moment of pleasure in an otherwise sea of misery.'

'I'm on lunch break. Pour me a glass, then. On second thoughts, we better go inside, away from prying eyes.'

They got up and moved inside and tucked themselves away in one of the corners.

Michael picked up the bottle of red and cursed; it didn't have much left, and now he had to give Karen some. He poured a half glass and put the bottle down.

'Michael, don't be stingy.'

She picked up the bottle and poured a full glass, which emptied the bottle. Karen drank half the glass in one go.

'Hmm, nice, thank you.'

Michael felt well pissed off that she had taken the last of the wine. Karen made eye contact with one of the waiters, who came straight to the table. 'Another bottle of red, please.'

Michael's face lit up. 'That's very kind of you.'

'I am kind unless you've committed a crime, and then I'm an obnoxious bitch. So, you wanted to speak with me about something? This seems as good a time as any, so shoot.'

Michael hadn't been prepared for Karen turning up and felt confused as to what to tell her.

'It's a long story, but the crux of it is that I'm certain I was professionally scammed out of that money.'

Karen was all ears. 'And you have proof?'

Michael sighed. 'Well, not real proof, as such, but it's out there. I just need to find it.'

'Michael, this is much more serious than you think. If someone, or a group of people, has swindled you out of seven hundred thousand, they are professionals and will not hesitate to protect themselves even to the point of committing murder. You are almost certainly not the only one, so the sums involved could be huge.'

'What do I do then?'

'If you have a shred of evidence, hand it over to me officially at the station, and we will investigate.'

Michael wasn't about to do that. As soon as he involved the police, the scammers would all go underground, and he would never get his money back.

'It's not really evidence, but more of a feeling that I was duped.'

'Surrey Police don't carry out costly investigations based on people's impressions. I'm sorry, but we need more than that.'

'Of course you do. I understand that. I've been a fool, but hey, it's nice to see you again, and let's enjoy the wine.' He filled the glasses. They finished the second bottle, and Michael felt decidedly drunk.

***

Karen felt tempted to order a third but should be going back to work. 'Michael, I'll have a police car here in a minute, and we'll take you home.'

Mick picked them up, and then dropped Michael back at Kingswood. Karen asked Mick to drop her at home, as she'd had enough for the day.

The phone rang in Karen's office at ten a.m. the next morning.

'Boss, James Bond is on the line.'

'Put him through.'

'James Bond here.'

Karen wished she had chosen some other code, as the name James Bond drove her crazy.

'Yes, Mr Bond, what can I do for you?'

'I've been thinking that bastard deserves all he gets. His name is Stanislav, and he's at 8 Hilltop House, Grange Road, Leatherhead. The guy who rents the flat is called Nartay.'

'Thank you, Mr Bond, we appreciate your assistance.' She put the phone down.

'Mick, let's roll. I have the address for our friend Stanislav. Get an armed response team ready. We leave in five minutes.'

They pulled out of the car park and headed to Leatherhead—six miles away. When they arrived around the corner from the flats, they parked up, and Karen jumped out of the car—well pumped up. The officers grouped together, and Karen took control. She pointed at three of the armed officers and told them to cover the outside of the building, while she, Mick, and the other armed officer would go in and arrest the suspect. Before they dispersed, Karen gave a few words of warning to the three officers who would be left outside:

'Look, this man is an animal and will kill to escape. If, for any reason, he makes it out of the building, you have my authority to use deadly force. In other words, if he's getting away, shoot the bastard.'

The armed officers nodded and looked as if they hoped hid did escape the building.

'Okay, let's go.'

Karen ran towards the front entrance, keeping hidden against the side of the building. The three of them entered the block of flats, and the armed officer in front scanned with his weapon. They made their way cautiously up the flight of rubbish-strewn stairs and along the landing. Outside number eight, the armed officer turned and put his finger to his lips, signalling them to keep quiet. Karen and Mick moved closer to the officer and got ready. The armed officer took a small battering ram off his back and prepared to swing it, counted to three, and smashed it against the door, which nearly came off its hinges, and the sound crashed all around them. They burst through the doorway into the hall. The armed officer charged through the small flat, looking left and right until he came to the lounge. He kicked the door open and prepared to fire. Nartay stood in the middle of the room, hands in the air, shouting, 'Don't shoot, don't shoot.'

The officer aimed the automatic machine gun directly at him and yelled, 'Get down on the floor. Lie on your stomach with your hands at your side. Do it NOW.'

Nartay did exactly as he was told, and Mick rushed in and handcuffed his hands behind his back. The armed officer continued forward to the bedrooms.

'What's your name?'

'Nartay.'

'Where is Stanislav?'

'He's gone.'

'Where?'

'Liverpool.'

Mick and Karen looked at each other in despair; they had missed the bastard.

Mick picked Nartay up and sat him on the sofa.

Karen took one of the chairs from the table, turned it round, and sat leaning on the back.

'So, Nartay, when did he leave?'

'Two days. He's on his way to Ireland. Could even be there by now.'

'How was he travelling to Liverpool?'

'Coach from Victoria. Reckoned it was low profile and the safest way.'

Karen glanced at Mick. She had nothing else to say. They would get CCTV tapes from Victoria coach station to see if he could be spotted. They would also interview the Liverpool-bound drivers and show them pictures. And they would inform Merseyside Police what had happened.

Two uniformed officers arrived at the flat and took Nartay into custody. Ten minutes later, crime scene turned up to, hopefully, find fingerprints and other incriminating evidence to prove Stanislav had been living in the flat. In fact, they found an abundance of DNA from his pillow, and fingerprints all over the flat.

\*\*\*

Stanislav wandered around Victoria coach station, making sure the cameras would pick him up. He then bought a ticket for Liverpool and again questioned the ticket clerk so that the cameras would get a good shot of him. He bought a take-away coffee in the café and boarded the Liverpool-bound coach at midday. He spoke to the driver so that he would probably remember him getting on. Stanislav had a plan of action, but it worked out even better than he could have hoped for. The driver saw a coach pull in, and he jumped from his seat, ran down the stairs, and jogged towards the other coach. He must have wanted to speak to the driver before departing. Stanislav, just as quick, darted down the length of the coach and jumped off. He walked away from the station and stopped just around a corner, out of sight. Then he removed his blue jacket and turned it inside out, so it was once again green. Next, he removed his baseball cap and took off his thick-rimmed sunglasses. With a smile, he walked back to the mainline station. He was a fucking genius. Ten minutes later, he walked down the steps and into Victoria tube station, where he bought a single ticket to Shepherds Bush, and soon sat on the train as it rolled and thundered along the dark tunnel—he couldn't help grinning.

\*\*\*

Karen and Mick returned to Epsom nick. Karen felt furious. They had fucked up the take at the ferry terminal, and now he was probably in Ireland. The chances of getting him were remote, to say the least. She went through the process of informing Merseyside Police and finished around four p.m. Frustrated, Karen went home early and sat in her lounge with a glass of red. She sat sipping it for some time, and tears rolled down her cheeks when she thought of Chau and Esme and now Francis. After she'd polished off the rest of the glass, she went to the kitchen for a refill and intended to get drunk—very drunk.

# CHAPTER 24

Seated in his office at nine-thirty in the morning, Michael felt calm and collected. He had made some notes, as he liked to be ordered—a throwback to his banking days. God, but that seemed like a lifetime ago now. He could tell Karen Foster everything he knew, but he just didn't trust the police. And felt sure that as soon as the police became involved, everybody would just disappear abroad and he would never get any of his money back.

Once again, he looked at the photo on the screen, and his anger grew. Oh, the thought of Francis swinging on that rope. He shut his eyes and shook his head in an effort to get rid of the image. Nothing in the world could be worse than what he'd seen that day when he opened the bedroom door.

His first course of action would surely be the easiest of the four. He had to play it so that the first person wouldn't talk—Michael could always terrify him, which would probably be the best way to get his cooperation. He thought again of losing his house—all the degradation, his wife, his children—his whole fucking life. Coated in sweat and breathing heavily, he swore. He needed—had to—remain cold, and had to keep the emotion at bay; otherwise, God knew what he might capable of. An hour later, he had mapped out the first payback.

\*\*\*

The couple sat eating dinner in their upmarket four-bedroom detached house. The rather domesticated wife had prepared an egg mayonnaise starter with homemade mayonnaise—one of his favourites, which he enjoyed immensely. She had just served the main course of Pork loin with cider sauce and red cabbage with apple when the doorbell rang. The man complained, 'Bloody hell. Can't even eat dinner in peace nowadays.'

The wife jumped up and made towards the front door.

'Whoever it is, tell them to bugger off.' He took a long slurp from his glass of chilled Sauvignon Blanc.

The man heard a few words spoken at the door but couldn't distinguish what was being said. About to get up to sort it out himself, he stopped when his wife appeared in the doorway. Something was very wrong.

'We have a visitor,' she said with a worried look on her face, and then Michael stepped into view.

'Hello, Graham. How are you?'

'Michael, this is awkward. You're no longer welcome here.' Graham left the table, walked towards Michael, took his arm, and tried to move him towards the front door.

\*\*\*

Michael felt like ice; he had come prepared for all eventualities. Calmly, he took the steel baton out of his right pocket and smashed it into Graham's face. He fell to the floor with blood gushing from his nose and a massive bruise already appearing around his left eye. Mary opened her mouth to scream, but Michael grabbed her and put his hand over her mouth.

'Shhhh.'

Scared, Mary couldn't move or speak. Michael took her to the dining table and sat her in one of the chairs.

'I don't have a grievance with you,' he said. 'Sit still and keep quiet.'

His face said it all: If she moved, he might kill her. Michael turned back to Graham, who sat wiping blood off his face, and the blood dripped over his clothes and down onto the carpet.

'You, get up and sit at the table.'

'I need to go to the bathroom to—'

Michael yelled at him, 'Sit at the fucking table, you cunt.' Michael had never used that word and hated it, but he felt so angry that he could easily have killed him there and then.

Graham staggered up and just made it to the table.

'Good.' Michael noticed the wine, topped up Mary's glass, and sipped it.

'This is what's going to happen. I'm going to ask the questions, and you are going to answer. I hasten to add, I will know if you are lying, and if you do, there will be repercussions. Do you understand?'

'Yes.'

Michael took a further sip of wine. 'Had you ever been to Kazakhstan before we went to Aqtau?'

'No, I promise, I told you I—'

Michael hammered the baton into Graham's podgy stomach. He doubled over in pain and could hardly breathe.

'Shall we start again?'

Mary couldn't hold herself any longer. 'He's never been to Kazakhstan before. Just the once, and I should know.'

Michael smiled at her. 'You think you know your husband?'

He turned back to Graham, 'Answer the question, or it will get a lot worse.'

Graham sputtered, 'Yes, I went once.'

Mary just looked at him.

Michael said, 'Question two, who did you meet up with while you were there? Remember, I know everything, and if you lie ...'

'I met up with friends.'

Michael spat the words out, 'Who, Graham? Who did you fucking well meet up with?'

'Sean King, Tony Morgan, and Bekzat Abdulov.'

'Well, what a fucking surprise, you bastard. How many have you helped stitch up?'

'A few. Not that many.'

'How many?'

'Six.'

Michael relaxed for a second.

'I don't understand. What the hell is going on?' Mary asked.

'Your husband is a fucking Judas. He helped to swindle me out of seven hundred thousand pounds. Isn't that right, Graham?'

'Yes, but I didn't get much. The others, they organised it all and kept most of the money.'

'How much did you get?' Michael said with a sneer.

'Twenty-five thousand.'

'You bastard. We were friends.'

Mary looked at Graham, 'Is this all true?'

'Yes, I tried to get out of it but they wouldn't let me. They threatened us—the family.'

Mary turned to Michael and looked as though she had taken charge. 'So, what do you propose, Michael?'

'I want my money and some extra for my aggravation.'

Mary turned to Graham. 'Go and get your laptop.'

He seemed about to argue but then decided against it. A couple of minutes later, he came back, plugged it in, and turned it on.

Mary, seething, said, 'Michael has every right to beat you to a pulp, you apology for a man. You disgust me. Transfer a payment to Michael of forty thousand.' She turned to Michael, 'Is that sufficient recompense?'

'Yes, but there is something else.' He looked at Graham. 'This needs to remain between us. If I find out you have warned the others, I will come back and kill you. Do you understand?'

Graham shook and said, 'You just need to put in your account number, sort code, and bank name.'

Michael put in the Metro Bank details, checked the amount, and clicked on pay. It went through.

'I don't want to hear from you, see you, or smell you.' Michael turned to Mary, 'You have my sympathy being married to this worthless piece of shit.'

And that was it. He walked to the front door, reflecting that he had let Graham off the hook, but smiled to himself thinking about what Mary would do to him. He didn't care about any of it, as he had forty grand back, which would help enormously.

The next morning, Michael got rid of the old banger and bought a three-year-old silver Mondeo. Although not much like his seven series BMW, it was a hundred times better than the old Fiesta. He also revisited the Western Union office in Epsom and sent a payment of eight thousand pounds.

# CHAPTER 25

Stanislav had booked into a grotty, cheap Bed and Breakfast in one of the back streets near Shepherds Bush Green. Although not much, it was clean and would suit him for the time being. He planned to lay low for at least two weeks, and then he would leave the country.

***

Karen had officers check the CCTV tapes at Victoria Station, which identified that the man named as Stanislav had arrived at the coach station, bought his ticket, and boarded a coach to Liverpool. When she read the report, she felt gutted and sure he had gotten to Ireland. The thought of him being free riled her beyond belief. She had asked Guildford to contact the PSNI Police Service and give them all the details but still didn't hold out much hope of him being arrested. In fact, she would be surprised if he was still in Ireland by now.

Karen's drinking had once again become a problem. The death of Francis had been hard to take, and she had only just gotten through the funeral without breaking down. Long and hard, she had thought about going back to Cannes to see Esme, but it could only ever be a short-term solution. Karen wanted something permanent. Something she could rely on. Maybe she should try male relationships again, as she never seemed to have much success with her female ones.

***

'So, Nartay, you do realise how much trouble you're in?'

'I am not in much trouble. Stanislav stayed in my flat for a few days. I had no idea what he was up to.'

Karen looked at Mick, smiled, shook her head, and then turned back to Nartay. 'You don't understand the law. You have been harbouring a murderer. You have been assisting Stanislav in murder, robbery, grievous bodily harm, and ... the list is endless. In the eyes of the law, you are guilty of a serious crime that could get you ten years in prison.'

Nartay jumped to his feet, 'Ten years, for what? I'm not a criminal.'

'Sit down,' Mick said in a stern voice.

Karen lowered her voice and became the concerned friend, 'Nartay, we know you were not involved in the actual crimes, but the law and, probably, the jury will not see it like that.'

'What Jury?'

'Well, this case will go to Crown Court with or without Stanislav, and you will be tried by jury and, if found guilty, will spend many years in prison.'

'It was him, that bastard Stanislav, he's the one who should be in court, not me.'

'I know. Look, I'm on your side. Why should you pay for his crimes? It's not fair.'

'No, it isn't.' Nartay looked liked he might burst into tears any second.

Karen took a deep breath. 'Well, we could help each other, of course.'

Nartay concentrated. 'What do you mean?'

'Stanislav murdered an elderly lady, killed a lovely married couple, and committed other terrible crimes. I want him brought to justice.' She paused for effect. 'If you were to help us, then maybe we could do something for you.'

'What do you want me to do?'

'Help us catch that bastard, and we'll make sure you get a reduced sentence.'

'Reduced to what?'

'Year or two at the most, and we could look at bail, which means you wouldn't go to Belmarsh.'

Nartay had heard of Belmarsh prison, and none of it sounded good.

'You mean I'd be able to go home today?'

'Well, not this minute, but as long as you agree, we'll see what we can do.'

'I'll help you, all right. That bastard has landed me right in it.'

'So, first of all, are you able to contact him?'

Nartay looked at the floor. 'I can call his mobile.'

'Good,' Karen said and nodded.

'We'll organise a cup of tea and a biscuit for you while we have a chat. We'll be back soon.'

Karen and Mick left the interview room and went to the canteen to get coffee. Karen felt happy at the small progress.

Back in Karen's office, they chatted.

'We need something to bring him back. As to what that is, I'm not sure. Any ideas?'

Mick said, 'Men like that are interested in two things: Money and safety. That means Nartay has to convince him that there's something worth coming back for. Something so easy and valuable that he can't resist the temptation. What that could be at this stage, I don't know.'

'You're right, but you're forgetting one other thing men like that are interested in, and that is—excuse my language—pussy.'

'So, all we need is money and—excuse my language, Boss—pussy, and he might come back?'

'Of course, that depends on where he is.'

'Nartay calls him to make sure he's safe and tells him he's got two gorgeous, sexy girls staying at the flat, who like shagging, and that they've been over here working as lap dancers for two years and are going home, and they have all the money they've made in cash, which could be thousands.'

'I like that. This Stanislav is such an animal; imagine two beautiful pussies on a plate, and when he's had his fill he takes all their money. Honestly, I think he might go for it. Now all we need are two young, sexy Russian girls to be there when he turns up.'

'That shouldn't be too difficult to arrange. It's not as if they're going to have to do anything.'

'I'll talk to my contacts at Guildford. I'm sure they'll be able to help. Let's go and talk this through with Nartay and see what he thinks.'

The discussion with Nartay proved to be positive. Stanislav's two passions in life were indeed money and women. Nartay just had to sell it in the right way.

# CHAPTER 26

Every day, Michael became more and more positive. His father had always said that a man needed to have a few bob in his pocket to have self-respect, and Michael couldn't agree more. He needed to recoup some more before he started sorting out his still-precarious financial situation, but at least he could eat properly.

He had chosen the second target and wanted to act as quickly as possible. No point in hanging around. And the longer he left it, the more money they would spend, and the likelihood they could disappear increased.

He knew where Tony Morgan lived, as he had been to some lavish parties at his two-million-pound house in exclusive Henley-on-Thames. He had heard that Tony had taken a year off to relax, and it grated that he had paid towards the man's high life. He had never liked Tony, but Michael had always been good at his job, so Tony had left him to get on with it. He wondered what Tony's cut had been for his small cameo role. However small, it had been an important part of the scam that added a certain gravitas to the proceedings.

Michael also knew Tony's wife Felicity—a right stuck up bitch, who had inherited millions from the sale of her father's printing business. Why Tony had felt it necessary to get involved in the scam, he couldn't understand. He definitely didn't need the money. Perhaps he was in it for kicks. Well, he wouldn't find it funny when next they met.

Michael felt wary, though. Tony could well have staff at his property, so he would have to choose carefully where and when to strike. The one thing he was sure of was that he wanted his ghastly wife to witness the humiliation.

Michael also thought about weapons; he'd bought the small steel baton online from the USA, but he felt he needed something else—something even more terrifying. Guns were out of the question, but a vicious knife. ... Yes, he would get one of those deadly-looking hunting knives.

Michael spent two of the most boring days of his life watching Tony Morgan's property. He chose a Monday and Tuesday, and didn't learn much, except to establish that an old boy pottered around in the garden 'til lunchtimes, and a woman who looked like a housekeeper arrived at nine and left at five.

At six p.m. the next Monday, Michael dressed in black and put on a balaclava, which had slits for his eyes and mouth. When he looked in the mirror, he scared himself. He now felt more like an SAS warrior rather than a staid, middle-class banker. When he practiced his tough-man voice, he felt a bit silly, but grateful he'd been such a good mimic in his youth. It would come in handy now for disguising his voice so he wouldn't be recognised. One of the men in particular would be especially hard to fool, given that they'd known one another for so long, but Michael felt confident in his impersonation abilities. He changed back into his normal clothes and packed the black kit into a small shoulder bag.

He drove down to Henley-on-Thames and arrived at six-thirty. Parked near the house, away from prying eyes, he waited. Darkness soon fell, and he changed into his black warrior kit. At seven, he clambered over the fence at the edge of the property and made towards the house. He could distinguish the lit up lounge and kitchen. Perhaps they were about to eat dinner. Scared and nervous, sweat coated his face, and the balaclava felt tight and itched his skin. He was also excited that payback time had come, and if it went according to plan, he would have a further substantial sum in his bank account at the end of the evening.

Stealthily, he moved like a cat through the darkness and arrived at the back door. He grasped the handle, turned and pushed, and, incredibly, the door opened. As quietly as he could, he entered and heard talking in the kitchen. It was the two of them, Tony and Felicity. Michael stood still and listened. They seemed to be talking about Christmas and whether to go away or not. Michael waited, and then, obligingly, Tony Morgan left the kitchen. Michael could hear his footsteps on the wooden floor.

The sweat dripped down his face, and his heart raced—time to move. Nice and slow, he crept forward, and could hear Felicity moving around. He moved forward some more and took a peek. Felicity stood washing something in the double sink and had her back to him. Now or never. He wanted to get as close as possible, so still tip-toed as close as he could. Almost on her, she began to turn, so he lunged at her and grabbed her around the throat with his left hand as he lifted his right, which held the hunting knife. He held it tight to her neck and whispered, 'Shhhh.'

Terrified, she could hardly stand. Michael felt good. He was in control. He turned her round, so she stood in front of him, and held the knife to her throat.

'One wrong move, and I'll slit your throat, you understand?'

She nodded. Michael walked her out of the kitchen and toward the lounge, where he thought Tony had gone. He got to the entrance and pushed Felicity in through the doorway.

Tony spoke, 'Hello, darling. Everything all right? Do you want a drink?'

Michael pushed her forward and entered the room. Tony sat on a single leather chair, sipping at a glass of red wine. He went white and sprang to his feet.

'What the hell is ... ?'

'Shut the fuck up, Morgan, and sit back down. Any trouble and, believe me, there'll be so much blood, you'll be able to bathe in it.'

Tony resumed his seat. Michael pushed Felicity onto the sofa and stood behind her, still threatening her with the knife.

'Go and get your laptop.'

'I don't understand. I—'

Michael yelled at him, 'You don't have to understand. Just fucking move and bring it here.' To emphasise who was in charge, he held the knife to Felicity's throat and cut her. She screamed, then said, 'Just do it and hurry up.'

Tony left the room and, a minute later, came back with his computer.

'Turn it on and go to your online banking.'

Tony tapped the keys, then said, 'I'm there.'

'Good. What is the total in all your accounts?'

Tony looked down and to the left, and then cleared his throat. 'Two hundred thousand.'

'Listen carefully to this question, and if you lie, I will know. How much did you get paid for the Kazakhstan scam?'

Tony's face registered shock.

Michael pressed, 'How much?'

'A hundred grand. Who *are* you?'

'Make a payment to the following account.' Michael gave him the Metro account number and sort code.

'How much?'

'The two hundred K. Now, get up, put the laptop on the table, and sit back down.'

Michael checked the transaction, pressed pay, and the money winged its way to his account. He smiled beneath the balaclava.

'Now, listen carefully, you fucking piece of shit. You tell anyone about this, especially the other members of your little team, and I will come back and rape and kill your wife, and then kill you. Have I made myself clear?'

Tony looked scared to death and nodded.

Michael raised his voice, 'Do you fucking well understand?'

'Yes, I understand.'

'Don't look at that bank account. Forget this ever happened, and you will never see me again. If you should fuck with me ...' Michael again held the knife to Felicity's neck. 'I will take great pleasure in cutting this pretty little neck.'

Michael wanted to take his balaclava off to show him. To show him who the clever one was and who the wanker was, but he didn't. Maybe one day he would let him know. Instead, he pushed Felicity onto the floor and walked out calmly.

***

Tony ran to Felicity and helped her up. She had peed herself, and he wasn't surprised.

'Just wait 'til I find out who that was, he's—'

His wife's strong voice stopped him, 'You'll do exactly nothing. He wasn't holding the knife to your fucking throat. I'm going to shower and change, and then you can try and lie to me about the Kazakhstan deal.'

***

Michael felt over the moon. He now had a substantial amount of money, which could change the situation dramatically. The next morning, he paid every single bill outstanding. He then paid one hundred thousand into his National Trust bank account, which wiped out the overdraft and left a tidy sum for future payments. Next on the list were the credit card companies, which he cleared, and then cut the cards into small pieces. He kept his Metro debit card for everyday use. The next payment was the one he would enjoy the most. Then he thought of Francis. It would have been wonderful if she'd been here to see the reversal in his fortunes. He contacted the bank's mortgage department and paid off the total outstanding arrears. Then he walked to the lounge and looked out of the large picture windows at the mess of a garden. He would get people in to sort that out. And then he cried and cried—some for Francis and some for himself—he was back.

# CHAPTER 27

Karen had decided to go ahead with the plan, and they had rehearsed the telephone conversation a dozen times. Although capable, they wouldn't know whether Nartay was skilful enough until they did the real call. At five o'clock, Karen sat in her office with Mick. Nartay would make the call at six. She felt nervous and excited at the same time. The thought of getting the scum known as Stanislav was all-consuming, and she couldn't think of anything else.

'Let's go for a stroll and try and kill some time.'

They left the office, toured the station, and then went outside for a bit of fresh air.

Karen asked, 'You think it's going to work?'

'Truthfully, it's a long shot. If he's still in Ireland, is he really going to risk coming back for a couple of girls and a few thousand quid?'

'Several thousand is a lot of money, especially for someone like that, and remember, it's on a plate—almost just waiting for him to pick it up.'

Mick checked his watch. 'It's ten to; let's go.'

Mick called through to the custody suite and asked for Nartay to be brought to the CID office. Karen arranged for an officer to stand at the entrance, as they didn't need any interruptions at the wrong time. Calls were not to be put through until Mick confirmed it was over. Nartay arrived.

'Nartay, you're ready?'

Nartay didn't say anything at first, then spoke, 'No. I need a drink. I must have some vodka. It will add to the scene.'

Karen looked at Mick, 'We'll have to send out for some.'

Mick held his hand up to say wait, and then strode out of the office. Three minutes later, he came back in with a half-full bottle of Smirnoff.

'I'm not going to ask,' Karen said.

Nartay opened the top of the bottle and drank heavily.

He sat in one of the comfy chairs and took a final swig of vodka.

Mick attached a wire to the mobile and turned on the tape machine. Karen picked up the phone connected to the tape machine and did a thumbs up to Nartay.

Nartay pressed some numbers on his phone and put it to his ear.

You could have heard a pin drop.

'Hey, Stan, it's me, Nartay. How you getting on?

'Good.'

'You away and free like a bird, eh?'

'Yeah, it's good to be going home.'

Karen smiled. He hadn't left Ireland yet.

'So, what's new, Nartay?'

Nartay took a slug of Vodka and laughed. 'Man, you missing out. Two sexy girls moved in, lap dancers, here for a week before they head back to Belgrade. Man, they are fucking it, and I had one already. Pussy sweet as sugar. Yeah, but not just that. They're loaded. All their dosh from two year's work. Must be thousands. All cash. I'm planning on marrying one of them.'

Silence held for a couple of seconds.

'I wish I could come back. Sounds like you need some help.'

Nartay laughed again. 'No. Don't need any help. You stay away. I can handle two sex addicts on my own, trust me. So, look, good luck. If you're ever around, look me up.'

'Yeah.'

Nartay pressed the 'end call' button.

'Shit. How did I do?'

Mick said, 'I thought you were going to invite him?'

'It would have seemed too obvious. Now we wait.'

Karen stood. 'Well done. It was good. We've dangled the bait. Let's see if he takes it.'

Mick went and got some coffees, and then the three of them sat together.

'We can't sit here waiting all night. What happens if he decides just to turn up at the flat? And what happens if there're no girls?'

'You worry too much. Nartay can always say they left early.'

'He won't just turn up. If—and it's a big if—if he decides he wants some of the action, he will let me know because he will want it to be just the four of us.'

Karen glanced at her watch: six-twenty.

'Okay, we can wait for an hour or two. Let's see if anything happens.'

Karen was used to waiting, as it was a part of being a police officer you had to accept, but it still felt tough at times.

The minutes dragged on, and on coffees came at regular intervals, but it didn't help that much. After what seemed like a week, seven-thirty came around. The atmosphere tensed, and Karen didn't think it was going to work. Then eight p.m. arrived.

'Okay, let's call it a night. Thank you, Nartay. Escort him back to custody, please, Mick.'

Mick and Nartay stood and made for the door. Nartay turned back to Karen. 'Sorry. Some you win, some you lose.'

He continued towards the door, which Mick held open. Just as he reached the door, his mobile rang, and he stopped. Nobody spoke or moved.

Nartay moved back to the chair and sat down. 'Hey, Stan. Back so soon?'

'This Saturday, about eight, the four of us—we have nice party, yes? I bring booze.'

'Eh, yeah, sounds cool. Just the four of us, then?'

'No one else. It must be just you, me, and the two girls.'

'Well, you better bring plenty of vodka. These beauties drink like fish.'

'Don't worry. Will be plenty booze.' Then he hung up.

Nartay had a huge grin on his face.

Karen jumped up. 'I could kiss you. Well done. Fucking hell, the bastard's hooked. Now all we have to do is reel him in.'

Mick smiled as well. 'Three days to get it organised. Better start first thing in the morning.'

'We need the girls, but I suppose we could take him outside. Let's discuss it all in the morning.' Karen nodded to Mick. 'Take Nartay back. He can keep the vodka as a well done present.'

Mick opened his mouth as if to protest, but then shut it again and did as asked.

# CHAPTER 28

On Wednesday, Michael finished sending an email and felt the happiest he had for months. At lunchtime, he went to the kitchen, opened the fridge, and took out the remains of a shepherd's pie ready-meal. It didn't look that appetising, and he prayed that it would look better after he'd heated it up. He stuck it in the microwave and turned on full power for five minutes. The doorbell rang, and the sound pleased Michael. He had bought new batteries only the day before. In the hope it was the delivery he had been waiting for, he rushed to the door. A van sat in the driveway, and he opened the door with a beaming smile.

'Welcome. Let's get unloaded, then.'

The driver went back to the van and opened the back doors. Michael followed and took a look inside, then he rubbed his hands together and couldn't wait to try some. Fifteen cases of good quality red and white wine. Now he was really back. They unloaded the wine into the cellar. Michael kept back a case of St Emilion and put it in the kitchen, then he opened a bottle and left it to breathe, ready for dinner that evening. Early that afternoon, the gardening team arrived. They went to work clearing weeds, trimming hedges, cutting back trees, and cutting the grass. They spent three hours at the property and when they left, the transformation was incredible. Michael walked around the gardens, front and back, as he wanted it to be perfect.

The next phase of the overall plan was Sean King—that green snake in green grass. Michael reflected on how he had done a good job sucking him into the scam. It would be such a pleasure to take him down, and it would be another chunk of his money back, plus interest.

First of all, he had used every ounce of charm he possessed and got Sean's address from National Trust Bank, saying he had urgent papers to send. Sean King lived in Brighton in a well-to-do area on the South Coast. Michael had been surprised to learn that he lived in a flat on the seafront and not some huge palatial property in one of the best areas. Michael didn't know whether he was married or not but assumed he was, so he prepared for all eventualities.

On Thursday afternoon, Michael drove down the M23 towards Brighton. He mulled over his situation and couldn't help but congratulate himself on a job well done, so far. Sean King was one thing; the big fish was that bastard Bekzat, and that was where the majority of his cash would be. Sean King might be able to help in other ways. Where could he find Bekzat? In Kazakhstan? When would the man be likely to travel abroad again, particularly to the UK? If Michael had to go to Kazakhstan, it would be complex and not easy.

For the moment, Michael was happy he had money in the bank, all his bills paid, and that he was going to visit the next rat that lived in the sewers. He drove along the seafront, noticing the Grand Hotel where the bomb had gone off during the Conservative party conference. Brighton was busy on this cool, balmy evening, and lots of people walked along the esplanades. Elderly couples held hands, and dog walkers, joggers, and young couples clearly in love enjoyed the evening air.

Michael parked in the multi-storey car park and headed back down the hill to the seafront. He felt for his knife and his steel baton. With both weapons, he felt confidence flow through his body. The flat stood in a block of twelve. He wanted number two, which would be on the ground floor. He found the flats—a block right on the front with what must be charming views of the sea—well, at least in the summer. He opened the main building door and walked into a gloriously decorated hall, with a black-and-white tiled floor that had the elegant feel of the fifties. Cream wallpaper decorated the walls, and it all just looked so lovely. Michael's heart raced. He had no plan as he stood outside number two and rang the bell. He heard someone shout, 'I'll get it,' and then the door opened. It wasn't Sean King, but some young Nancy-boy in a pink dressing gown.

'Hello, handsome. What can I do for you? Or shouldn't I ask?'

Michael had the knife at his throat in a split second, and the smile disappeared from his face, replaced with a look of sheer terror.

Michael pushed him back into the hallway and kicked the door shut. Sean's voice came from one of the other rooms. 'Who was it?'

Michael stood still with the knife at the young man's throat.

Sean came out of the lounge and almost collapsed on the spot.

'Don't hurt him, please, God. What do you want? Take anything, but leave him, please.'

The sight of Michael dressed all in black finished off with the balaclava must be a terrifying sight, and King sobbed and muttered, 'Please, don't hurt him.'

Two seconds later, the young man broke out blubbing as well.

'Get back in the lounge and sit down, you piece of shit. Move.'

King rushed back and plonked himself on the two-seater pink sofa. Michael pushed the fairy godmother onto the seat next to him. They huddled together and held hands.

'Well, well, a right couple of Nancy-boys, eh.' Michael shook his head in disbelief. Sean King, a right woofta? He never would've seen it.

'Don't think about moving. If you do, I'll cut your genitals off. You understand?'

The young man crossed his legs and blubbered even more. King comforted him in a whisper, 'Don't worry. Everything will be all right.'

'Nothing will be all right unless I get what I came for, so shut the fuck up and listen. Simple questions. I want simple answers. I'm not interested in what you think, and don't bother asking me anything. So, we'll start. How much did Bekzat pay you to be involved in the scam?'

'I—I don't ...'

Michael got close and stuck the knife against King's throat.

'Have you ever seen a man with his throat cut? Blood shoots up like a fountain, he bleeds to death, and chokes on his blood. Not a nice way to go. Now, answer the fucking question. How much?'

'A hundred thousand.'
'That's better. Where is Bekzat?'
'He's in Kazakhstan.'
'Does he travel much?'
'Constantly.'
'When is he coming to the UK next?'
'I've, ... he mentioned next week sometime.'
'Get your laptop and plug it in.'
'What do—'
'Just fucking get it.'

King jumped and rushed out. He came back a few seconds later, plugged it in, and started it up.

'Good. How much do you have in your online accounts right now?'

King took his time and obviously wanted to lie. 'About sixty thousand.'

'Put the laptop on the table and sign in to your online banking, and then sit down.'

King did as he was told.

Michael sat in front of the computer and checked the accounts.

'You can't count, you lying toe rag. I make it one hundred and sixty thousand.'

Michael put in his bank details and transferred the entire amount.

'Very helpful, thank you, Sean.' Then he turned and looked at the young man. 'And what might your name be?'

'Steven, but Sean calls me fluffy.' He fluttered his eyelashes and smiled.

'How lovely. Now, both of you listen carefully, I'm going to walk out of here in a minute, and you will never hear from or see me again. If you should choose to try and find out who I am, I will come back and cut you both into pieces. Do you understand?'

Fluffy gasped in horror and trembled even more.

'Last thing, Sean, do not talk to Bekzat or the others, or it will be the worse for you.' He swung the knife to and fro in front of their faces, and fluffy couldn't take his eyes off the knife point.

'Good, so we understand each other.' And with that he walked out of the flat and shut the door. As he sped towards the main door, he pulled the balaclava off. Perspiration soaked his face, and he couldn't wait to get out in the fresh air.

Michael now had another sizable sum in his account. The next thing he did was to close all his accounts at National Trust bank. The only payment he made to them was the house mortgage, and he'd had already started the process of transferring that to a new lender.

Later, in his office, he got a phone call that made his day.

'Michael Fletcher.'

'Michael, it's Andrea Houlihan from the National Trust Bank. How are you?'

Michael smiled. The bitch had some front.

'What can I do for you, Miss Houlihan?'

'I see you cleared all your debts and closed your accounts. There was no need for that. Obviously, your circumstances have changed, and we would welcome you back. Why don't we have a spot of lunch—my treat?'

'Listen carefully, I would rather have lunch with the devil. You are a disgusting human being. Do not ever contact me again. Now fuck off.' He ended the call. God, but he enjoyed that.

That afternoon, he paid a visit to the Western Union shop, and then pottered around Epsom, where he did some shopping and bought some books.

At four, he got back home and went straight to the office. He needed all his charm again when he called National Trust Bank's head office.

'Good afternoon. Can I speak to Mark Heenen, please?' Michael had already established that Mark was the new commercial director and had been brought in from KPMG.

'Who's calling, please?'

'Sean King.'

'I'm putting you through to Mary Fish, his PA.'

'Thank you.' He breathed a sigh of relief. He'd never heard of her and guessed she may well have come with Mark from KPMG.

'Mr King, it's Mary Fish.'

'Hi Mary, Sean King, how are you?'

'Great.'

'Good, look, I know Mark hasn't been in-situ long, but I've got some Russian bankers coming over next week, and they're looking to invest over here and need someone to hold their hands. It could be considerable business for the bank.'

Mary wouldn't know Sean King personally, but he would be in the files as a facilitator and a grade A friend of the bank.

'Let me have a look at Mark's diary and see if we can fit you in—an hour do?'

'The longer, the better. By the way, have you heard from Bekzat? I was trying to get hold of him the other day. Goodness knows what country he's in at the moment.'

'Mr Abdulov? Yes, I spoke to him recently, and he's in next week. With any luck, you might bump into him.'

'Oh no, if I do I'll have to pay for dinner, it's my turn, and he loves vintage champagne.' Michael laughed. 'What day is he coming in?'

'Okay, Mr King, you're booked for Thursday at two p.m. Mr Abdulov is in on Tuesday.'

'Thank you so much. Does he still stay at the Savoy? I want to surprise him.'

'Don't quote me, but I'm fairly certain he's booked in at the Hilton Park Lane for two nights. Thank you, Mr King. We look forward to seeing you next week.'

'Thank you, Mary.' He put the phone down, jumped out of his chair, and shook his fist in the air. 'Got you, you bastard.'

Michael grabbed the open bottle of St Emilion and poured himself a full glass, took two mouthfuls of the nectar, and shouted, 'Life is just getting better and better.'

Later, he got back on the phone. 'Hello, yes, this is Mr Abdulov's diary assistant. Can I confirm the room for two nights next week, please? I don't want any issues on arrival.'

'Yes. Mr Abdulov is booked in for Monday and Tuesday night.'

'Excellent, thank you.'

If you spoke and acted like you owned the world, people would tell you anything. So, now he had to come up with a plan. Bekzat would be the most difficult of the four, particularly because he would always be in public places. He would have to take him in his room at the hotel.

The next day at ten a.m., Michael got in his Mondeo and headed for Epsom. He drove down East Street and took a left at Sainsbury's. Past the supermarket, he kept going, and down into the industrial estate. He passed the Vauxhall and then the Mercedes dealers, drove on, and then saw the location he was after. He eased into a parking space reserved for customers. The Mondeo looked more than a little out of place, but he couldn't have cared less. Then he noticed that he wore scruffy old trousers and a shirt that had seen better days, and made a mental note that he needed to buy some new clothes, and definitely before his visitor arrived. Out of the car, he hesitated—this was a big moment for him, and he wanted to enjoy every second. He shut the door but didn't bother to lock it, and then strode into the building.

The head of sales sat at his desk. Michael made straight towards the thirty-thousand-pound, jet-black option. The sales manager looked around for one of his staff, but no one seemed to be free. He rose and crossed to Michael.

'Good morning, Sir. I'm Matthew. Can I help you today?'

Michael did not like the condescending speech of the man but smiled.

'Yes. I'll take this one. When can it be ready?'

Matthew tried to remain composed but still looked flabbergasted. 'It's the top of the range, Sir. Thirty-five thousand. How will you be paying?'

'Cash.' Michael opened the driver's door and sat down. The delicious smell of new leather hit him as he admired the panelling and gadgets.

'We could have her ready to go in two hours, Sir.'

Michael shut the door and pressed the electric window button. The window slid down quietly, and Michael leaned out of it. 'Well, you better get a bloody move on then, sunshine.'

Matthew frowned, then swallowed his pride, smiled, and rushed off to prepare the paperwork.

Two hours later, Michael drove out of the BMW dealers in his brand new, sleek, jet-black seven series BMW with every extra imaginable. He drove straight home and pulled into the driveway in front of his house, got out, and walked around the car, just looking at it. Loving it. Then he walked to the front door and turned. The car looked sensational, especially with the backdrop of the immaculate plants and garden. She would love it.

Michael took it easy for a couple of days, and then the weekend arrived. Every day passed pretty much the same, but this Saturday would be a special day. He got up at the crack of dawn and made sure everything was perfect. A team of Molly Maid cleaners had come in for a day, and the house had never looked so clean.

At ten-thirty, he slid behind the wheel of the new BMW and glided out of his drive. Forty minutes later, he parked in the short-stay car park at Heathrow's terminal five and walked towards arrivals. Scared but excited, he could barely contain his composure. A moment to savour and remember forever. Hard work lay ahead, no doubt of that, but it could work.

He had spent a great deal of time showering, and then covering himself in Lynx deodorant and Paco Rabanne aftershave. He wore some of the new clothes he had bought in TK Max and Burtons: A pair of cream chinos matched with a plain blue shirt, and new, casual loafer shoes finished off the look. He felt confident and cool. The plane was due in at eleven-forty. He'd arrived early but that just formed part of the event, and the anticipation felt excruciatingly delicious.

Michael had a coffee in Costa, directly opposite arrivals, and when he'd finished, he moved to the silver barrier and stood opposite the doors. Tense, he kept looking at his watch. By the time she had retrieved her luggage, it would be about twelve-fifteen. Another glance at his watch showed ten past.

His eyes glued to the doors, he watched passengers pour through from around the globe. And then it happened. The doors swung open. Here she came, pushing her trolley. He froze for a second when she saw him and their eyes met. Then it all happened so quickly.

He jumped the barrier. She ran to him. They embraced tightly. Then shared a long, lingering, passionate kiss. Michael couldn't stop saying her name.

'Ainalayin, Ainalayin, you're here at last.' Tears flowed from them both, and they refused to let go of each other. After what seemed an eternity, he finally parted from her, grabbed the trolley, pulled her close, and refused to let her go for a second.

'Michael, you look so handsome today for me.'

'Wow, your English has improved so much.'

'I try hard. It is very difficult.'

'You are doing brilliantly. Let's sit down for a minute. It's an emotional time for me.'

They moved to the Costa Coffee and sat at the edge away from the crowds.

'Michael, Michael, I never thought we would see each other again. It's a miracle, and now I am here in London.'

'Things have been terrible. My wife ...' He couldn't finish.

Ainalayin held his hand. 'I know, my love. I'm so sorry. It's been awful for you. It will get better.' She smiled.

Michael beamed. 'Now you are here, and I am so happy. We will have to work hard to make it work, you understand?'

'Of course. I am ready for anything. Now, tell me everything that has happened. Everything.'

They sat for ten minutes in the coffee shop, and then made their way to the car park. Michael zapped his key and, when Ainalayin saw the flashing BMW light, she screamed with delight.

'Oh my God, Michael, such a beautiful car. Is it yours, or have you borrowed it?'

He looked at her. 'It's our car. Is that okay with you?'

'Yes. I just have to learn to drive.' They shared a laugh.

The journey home took an hour and, for that whole hour, Michael didn't stop talking. He told Ainalayin everything that had happened. She already knew about the scam but not the results of Michael's investigations. Michael had been waiting for the right opportunity to thank Ainalayin. A moment of silence fell, and he spoke from the heart, 'If you hadn't sent me that photo, and then the eight thousand pounds, I wouldn't have made it. I owe you my life.'

'It was all I could do. When I saw how they were stealing your money, I felt ashamed, and I liked you so much.'

'You took a huge risk sending me your life savings. When I went to the Western Union office to collect the money, I was shocked how much you had sent.'

'I wanted to help and to show my commitment to you.'

'Well, you certainly did that.'

'Yes, but you're forgetting, not only did you send me the eight thousand back, you then sent ten thousand extra. It was more than kind of you.'

They pulled into the driveway, and Ainalayin sat in shock.

She said, 'D-do, do you own this house? Or ... ?' She laughed. 'Have you borrowed it to impress me?'

'*We* own this house.'

She jumped out of the car. 'My, my God, it's fabulous, lovely, gorgeous.'

'Well, I like it too, so that's good.'

She jumped into his arms. 'You are, I think they say, a good catch, no?'

'Listen, I am the lucky one. Let's go inside.'

He opened the front door and, before she could say anything, he swept her up in his arms and carried her over the threshold. A musical chuckle escaped her lips.

'What are you doing?' She kicked her legs and squealed, but loved it. 'Put me down.'

He brought her down tight to his body, their faces inches apart, and kissed her passionately. He felt happier than he had for a considerable time.

Michael took her bags in and put them in the spare room, unsure of the sleeping arrangements and not wanting to presume too much. Michael gave Ainalayin a grand tour of the house, and she loved every bit of it. They eventually sat down in the lounge and both fell quiet in a pleasant sort of way. Michael then told her that Bekzat would arrive in the country on Monday and would stay in a hotel in central London. He explained how he was the last and the most important because he still had most of the money. He then explained how he planned to get his money back.

Ainalayin said, 'He travels with a bodyguard. A nasty piece of work called Dosken Mustafin. Ex-army. Big man. What about him?'

'Truthfully, I don't know.'

'Let us think and see if we can come up with any ideas.'

# CHAPTER 29

'Come in, Mick, and take a seat. Coffee?'

'Just had one, thanks.'

Karen sat opposite him and opened her notebook at a clean page.

'Right. God, it took me ages to get to sleep last night. I couldn't stop thinking about our meeting with this Stanislav bastard.'

'I was the same. I'm so looking forward to locking him up for a long time.'

'Agreed, so let's go through how we're going to play this. First, do we take him outside the property or in?'

'Tidier if we get him on the way in, and less chance of someone getting hurt.'

'Agreed, but we still need the girls just in case something goes wrong. I'll talk to Guildford later. Stanislav won't have a car?'

'Hmm, well, he might hire one. If not, my bet is he would come by train.'

Karen threw ideas into the pot, 'Is he coming by plane? Ferry? We could try and track him from the airports and ports, but it's a massive job. Is he going to be using his own passport? The list is endless.'

Mick leant forward to emphasise his point. 'Let him come to us. Less can go wrong.'

Karen looked at Mick for a second. 'I agree. We have armed units outside and in the flat. We take him as he arrives, whether from a taxi or on foot. I want the entire area mapped. He could sneak in from the rear, so we need to cover all angles. You see how far people will go for money?'

'Well, and the ...' He stopped.

Karen raised her eyebrows. 'Yes?'

'The girls.' He smiled. 'He does like the girls.'

'He certainly does, and they and greed will be his downfall. Now, let's get down to the details. How many officers, etc.'

Two hours later, the job done, the police drew up the operational papers and notified the task team. They would meet one mile from the property at a golf course, at midday on Saturday, followed by deployment at six p.m.

*** 

Stanislav caught a train to Leatherhead, and then got in a minicab and gave the address for the flat. They soon arrived, and he told the driver he was early and that he should drive slowly past the flats to the end of the road. He held out a twenty-pound note, which disappeared into the driver's pocket in record time. Stanislav glanced left to right but couldn't see anything out of place. Pitch blackness draped the road, and the only light came from the street lights, of which, two outside the flats weren't working. He glanced up at the windows. Most of them had lights on, but he couldn't detect a single person or even a shadow. It didn't mean anything, but he liked to be careful. They got to the end of the road and stopped. Stanislav looked back. Still nothing happening. He took out his mobile phone and pressed some numbers.

'Hey, Nartay, sorry, man. I can't make it.'

'That's a shame. The girls are here all ready and waiting.'

'Shit, man. They cancelled fucking flight at last minute.'

'Where are you, then?'

'Belfast, and I can't swim.'

'Go and have a few pints of the black stuff while I look after the girls for you.'

'I might just do that. We'll catch up another day, okay.'

'Yeah. See ya.' They both clicked off at the same time.

\*\*\*

One of the armed officers hidden outside watched the taxi with keen interest, which faded when the vehicle drove on by without stopping until way down the road, at the far end of the street. He shrugged and sighed. It looked like this might all turn into a no-show.

\*\*\*

'Shit,' Nartay shouted.

Karen and Mick stood in the bedroom. The mobile had been attached to a recording and listening device in the spare bedroom for just such an occasion as this. Karen had heard it all. They left the bedroom and joined Nartay and the two Russian girls in the lounge.

'Don't worry. Sometimes it just doesn't fall into place.' She turned to the two attractive young girls. 'Might as well get packed up. We're leaving.' Karen pulled back the curtain slightly and looked outside. She scanned up and down the street. Nothing but blackness. All she saw was a car parked up right at the end of the road. 'Mick, make sure those street lights are put back on, and stand everybody down.'

Natasha, the eldest, spoke up for the girls.

'We get paid, whatever, and we like Nartay, so thought we would stay and have a good drink with our new friend.'

Nartay answered before Karen could speak, 'Sorry, girls, I have to go with the police officers. Another time?'

Karen smiled. 'It's your lucky night.' Then she produced a document from her pocket. 'Your conditions of bail.'

Nartay looked stunned.

'It was meant to be a present for a job well done, but it wasn't your fault.' She handed the paper to Nartay, who couldn't believe his luck.

Nartay smiled at the two girls. 'Party time.'

'Whoopee.'

Karen looked at the two girls. Long legged and so bloody sexy, they tempted her. Mick interrupted her dreamlike state.

'Men are being stood down now.'

***

Stanislav sat in the front passenger seat, watching and waiting. Desperate for a good fuck, he thought about the two girls and prayed he could have them. The street looked quiet, and then he focussed. Police officers, dressed in black and wearing balaclavas, appeared from the shadows. So many of them he wouldn't have stood a chance. That bastard Nartay would pay for this. He continued to watch while two police vans arrived and took the officers away. They drove up the road and away.

Still he didn't move. There would have been officers in the building, if not in the flat, and no one had left through the doors as yet. He didn't have to wait long. Two plain-clothes officers exited the building and got into a black Audi car. Stanislav could smell that they were filth. He took a wedge of notes out of his pocket, peeled off another twenty, and gave it to the driver.

'We wait little longer, and then is time.'

# CHAPTER 30

Michael felt nervous. They arrived home from the Chinese restaurant, and the sleeping arrangements concerned him. He poured wine for the two of them, and they sat in the lounge. They chatted about this and that, and then Ainalayin excused herself, saying she would be back in a minute. Michael assumed she'd gone to the loo, topped up his glass, and sat back. He still couldn't believe she was here, and that he had sorted out his finances and his life. He began to relax. Ainalayin seemed to be taking a long time. Almost on cue, she came back into the room, carrying a small bag.

'Everything okay?'

'Everything is more than fine, thank you. Will you do me a favour, please?'

'If I can, of course.'

'Go and get ready for bed. I'll be up in a minute.'

He just looked at her. What was going on?

'Michael.'

He jumped up. 'I'm already gone.' Then he strode out of the room. He got to the main bedroom, opened the door, and stepped in. He sipped his wine and looked around. One of the drawers hung open a little way. When he went to it and pulled it open, he saw that knickers filled it. Ainalayin's clothes filled the other drawers too. He heard the door open and turned. Ainalayin stood in the doorway. His jaw hit the floor. Dressed in a beautiful set of black underwear and stockings, she looked like a supermodel.

'Michael, we do not know each other that well yet, and there are one or two things I want to tell you.' She paused for a moment. 'I am yours to do with as you wish. I am here to please you.' She reached behind and undid the bra, which released her magnificent breasts. 'I will always try to please you. And you can do whatever you want to me. I am yours. Do you understand?'

Michael understood that Ainalayin had given herself to him totally. Not half-heartedly but fully, completely, and without reservation.

'I understand. I—'

'Shhhh. Wait.' She slipped her black panties down and removed them with a flourish, to reveal her smoothness, which he loved.

'I want you to feel free to have me any way you wish, at any time you wish. Nothing is out of bounds for you.'

She took off her stockings. Michael became tearful. No one had ever said anything like this to him before. She left him mesmerised.

'We start tonight. I am going to give you so much pleasure, and I will love doing that. I am to be enjoyed like ripe fruit and delicious wine. Take your fill of me until you can take no more. And, after you have rested, you will take me again, and again, and again.'

The stockings off, she kicked her black high heels to the side of the bed.

Then, slowly, she approached Michael and knelt, undid his belt and trousers, and pulled them down. His boxers couldn't hide the massive erection he had. She gripped the sides of his shorts and pulled them down. His cock shot into the air, and she took him in her hand, and then licked him and ran her tongue up and down his shaft while smiling up at him. He hardened and grew even more. In ecstasy, he closed his eyes, and she turned her attention to his balls, and sucked and stretched them. Oh God, he'd gone to heaven.

He held her shoulders. 'It's going to be over too quickly if you don't stop.'

She paused for a second. 'I want to taste you, and we have all night.'

Ainalayin continued to suck and increased the speed and pressure. He couldn't stand it.

'Ainalayin, yes, now.' He jerked and pushed. She swallowed hungrily.

Spent, Michael collapsed onto the bed, and Ainalayin curled up next to him. A few minutes later, he whispered in her ear, 'Now it's time for me to taste you.'

He sat up, moved her into position, went down on her, and soon heard her moaning in pleasure. As he continued to pleasure her, he had only one thought: It would be a long night.

# CHAPTER 31

Stanislav waited a further thirty minutes and decided it was time.

'Drop me just before flats, and then can go.'

The driver nodded and pulled away from the kerb.

Stanislav scanned in all directions and couldn't see anything of note. It should be safe. Would they have left an officer in the flat just in case? He didn't think so. Cap pulled down over his eyes, he kept in the shadows and made his way to the building's front door. On edge, he fully expected a burly police officer with a machine gun to challenge him at any moment. The quiet was deafening as he opened the doors and slowly entered, listening intently for any sound. He stopped—nothing—he tip-toed and soon stood outside Nartay's front door. Again, he listened, and could hear laughing and loud rock music. Good, it would cover any noise he made. He rang the bell.

*\*\*\**

'Oh God, I told you the neighbours would complain if we had the music on too loud.'

'Who cares,' the girls shouted, knocking back more vodka.

Nartay opened the door, but saw no one there. He started to shut it, and Stanislav launched a punch, which connected with Nartay's jaw and broke it. He tried to scream but couldn't—the pain felt terrible. Stanislav grabbed him by the neck and threw him onto the floor in the small hall, and then he shut the door and brought his leg back. He kicked Nartay hard in the stomach, and he doubled up in agony and thought that he was having his last few moments of life. Stanislav grabbed a handful of hair and pulled. Nartay pushed himself forward, trying to reduce the pain. Stanislav kicked the lounge door open and dragged Nartay to the centre of the smallish room. The two girls sat on the sofa, covering their naked breasts.

'I arrived just in time.'

Stanislav then beat and kicked Nartay half to death, his face a red mass of cuts and bruises and, no question, he had multiple broken limbs. Stanislav finally finished and ended by spitting on his face and shouting 'Traitor.'

***

The two girls cowered, terrified, and being half-undressed made it even worse.

'So, which of you bitches wants to get fucked first?' Stanislav asked.

Natasha took responsibility.

'Look, we were hired to make sure a visitor had a good time. We know nothing else and, to be honest, don't care. We are on our way home.'

'Bring me the money.'

'What money?'

Then Stanislav understood there was no money. Of course, it had all been a set-up from start to finish. What to do was the question? He didn't want to hang around too long.

Angry and frustrated, he grabbed the youngest girl and ripped off her short, blue, pleated skirt, followed by her black satin panties. She cried and begged him to stop. Natasha shouted at him to take her instead and to leave her sister alone. Stanislav grabbed the girl by the neck, spun her round, undid his belt, and lowered his trousers and underwear. His erection sprang free—huge. At that moment, Natasha attacked and scratched at his eyes with her sharp nails. Although unable to move freely, Stanislav brought his fist up and smashed her hard on the nose. Natasha screamed when the bone splintered and her eyes filled with tears. Brave, she continued to scratch and punch. This time, Stanislav got mad and hit her in the face four times with pile-driver strength. Weak, she collapsed in a heap on the floor. He went straight back to the younger girl, got her in position, and entered her roughly. She gasped.

\*\*\*

Meanwhile, Karen and Mick made their way back toward Epsom. The day had started so positively and had ended in disaster. You could have cut the silence in the car with a knife. Finally, Karen spoke, 'Fuck it. These things happen. I just wanted that bastard so badly. Cancelled fucking flight. Perhaps we should blame BA or whoever it was.'

Mick felt pissed off as well. 'Don't worry. He'll make a mistake. They always do.'

'You mean most of them. What about all the ones in Spain, sunning themselves in retirement? The way things work out sometimes, it's just not fair. We did everything we could, don't you think?'

'Shit, Boss, he could have phoned from Ireland. And he could have been sat in a car at the end of the road saying he missed his flight and we would be none the wiser.'

Karen took in the words and froze, ... *the car at the end of the road* ...

Karen lost control and shouted, 'Turn around, quickly. Get back to the flat. Fucking hell. Of course, he's so fucking clever. Step on it, for God's sake.' Karen fumed. 'The girls and Nartay. Oh God, I hope we're not too late.'

In shock, Mick concentrated on one thing—driving as fast as he could without killing anyone. Karen got on the radio and called for armed backup, and thanked the Lord that she and Mick had booked out weapons. Although a hair-raising journey, it seemed over in a minute. They pulled up outside the flats, jumped out of the car, and headed in. They listened at the door. For certain, there was no party going on. The flat sounded deathly quiet. Karen then noticed the door stood open about half an inch and pushed it slowly. It creaked ever so slightly.

\*\*\*

Stanislav stood in the main bedroom, trying to find anything of value. So far, he'd found fuck all. Nartay was hardly a wealthy man. He'd pocketed three good mobiles and a bit of cash from the girls, but it was a paltry haul. When he heard the front door creak, he froze and listened. Someone came in. He assumed it was the police, and took his long knife out and hid behind the door. As soon as the opportunity arose, he would make a run for it.

\*\*\*

Karen and Mick took the few steps down the hall. Karen immediately recognised the smell of blood and gore. She pushed the lounge door, and a hideous sight greeted her. Nartay and the two girls all looked dead.

Blood covered the walls and large puddles lay on the floor. She closed her eyes for a second, and then became scared. His presence lingered in the flat—he was still here—Mick had seen the bodies, too, and held his pistol in front of him, also scanning for danger. Karen held her finger to her lips and took a step down the hall. Then, with her mouth close to Mick's ear, she whispered, 'He's still here.'

The two of them inched down the hall—Karen on the left and Mick on the right. Terrified, Karen came to the kitchen, and her gun-hand shook. Mick took her arm and squeezed it, then looked her straight in the eye and smiled. It gave her renewed confidence, and she swung into the kitchen, gun first, ready to blaze away at the sight of any human being. The room stood empty. They moved like snails further down the hall. The two bedrooms lay ahead. If he *were* here, he would be in one of them.

# CHAPTER 32

She had begged and begged him to let her go with him, but Michael had insisted that Ainalayin stay behind with the car, and that she did, though with protest. Michael wasn't sure if he would go through with it. He had promised Ainalayin that he would take no risks and would come back if he couldn't get Bekzat on his own and retrieve the money. If he couldn't get the money, he would take great pleasure in ending Bekzat's miserable fucking life.

He parked at the underground car park in Park Lane and walked to the Hilton Hotel. He thought of all the Hollywood movies he had seen. It all looked so easy but when it was real, and it was you … his heart pounded, sweat soaked him, and his breathing came laboured. He slowed down—he had to get control of himself before he got to the hotel. The hotel looked busy, and cars continually stopped outside the main entrance and deposited glamorous couples and high-powered businessmen. Michael took a final, long breath, and walked in through the huge glass doors. When he walked forward, a floor greeter smiled at him.

'Good evening, Sir. Can I help direct you?'

Michael felt flummoxed but recovered. 'The à la carte restaurant. I have a booking.'

'Very good, Sir. Please, go to the lifts at the left-hand side of the lobby and go to the tenth floor.'

Fuck. What to do next? Nine o'clock, so if Bekzat were staying in the hotel, he would be eating dinner. Could he risk going and seeing if he was in the restaurant? He kept walking to the lifts and decided it was worth the risk. At the tenth floor, he headed to the World's End Restaurant. A superior-looking Maître D approached him.

'Good evening, Sir. Can I help you?'

'Yes, I'm looking for a friend of mine. I'm not sure if he is in the restaurant or the bar. My first port of call is here.'

'And his name, Sir?'

'Bekzat Abdulov.'

'I can tell you that Mr Abdulov is eating in his room tonight.' He leant forward and lowered his voice, 'Between you and me, Sir, I believe he is entertaining in his room.' He smiled the *'if you know what I mean'* kind of smile.

Michael nodded. 'Yes, of course, thank you so much.' A twenty-pound note changed hands in a switch that Paul Daniels would have been proud of.

Michael went to the bar and thought about his predicament. Where would the bodyguard be? Definitely not in Abdulov's room if he had a woman with him, but probably in a nearby room, and maybe even next door. It would be risky, but he felt he could do it.

He got the room number from a concierge for another twenty-pound note—third floor, room 321, and Dosken had room 322. Michael got in the lift and pressed three, and planned to put on his balaclava as soon as he got to the room. More nervous than ever, he took comfort that this was the last time. This would be the one that would make a huge difference to his and Ainalayin's future. If he had to, he would be vicious and torture the bastard.

The lift opened at the third floor, and he followed the signs to room 321. He turned the corner. No sign of the bodyguard, and the corridor looked clear. The expensive carpet felt thick and soft beneath his feet and nullified the sound of his shoes. Soon, he stood outside the room. What was the plan? How could he get in? Without realising it, he knocked and said in as quiet a voice as he could, 'Room Service.'

Then he put on his balaclava. Footsteps approached, and the door opened wide. Michael stared for half a second at the beautiful woman who stood in front of him. She looked Middle-eastern, maybe from Iran, and was absolutely stunning. He grabbed her throat and forced her back into the room—all thoughts of her beauty disappeared quickly—then he kicked the door shut and held her still. He could hear the shower. It must be Bekzat.

'You speak English?'

'Yes.'

'Go. I will not hurt you, in exchange for your silence.' He fumbled in his pocket, brought out a hundred pounds, and pushed it into her hand. She smiled at him and most likely hadn't been looking forward to sex with the man in the shower.

The woman disappeared, and Michael prepared. Bekzat's laptop sat on the table, so he plugged it in and pressed the start button. It purred into life and just needed the password to open all the functions.

Boy, Bekzat took one hell of a long shower. At last, Michael heard it stop. He felt for his knife and baton, and when he touched both, he felt better. Positioned near the door, so Bekzat could not escape, he tried to relax. Then Bekzat brushed his teeth. It wouldn't be long now. Michael took the hunting knife out of the scabbard hidden under his black jumper, and then took two steps to the side of the bathroom door. It opened. Michael got the shock of his life as a huge bear-like man appeared. This had to be the bodyguard. Michael had no choice, so he held the knife to the man's throat and pushed him forward onto the bed. The man sat still and showed no nerves.

'What do you want?'

'Where is Bekzat?'

'Next door, of course. Part of our security is that we stay in the room under the other's name. You realise you have made a huge mistake. That knife will not save you.'

Michael fought to control the panic trying to overcome him. 'I'm going to give you a chance.'

Dosken said, 'No, listen to me. Leave now and I'll let you live. I'll count to five: one, two, three ...' Dosken didn't finish but lunged and grabbed Michael's wrist with incredible strength. Michael kicked out at Dosken's legs and stomach to no avail, and then fell back and dropped the knife. Dosken fell on him and closed his hands around Michael's throat and squeezed. It wouldn't be long before he lost consciousness. In this fight for his life, he could do only one thing.

As a last resort, he pushed his hand down and felt for the man's genitals. When he found them, he took the balls in his hand and dug his nails into them, squeezing as hard as he could. Dosken screamed and leapt up, holding his damaged balls. Michael had to take advantage. This might be the only chance he got. He charged at Dosken and knocked him flying. The man hit his head on the corner of the bedside cabinet, which stunned him, and then he fell unconscious onto the carpet. Michael had felt terrified, and gasping for breath, he couldn't believe he had fought the bodyguard and won. He collected his thoughts, picked up his knife, and opened the room door. The corridor remained empty. Still trembling from the adrenaline rush, he strode to the next room and gave a loud knock. 'Room Service.'

The door opened, and Bekzat attacked. He must have heard the commotion. A knife flashed an inch past Michael's face, but he ducked and swung his knife and nicked Bekzat's arm. He gasped in pain. Michael pushed forward into the room and swung the knife viciously in front of Bekzat. Michael got lucky, and Bekzat backed off, tripped on his sandals, and fell. Michael jumped on him, pinned his wrist to the floor, and forced him to let go of the knife. Michael held his knife to Bekzat's throat.

'Enough. Enough. What do you want?' Bekzat sounded scared.

Michael glared at him. 'I will let you live if you do exactly as I say. No comment, no discussion, and no chat. You understand?'

'Yes.'

'Get your laptop and turn it on.'

Bekzat got up and went to the table, plugged in the laptop, and waited.

'Go to your online banking. How much do you have in your accounts?'

'About six hundred thousand dollars.'

'Good.' Michael took a piece of paper out of his pocket and handed it to him. 'Transfer the full amount to this account.'

Bekzat started to argue, but then shut up and typed one-handed on his keyboard. Then, in a lightning-quick movement, went for the paper-knife next to the laptop and lunged at Michael. He sank the knife into Michael's shoulder, who had never felt pain like it. Unable to control his grip, Michael dropped his knife to the floor. Bekzat pulled the knife out of Michael's shoulder, and more searing pain shot through his body.

He had failed. And if he didn't get help, he could bleed to death. Bekzat approached and ripped off the balaclava.

'Well, well, well. Michael Fletcher, if I remember correctly?'

'That's right, you fucking scumbag. I want my money.'

'I don't think you're in a position to ask for anything, do you?'

Michael didn't wait. He kicked at Bekzat, and then jumped at him. He only had enough strength for one final assault. The pain in his shoulder felt unbelievable. He fell back again—finished. Bekzat came at him with his knife held high.

'An obvious case of self-defence, don't you agree?' He laughed as he brought the knife down towards Michael's stomach. Michael readied for the pain, but something happened. A shadow fell over his shoulder. Someone else had come in. A loud thwump sounded next to his ear. He dove to the side and turned. A woman. Ainalayin. She held a small pistol fitted with a silencer.

Michael glanced back at Bekzat. Half his face had disappeared, and blood had splattered everywhere—on the walls, the carpet, the furniture, and all over Michael.

'Are you all right?' Ainalayin gasped.

'I am now, thank you. Thank you. It's a miracle.'

Ainalayin smiled. 'You know what they say: Behind every successful man is a strong woman. And with you, it's me.' She knelt down and looked at his wound. 'Nasty, but we have to go, and quickly.'

She helped Michael up and stepped towards the door.

'Wait.' Michael rushed to the laptop and studied the page. 'Thank God,' he muttered and pressed transfer. Then he picked up the laptop with his good hand and rushed to the door. They went down the service stairs and left by the delivery entrance.

# CHAPTER 33

Karen felt just plain terrified and had an awful feeling that something wasn't right. Unlike her, Mick seemed so sure of himself. They got to the end of the hallway. He smiled at Karen and pointed at the left door. She nodded and took the left. When Karen pushed, the door opened slowly and creaked. Mick opened the other door, and for some reason, she turned to watch him. He disappeared into the bedroom, and Karen turned back. She had lost concentration for a split second.

All at once, she relaxed, thinking Stanislav had probably gone. She took one step into the room, and then her gun-hand got knocked to the side. She fired and, at the same time, felt a knife enter her chest. Unbearable pain hit her, and she collapsed to the floor. The handle stuck up, out of her chest, and she had difficulty breathing. Had her lung been punctured? The pain grew worse. Stanislav rushed through the door and hurtled towards the front door, and from the floor, Karen watched Mick sprint out of the other bedroom.

Then he yelled, 'Stop or I will shoot.'

They wanted the bastard alive, but if not ...

Stanislav stopped and turned, ready to attack.

Mick held the Glock pistol at head height, and as Stanislav turned, he fired three shots in succession. Each slug hit him in the face and obliterated it. Mick ran to Karen, knelt down, and gawped at the knife embedded in her chest. She fought for breath. He called for an ambulance and screamed at them to hurry. Armed colleagues dragged him back. The ambulance got there in minutes and, sirens blazing, they rushed her to Epsom General Hospital. They took her straight into the operating theatre upon arrival.

*\*\*

Six days later, Karen lay in intensive care, still on the critical list. Until now, the doctors had kept her in an induced coma to help her get over the worst of the injuries. Today, they turned off the medication drip, and, slowly, she came to. Her eyes blinked open, and some slight feeling came back to her. *Thank God,* she thought, *I'm alive.* She felt squeezes on her hands and looked up and from side to side. Chau and Esme and Mick stood there. The tears flowed from all four as they hugged and kissed. Happy, she closed her eyes.

THE END

OTHER TITLES AVAILABLE FROM AUTHOR CHRIS WARD

**SERIAL KILLER: DI KAREN FOSTER BOOK 1**
http://tinyurl.com/p5ld9dx

**BLUE COVER UP: DI KAREN FOSTER BOOK 2**
http://tinyurl.com/mzy5f2f


**THE BERMONDSEY THRILLER TRILOGY**

**BERMONDSEY TRIFLE**
http://amzn.to/1l3B3up

**BERMONDSEY PROSECCO**
http://tinyurl.com/nebwtys

**BERMONDSEY THE FINAL ACT**
http://tinyurl.com/nbuahoj


VISIT THE www.authorchrisward.com WEBSITE AND JOIN THE MAILING LIST.

SOON TO BE PUBLISHED: 'RETURN TO BERMONDSEY' FEATURING PAUL BOLTON, LEXI, DI KAREN FOSTER, AND SERGEANT JEFF SWAN.

Printed in Great Britain
by Amazon